Donors

An Agent Jade Monroe FBI Crime Thriller
Book 3

C. M. Sutter

AUTHOR'S NOTE

This book is a work of fiction by C. M. Sutter. Names, characters, places, and incidents are products of the author's imagination or are used solely for entertainment. Any resemblance to actual events or persons, living or dead, is entirely coincidental.

ABOUT THE AUTHOR

C.M. Sutter is a crime fiction writer who resides in the Midwest, although she is originally from California.

She is a member of numerous writers' organizations, including Fiction for All, Fiction Factor, and Writers etc.

In addition to writing, she enjoys spending time with her family and dog. She is an art enthusiast and loves to create handmade objects. Gardening, hiking, bicycling, and traveling are a few of her favorite pastimes. Be the first to be notified of new releases and promotions at: http://cmsutter.com.

C.M. Sutter

http://cmsutter.com/

Donors:

An Agent Jade Monroe FBI Crime Thriller, Book 3

It's the dead of winter, and FBI Agents Jade Monroe and J.T. Harper are asked to assist the Gary, Indiana, police force in a possible serial killer case that has everyone stumped.

A body, frozen stiff and drained of blood, is found by children playing near an old quarry. Several weeks later, a second body is discovered in an abandoned house, and the manner of death is identical. The agents race to Gary when word of a third victim comes in.

With no clues and multiple frozen bodies, the agents have no idea when these women died or what the FBI is facing, yet the body count rises and the manner of death remains the same.

Jade wonders whether they're heading into the dark, unknown world of the occult, a place she knows nothing about—and has no desire to.

The most well-known occult leader in the area is in their sights and currently their only lead. Are the agents and local law enforcement heading down the wrong path? The final blindside shakes Jade to her core and leaves the entire police force stunned.

Stay abreast of each new book release by
signing up for my VIP e-mail list at:

http://cmsutter.com/newsletter/

Find more books in the Jade Monroe Series here:

http://cmsutter.com/available-books/

Chapter 1

"Mom, please. I have to get ready." Sam checked the time on the antique mantel clock perched on the shelf above the TV. Flanked by ivory pillar candles on carnival glass saucers, the clock had just chimed the half hour. It was five thirty. "Heather is going to be here in less than an hour. We'll get you feeling better in no time. Just let me do what I need to do."

He lifted his mother off the couch, slung her arm over his shoulder, and helped her into the wheelchair. She settled in with a painful groan. The wheels on the second-hand chair squeaked grudgingly against the nappy carpet as he pushed her down the hallway toward her bedroom.

"Okay"—he patted the back side of her bruised wrist— "let's get you comfortable, and then I'll set up a movie on the laptop. What do you want to watch tonight?"

"Let's go with *The Other Woman*."

"Sure, no problem. I'll get your dinner and juice ready then set up the movie. You'll be settled in and good to go in no time."

"Thank you, honey."

Sam noticed her eyes tearing up. There wasn't time for that. "It's all good, Mom. Let's get you into bed." He positioned the wheelchair with the front facing the foot of the bed and locked the wheels. With his mother's feet out of the way, he lifted the wheelchair footrests. He circled to the back of the chair and lifted her by the armpits then positioned her on the bed. "There you go, Mom." He fluffed three pillows behind her head and pulled the blankets up to her chest. "Comfortable?"

She nodded.

"Good. I'll be back in a few minutes."

He rushed out of her bedroom, cursing the time, and headed to the kitchen. Kneeling down, he browsed the microwave dinners that lined the lower freezer compartment of the refrigerator. That night, she'd get the meatloaf, mashed potatoes, and green bean dinner with a quarter-cup portion of apple crisp for dessert. He folded back the corner of the cellophane and tossed the tray into the microwave for four minutes. Back at the stove, he lifted the glass lid of the pot and gave the canned spaghetti sauce a gentle stir with the wooden spoon. With a few taps against the edge of the pot, he set the spoon on the ceramic spoon rest and replaced the lid. He watched as the red concoction bubbled gently on low heat. Sam pulled the bottle of red wine from the rack. That 2009 Chianti Classico from the liquor store near the hospital had set him back twenty-five bucks yesterday. He plunged the corkscrew deep into the cork, gave it a few twists, and popped it out. He left the opened bottle on the counter to breathe next to two wineglasses.

The microwave buzzer sounded. Sam opened the door and pulled out the steaming dinner. He gave it a stir and placed it back in the microwave for an additional two minutes. Meanwhile, he sliced the loaf of garlic bread lengthwise and dropped pats of butter into the opening. He wrapped the loaf in foil and set it on the counter. He'd put the bread in the pre-heated oven fifteen minutes before dinner. He looked around. Other than boiling the noodles and dumping the premixed bag of salad into a bowl, everything was taking shape.

The microwave buzzed a second time. Sam pulled a plate out of the cupboard and set it on the Formica countertop. He dropped the cardboard tray onto the plate and carefully pulled the cellophane wrapper toward him to avoid being burned by the steam. He threw the wrapper in the trash can. His floppy blond mane fell into his face again, and he pushed it back with his forearm as he prepared his mother's dinner. He reminded himself to trim his hair if time permitted, although from what they had said, the ladies seemed to like his appearance just the way it was. He relived those days when he had chosen his victims.

Corrine said my hair was rad, and Taylor said I looked like a sexy surfer. Typical women who are only interested if a guy comes across as polite and handsome and says he owns a house. Reality check—this house will be foreclosed on by the bank pretty damn soon.

He had met the girls at coffee shops on the opposite sides

of town. Small talk and flirtation led to lunch dates that neither woman ever returned from. Naively putting their trust in someone they barely knew had cost them their lives.

Sam carried the tray with his mother's dinner down the hallway to the second bedroom on the right. A bottle of apple juice, a plastic cup, a napkin, and silverware sat alongside the microwave dinner. He pushed the door open with his foot and placed the tray on the roller table that spanned the bed.

"Here you go, Mom." He forced a reassuring smile, just as he did for every meal he prepared and delivered into her weakened hands. Her recovery was taking too long, and every donor he snagged posed a risk. "Dinner is served. Are you feeling okay? Can you get by for another few hours?"

"I think so. Dinner looks good."

"Wonderful. I'm going to shower now and get changed. Company should be here in forty-five minutes. I have to be ready when she shows up."

Adeline's forehead furrowed.

"Mom, we've gone over this a million times. It won't be long now."

She waved him out of the room. "Go along, then. Do what you need to do."

"I'll get your movie and headphones set up after you eat."

Sam closed the door at his back and crossed the hall to the master bedroom and bath. Twenty-five minutes later, showered and dressed, he slicked back his chin-length hair with styling cream, patted aftershave on his cheeks, and gave himself a final once-over in the mirror.

Who could resist this?

He walked to the kitchen and pulled out a large kettle from the lower cabinet shelf. He filled it with hot water then set it on the stove's front burner. He turned the knob to High, pulled the package of spaghetti noodles out of the pantry, and set them next to the foil-wrapped bread.

The clock played the full Westminster chime. The melody indicated six o'clock had arrived. Heather would be there in twenty minutes.

Sam returned to his mother's bedroom and moved the tray table away from her bed. "Are you ready for your movie?"

"Sure am. It's two hours long, but I'll find something else to watch after that. I don't want to interrupt your evening."

"Thanks, Mom, and I'll check in on you in a few hours. Here are your headphones." Sam removed them from the side drawer and snugged them over his mother's head. "Make sure you keep them on during the movie."

"I will, dear. Have fun."

With the tray balanced across his bent arm, Sam placed the half-full juice bottle on the nightstand. He kissed his mother's cheek and closed the bedroom door behind him. He slid the tray into the three-inch-wide opening between the refrigerator and wall, then he stacked the dishes in the dishwasher. Gripping the package between his teeth, he tore open the bag of spaghetti noodles and dropped them into the rolling water. He didn't have much time. Sam popped the bread into the warmed oven and set the table. The loaded syringe with the safety cap on was ready and waiting in his back pocket.

The doorbell ringing made him look toward the foyer. "Here she is." He dried his hands on a dish towel, draped it over the oven handle, and turned the radio to a blues station. The doorbell rang a second time. Sam took a deep breath before answering. The large mirror hanging in the entryway confirmed what he already knew—he looked handsome and approachable, and that always worked in his favor.

He pulled open the door of the older Cape Cod and smiled widely. "Heather, I'm so glad you came."

Remember to emphasize your gentle nature and warm personality.

"Please, come in." He motioned for her to enter and closed the door behind her.

"Thanks for the invite, Sam. I'll admit, I was a bit surprised when you asked me over for dinner since we haven't known each other that long. It's odd that a single guy your age lives way out in the boondocks like this." She shrugged. "Thank goodness for GPS, right?" Heather glanced beyond the foyer. "This place doesn't look like a typical bachelor pad."

He cocked his head and smiled as he cracked his knuckles. "So, you've seen a lot of bachelor pads, then?"

"No. I guess that came out wrong. Anyway, something smells wonderful. I like the music too."

"The kitchen is right this way. Dinner will be ready in

about ten minutes, but I think a glass of wine sounds good, don't you?"

"Sure, lead the way." She giggled coquettishly. "Are you going to give me the nickel tour?"

"Maybe later, and I'm sure you'll like my man cave. There used to be a storage room off the garage, but now it's reconfigured to my liking."

"That sounds cool. I'm eager to see it."

Sam brought the bottle of Chianti to the table and poured. "I took it upon myself to buy red. I hope you like it." He pulled out a chair for Heather and one for himself then nodded.

She took a seat and reached for the glass. Sam watched as she gulped the wine.

Such a novice. You don't even know how to drink wine properly.

"I didn't see you at the hospital this week, so I was surprised to get your text yesterday. Where have you been?"

"I needed a little personal time off, but I'll be back next week. I took a short trip to Atlanta to visit my mom. She's suffering from an aggressive cancer that's causing infections and anemia. I needed to check on her."

"I'm so sorry to hear that. Sounds like you're close."

"As close as two people can be. I feel her presence all the time." Sam's eyes darted down the hallway. He needed to confirm that his mother's bedroom light wasn't noticeable beneath the door. "You didn't tell anyone you were coming here tonight, did you?"

"No." She gave him a look of disappointment. "I would

have liked to, though. I'm sure some of the women would have been jealous, but they don't talk to me much, anyway." She took another gulp of wine. "And because of the hospital's fraternization policy, I knew better."

"Thanks, I appreciate it. St. Mary's is very strict about that, and I'm sure we'd be easy to replace. I don't know about you, but I need the income."

She nodded. "I understand, and I do too."

"Good, so let's keep this budding relationship on the down low."

The timer on the stove beeped. Sam slid his chair back and stood. "Spaghetti is done." He carried the kettle to the sink, where he dumped the noodles into the colander and rinsed them. He turned off the stovetop burner, poured the sauce into a bowl, and placed it on the table. He did the same with the noodles. Sam reached into the oven and slid out the warmed bread. "Would you mind grabbing the salad out of the refrigerator and putting it in a bowl?"

"Sure, no problem." Heather stood and took three steps to the refrigerator. She gave the handle a pull and reached in. "What in the world is—"

She screamed and spun toward him as she swatted her shoulder. Confusion was written across her face when she saw the syringe in his hand. Sam had already sunk the needle deep into her muscle and pulled it back out. He dropped it to the floor and waited as Heather stumbled to the table. She tried to hold herself up, but her legs quickly folded beneath her.

"That didn't go according to plan—damn it. I totally

forgot about what was in the refrigerator. Sorry, Heather, but I did it for the greater good. My mom is far more important than you are." Sam watched as she fell to the floor, still clenching the bag of salad.

Grasping her wrists in his hands, Sam dragged her across the kitchen and through the laundry room. He shook his hair out of his face as he heaved her along the floor. "Hang on. We're almost there."

He opened the garage door and hit the light with his shoulder. The back of Heather's shoes scuffed against the concrete as he pulled her down the two steps and continued through the garage. His workroom was tucked at the back of the space, which was not the best location, but at least it was out of his mother's sight. He dropped Heather's arms, unlocked the door, and pulled her in. Once he stripped her naked, Sam bent to the floor. With a grunt, he heaved her onto the gurney he had used as a table. He fastened the straps across her upper chest, hips, and calves. The drug she had been given didn't knock her out, only made her unable to move. Sam snugged the straps tightly across her and secured her forearms and head so she couldn't budge once the drug wore off. He covered her mouth with tape so she would be silent. He gave Heather a quick glance. Her wide-eyed expression showed her fear.

"Yeah, I know, we didn't have dinner and you missed most of the nickel tour, but you are seeing my man cave now. At least I came through with one of my promises."

Sam immediately began the process—he had to work quickly. The paralysis drug, SUX, would render Heather helpless for only a short period of time. He pushed the thick needles into her carotid and femoral arteries and taped them down. After making sure there were no kinks in the lines, he followed them to the floor and placed each tube end into the neck of a sterilized half-gallon milk jug. Sam taped the tubes to Heather's skin and to the gurney legs so she couldn't jostle them loose. He flipped the valve and watched as blood began to move through the clear plastic tubes. Once her heart stopped beating, the blood would stop pumping out of her body. The entire process would take less than a half hour. She'd be dead before he finished dinner. He returned to the kitchen and ate. A long night lay ahead.

Sam returned to his workroom at seven forty-five. He glanced at the jugs—each was half full. Tubes once filled with dark red flowing blood were now empty save a few droplets here and there that clung to the inside walls of the tubes. He assumed Heather was dead. Sam approached her body and stared down at her face. Her eyes, wide open, were unblinking. She lay motionless. He rounded the gurney and opened the drawer in the old desk along the wall. He pulled out the stethoscope and hung it around his neck before returning to her side. With the earpieces tucked in his ears, he placed the diaphragm against her chest and listened—silence. He placed it against her neck and wrists too and heard nothing.

Thanks for the donation, Heather. Mom will appreciate it.

Sam crossed the garage and reentered the house. He checked on his mom before leaving.

Adeline pulled the headphones off and paused the movie. "Is it done?"

"It's done, and I'll be back in a few hours." Sam gave her a reassuring nod and walked away.

Heather's purse still hung from the back of the chair in the kitchen. Sam took it into the garage, sat on the step, and unzipped it. He found her keys inside. He pushed up off the step and opened the overhead. He pulled out the van then backed her car in. With the trunk popped open and waiting, he removed the tubes from Heather's body. He carried her into the garage and lowered her into the trunk. She was about to take her final journey. Sam climbed in behind the wheel, set her purse on the passenger seat, and drove away. He wouldn't be back home until after midnight.

As with the others, he dumped Heather somewhere in the Gary area and abandoned her vehicle in the worst neighborhood of South Chicago. He knew it would be dismantled quickly with no trace of its existence left behind. He always dropped off the cars and purses, void of any ID and cash, in that same Chicago area. A local bus frequented a stop two blocks away, and it took him within walking distance of the Illinois and Indiana Freeway Flyer. That city-to-city bus dropped him off within two miles of home. Sam walked the rest of the way. He was careful never to leave a trail or use a toll road that had cameras and plate readers.

Finally back home, Sam checked in on his mom one last time that night. She was sound asleep. He powered down the laptop, placed it on the side table, and turned off her light. In his workroom, he tightened the caps on both half-gallon jugs of blood and placed them in the refrigerator. He'd deal with the cleanup tomorrow.

Chapter 2

Our normal workweek began early on Mondays. Weekend incidents had to be reviewed, and we needed to determine whether any law enforcement agencies had requested our assistance. Spelling sat at the head of the table and conducted the usual back-and-forth with us about everyone's weekend activities before beginning our morning meeting. He opened the black folder his hands had been resting on. All of us had matching folders. He nodded, and we opened ours and followed along.

Inside were three files, each with a photograph paper clipped to the first of four pages of notes, including the initial police report, ME field exam, forensics report, and final autopsy reports. The photographs showed three deceased young women, each with the pads of their fingers burned away, most likely with some type of acid. Their nude bodies had unusually white skin.

Spelling put his fist to his mouth and cleared his throat. "Let's begin. Take your time reading the full reports after the meeting. These cases were called to my attention because of the similarities between them. At this point, we're assuming these three ladies met their deaths at the hands of the same individual because of their condition and the proximity of where they were found. All three were discovered within a twenty-mile radius of Gary, Indiana. The skin on their fingertips was burned off postmortem, and most noticeably, nearly every drop of blood had been drained from the first two bodies for sure, according to their autopsies. We're assuming the third will be the same. Each woman had bruising at their femoral and carotid arteries."

I shook my head. "That explains the freakishly white skin, and the bruising means their blood was drained while they were still alive."

Spelling continued. "That's correct, Jade. The first two women discovered, in order, were"—he looked at the contents of the folder—"Corrine Lionel and Taylor Dorsey. They were found two weeks apart, seven miles from each other, and both in December."

"Wouldn't the winter temperatures interfere with determining the actual TOD?" I asked.

"Absolutely. The killer could have kept them alive for months or killed them immediately and had them stashed in a freezer until winter to dispose of them. There wouldn't be an odor from decomposition or a way to tell when they actually died."

Cam spoke up as he flipped each page. "So you're saying they've been missing for a while?"

"The missing persons report was filed on Corrine in late October and on Taylor right around Thanksgiving. Corrine was located in tall brush near a quarry on December fourth, and Taylor was found on December seventeenth in an abandoned house in one of the worst neighborhoods of Gary."

"What about Heather Francis?" Val asked as she looked at Spelling.

"She was reported missing Saturday morning and found yesterday along a path at Marquette Park."

"Marquette Park?" J.T. flipped to the last page with the rest of us. "I've never heard of it." He took a sip of water then rubbed his nose.

"It's supposed to be very scenic. It's a large park along Lake Michigan with paths, beaches, and a pavilion for weddings, that sort of thing," Spelling said.

"Are any of the locations near each other? Could we possibly draw those parameters in a little tighter?" Maria asked.

"I'm afraid not. Each location couldn't be farther away or less similar to the other. Seven miles was the closest, and that was between Corrine and Taylor. Heather's body was found twelve miles from Corrine's location and nineteen miles from where Taylor was found. Of course, the areas are too remote, or in Taylor's case, too impoverished, to have CCTV cameras installed."

"Smart guy," I said. "He isn't establishing a dump pattern or location. He could live anywhere, but he's obviously familiar with the different areas of Gary. How were the girls identified without fingerprints, boss?"

"Not everyone is in the system, especially at that age,

unless they've been caught in criminal activities. Removing their prints was an odd act to begin with, but the perp was likely trying to buy some time. He wasn't counting on the DNA profiles. The samples taken from the bodies were matched against the DNA in the missing persons profiles of Corrine and Taylor. At least with them being frozen, their features hadn't decomposed yet. The parents were able to make positive IDs through photographs too. As far as Heather was concerned, she had only been missing for thirty-six hours before she was found. Other than the obvious injuries and unusual coloring, she still looked like Heather. All three ladies are being held at the government complex building where the medical examiner's office and morgue are located. Heather's autopsy is scheduled for today." Spelling stood and closed his folder. "Gary, Indiana, is requesting our help. Jade and J.T., familiarize yourselves with the information contained in your folders. Val, schedule meetings for Jade and J.T. at the police department in Gary and with the Lake County coroner in Crown Point. Get contact names for them. Let the PD know that two FBI agents should arrive by twelve thirty." He pushed up his sleeve then looked at both of us. "Yeah, that will give you time to take traffic into consideration and grab a bite to eat."

J.T. nodded. "Thanks, sir."

Spelling continued. "Val, set up hotel rooms for them in the area. Text all the information to their phones when it's done."

"Got it."

"Okay, you'll be leaving immediately. Good luck, and update me every chance you get."

J.T. and I grabbed our go bags and coffee and climbed into a fully fueled government cruiser that sat in the lot just for these occasions. Gary, Indiana, was close enough to justify the drive since it was only two and a half hours away by car.

I read and took notes as J.T. drove. Every so often, I'd run ideas by him.

"What do you think of demonic cults? Is that still popular with youths?"

J.T. rubbed his chin, as if in thought. "What was the age range between the girls?"

"Hang on a sec." I opened the folder and double-checked. "Okay, Corrine was twenty-three, Taylor was nineteen, and Heather was twenty-one."

"Yeah, still pretty young. Even though kids that age think they're smart, they don't have the best judgment yet. They're impressionable, and if the perp was close in age, well—"

"Well, what?"

J.T. raised his brow at me. "Have you ever known a millennial that didn't trust another millennial? That's like expecting a pup to be afraid of a car by instinct. Why would they if they've never been hit?"

"Good point." I took the final sip of my lukewarm coffee and jotted down notes. "So back to the cult thing."

"Sorry, I got a little sidetracked there. So based on the ages of the girls, their closest peers would likely be between eighteen and twenty-five. The outer range could be from seventeen, but probably not younger, up to possibly twenty-eight. And yeah, I do believe demonic cult activity is still popular across the country."

"So that could include blood sacrifices?"

"Uh-huh, although that would lead us into a really dark culture, Jade."

"But we have to go where the clues take us, right? Anyway, I'm just throwing possibilities out there, partner. You never know what goes on in this messed-up world anymore." I paused and thought about my next comment. "Don't laugh at me."

J.T. laughed, and I gave him a left eyebrow frown.

He raised his hand in protest. "How am I *not* supposed to laugh when you just said not to?"

"Whatever. So, what's your take on vampirism?"

He held back the second laugh. "It's Gary, Indiana, Jade, not LA."

I smirked. "Was there a point to that comment? Messed-up people can live anywhere. Look at the freak shows I've dealt with in North Bend."

"All right, you've got me there. I concede. Write that down too."

I did. "What about selling blood on the black market?"

"That's a good point. We'll check that out as well. I'm thinking since the police have had several months to conduct investigations on the first two girls, they might have covered those bases already, but it doesn't hurt to cover them again."

Chapter 3

"Sam, that stack of mail is really piling up, and it doesn't look like you've opened any of it. No reply from the state-funded health care department yet?" Her hopeful expression quickly disappeared when she saw him shake his head.

He punched the straw through the tiny foil circle on the juice box and handed it to her. "I checked for that letter first, and like every other day, no response." He knew what the rest of it was without opening it, and there wasn't much he could do. The bank had been threatening foreclosure for six months, and warning letters came in the mail constantly. Sooner or later, Sam and his mother would be kicked out onto the street. The electric company had turned off the power three times before Thanksgiving, spoiling everything in the refrigerator. At least they weren't allowed to do that anymore in the dead of winter. The thought of it all made Sam even more anxious. "Look, Mom, I'm trying to take care of you *and* go to work. I've missed a lot of days because you're getting sicker."

Adeline buried her face in her hands. "Why don't you

let me die? It would make your life a lot easier."

Sam took a seat on the couch and carefully embraced her. She was thin and frail. Her bones poked him when he held her close. "Don't talk that way. Let me check your veins, Mom."

She held out her arms. Bruises covered both of them between her elbows and the back of her hands.

"You need to drink more water so your veins don't collapse. I'm going to leave the IV ports in from now on." When the clock chimed on the half hour, he checked the time. "It's almost time for your transfusion. I'll grab you a snack before we get started." Sam pushed off the couch and walked into the kitchen. He took a package of almonds out of the cupboard and two individually wrapped cheese sticks from the refrigerator.

"Will you set the bag of blood on the counter as long as you're in there? I don't like the way it feels when it's too cold."

"Sure, Mom." He did as asked then returned to the couch and handed her the snacks. "Here you go—plenty of protein."

"I watched the news today, Sam. They found that Heather girl way too soon. Isn't she the one that came over Friday night?"

He waved away her comment. "You don't need to worry about that. The only connection I have with her is that she works at the same hospital as me. They employ over seven hundred people. The others were random girls, no connection at all. I'll be more careful from now on, I promise."

Adeline patted Sam's knee. "You take real good care of me, honey. What would I do without you?"

"Don't know, but we'll get through it together. I promised you that years ago and don't intend to fail you now. I did my research before we started this process. I know whole blood isn't the best thing for you, but look on the bright side. Your blood type is compatible with everybody's blood. I'm going to start giving you two smaller transfusions a week. It might be easier on your body. I know we can turn this around."

Sam mentally calculated how much blood he needed. At the halfway point of blood loss, his victims usually died. When their hearts stopped pumping, they were useless. No more blood flowed out, and the blood that remained clotted. He was determined to keep his mother alive.

"Anyway"—he turned to his left and smiled—"stop frowning. It wrinkles your fragile skin. Eat your snacks, then we'll get started."

After that light lunch, Sam helped his mother into the wheelchair and back to her bedroom. He lifted her to the bed, raised the back slightly, and arranged the pillows as she liked them. With several taps against her skin, he checked to see which veins popped up. "How about the back of your wrist? The port won't be in the way, and I'll tape it down really good. That's where I'll leave it."

"Yeah, go ahead." Adeline braced for the poke with the needle. Sam had become proficient at finding a viable vein on the first try.

"There we go." He placed the IV bag of blood on the

hook. "I'm going to change it to a half a pint, twice a week, so you won't have to be hooked up for so long. How about a TV show?" He reached for the remote and handed it to her. "I think your favorite soap is about to start. Need anything?"

"I'll take water and a straw."

"Sure thing." Sam checked the IV bag and left the room. He returned with a tall insulated cup with a straw poking out of the lid. "Here you go. I'm going out for a bit."

Adeline gave him a look of concern and swiped her bangs out of her face. "Be careful, honey."

He placed her cell phone within reach. "You know I will." Sam closed her bedroom door at his back. He changed into warm, winter jogging pants. As much as he hated the cold, he knew where diehard females ran along the public paths, often with their dogs. He had become acquainted with a few ladies who frequented the trails and knew at some point they'd come in handy. Plus, there weren't any cameras nearby. Sam pulled two bottles of water out of the refrigerator. One had a nearly invisible needle hole poked through the label and into the bottle, and the other hadn't been tampered with. He placed a black dot on the label of the bottle that wasn't laced with GHB and headed out.

Chapter 4

With our lunch finished, we were back in the car, and J.T. merged onto the Indiana Toll Road, also known as Interstate-90.

"Okay, ten miles to go. You'll take the Buchanan Street exit and go south to West Sixth Avenue, then turn left. No, scratch that. It's a one-way street. We'll go to West Seventh, turn left, then backtrack a few blocks to Polk. The police department is at 555 Polk Street, and it must be on the fourth floor. I'll go over it again once we exit the freeway. It seems simple enough."

"Yeah, okay. Did you get the texts from Val? There's plenty of time to check into the hotel first if it's close enough to the police station."

I pulled up my phone again and read the text Val had sent an hour earlier. I hadn't even thought of it until J.T. asked. I'd been busy trying to come up with reasons somebody would drain blood from their victims. In my mind, removing the blood seemed more important than the actual kill.

"Looks like we'll be checking in later, after we pay the ME a visit. The nicer hotels are near Merrillville, south of Gary. Actually they're just over halfway to Crown Point. Val booked our rooms at the Fairfield Inn and Suites off of I-65."

J.T. clicked his blinker when he saw the sign for the Buchanan Street exit a mile ahead. I craned my neck and looked over my shoulder. "You're okay to get over."

"Thanks." J.T. crossed two lanes of traffic and stayed to the far right. "So who do we ask for when we get to the PD?"

"Looks like Captain Mark Sullivan is the man in charge. I imagine he's our initial"—I made air quotes—"'go-to guy,' but he probably has a slew of detectives on the case."

J.T. took the exit ramp and turned right onto Buchanan Street. "Now where?"

"Go south until you get to West Seventh Street. Turn left, then another left a few blocks later on Polk. We'll head back north until we see the building."

"That's confusing."

"Nah, it's just because of the one-way streets. You live in Milwaukee. You should be used to it." I spread my fingers across the phone screen and enlarged the picture of the police department. "It looks like that building has a gated parking structure. That's probably our best bet."

J.T. turned left on Polk. "We're almost there."

I stared through the windshield and lifted my sunglasses. In the downtown area, the large buildings blocked the light, anyway. "We should see 555 Polk Street coming up in a minute."

We found the building and the entrance to the parking garage. Luckily, it was a manned booth. I'm sure that was only because the building housed government offices. J.T. pulled forward. When we approached, I saw the guard glance down at our government plates.

"Get your badge ready. You know he'll want to see it," J.T. said.

I unclipped my FBI badge from the lanyard and handed it to J.T. He shifted the car into Park, leaned forward, and pulled the bifold badge wallet from his back pocket.

"Afternoon, sir," J.T. said as he passed the badges out the car window.

"Here to see anyone in particular, Agent…"—the guard looked down at J.T.'s badge— "Harper?"

"We have a meeting set up with Captain…" J.T. looked at me.

"Um, give me a second." I checked the text again then leaned toward the window so the guard could see me. "Captain Sullivan, sir."

"One moment, please."

We waited as he made a quick call and mentioned our names. He held our badges then hung up. "You're good to go. The police department is on the fourth floor, so I'd look for an open parking spot on that level. There's an enclosed footbridge that will take you directly into the building. Have a nice day, agents." He handed our badges back through the window, pressed a button, and lifted the gate. He gave us a nod as J.T. drove through.

"Humph. They've got good security here."

"Don't be that impressed. It's only because this is a rough neighborhood. That's why Val couldn't find any decent hotels around here. I don't know if you noticed or not, but that guard was armed."

"Yeah, I saw that too." Once J.T. reached level four, I watched for an open parking space. I pointed at taillights backing up. "It looks like that car is leaving."

"Perfect timing." J.T. waited until the vehicle pulled out and drove away, then he slipped the cruiser into that designated visitors' spot.

"Hang on a sec. I want to call Spelling before we get out."

J.T. reached for his phone and checked emails while I made the call.

"Hello, sir. Just wanted to tell you we're about to head into the police station. We had an uneventful drive, and I'll call you back as soon as we leave here to go to the medical examiner's office. Okay, talk to you later." I clicked off, and J.T. silenced his phone and slipped it into his jacket pocket.

"What did Spelling say?"

"Nothing except to call him again after our initial meeting here."

J.T. pulled the keys out of the ignition and hooked them on his index finger. "Ready?"

"Yeah, I have the folders."

We exited the car, and J.T. hit the lock button on the fob. He pocketed the keys, and we crossed the footbridge into the police department. Inside, we approached the long counter that spanned the width of the waiting area. Four officers, two male and two female, sat behind the counter, busy with various duties.

A female officer stood and called us over. "May I help you?"

J.T. spoke for both of us. "Yes, thanks. We're FBI Agents Harper and Monroe, here to see Captain Sullivan. He's expecting us."

We automatically pulled out our badges because showing them to her was likely the next thing she'd ask us to do.

She smiled. "Reading my mind, are you?" She compared our faces to the images on the IDs then asked us to sign in. "Captain Sullivan should be out to greet you in just a minute." She pointed at the waiting lounge. "There are beverages and magazines over there if you'd like to have a seat."

I thanked her, and we poured ourselves coffee and paced. I had sat enough during the last few hours.

"Agents Harper and Monroe, I assume? I'm Captain Sullivan."

We turned to see a tall man, possibly twenty pounds overweight, heading toward us with his hand outstretched. He looked to be in his mid-forties with balding brown hair and a thin mustache.

I pocketed the sunglasses that were still on the top of my head and gave him a firm handshake. "I'm Agent Monroe, and this gentleman is Agent Harper. It's nice to meet you, sir."

"Likewise." He shook J.T.'s hand and pointed at the hallway. "Right this way, agents. My office is around the corner."

We walked the glossy tiled hallway with Captain Sullivan to a large glass-walled office. Two comfortable looking guest chairs faced a desk stacked sky-high with paperwork. He tipped his head toward the mess.

"See why we need your help?" He gestured toward the chairs. "Please, have a seat. I'll summarize what we know so far." Captain Sullivan plopped down on his desk chair. The leather let out a long objecting hiss. "I have two detectives working this case exclusively, and they can go over details more thoroughly with you. They took the witness statements, they've spoken with the families, and they've gone over the autopsy results with the medical examiner."

"You said witness statements?"

"Well, by that, I mean the person who called in the discovery in each case. We don't actually have witnesses, per se, who saw an assailant or anyone disposing of the bodies at the locations where they were found."

"Understood," J.T. said. "Are there any theories bubbling in your, or the detectives', minds?"

"Nothing that has panned out. We've had time, agents, since the first and second girls were discovered in December several weeks apart. Originally, we thought the first girl was an isolated murder until the second girl was found in that abandoned house. The manner of death looked identical in both cases. The serial factor didn't come into play until the third girl was found Saturday." He rubbed his head with both open hands.

I offered my two cents. "It seems like the MO has changed a bit. According to the missing persons reports filed by the families, and the dates that the first two girls were discovered, there was a span of a few months before they were found. But this last young lady was discovered in less than two days. That could tell us a number of things."

"Such as?" Captain Sullivan looked at me with what appeared to be renewed hope.

"One scenario could be that he waited to dump the first two victims because the outside temperature was still too warm when they actually died. It seemed like he tried to throw off the TOD by keeping those girls frozen. Otherwise their remains would have been decomposed. Now that the weather is below freezing, anyway, it doesn't matter. He can dump his victims right away. Another theory could be that the living arrangements have changed for the perp. He, or she, may not have a secure place to hide their victims anymore."

J.T. added, "Or, they may feel remorse and want to get the body out of sight. Another scenario could be they got word of unexpected company stopping by and had to dispose of the last girl quickly. See what we're getting at? Every new piece of the puzzle we find and put together leads us one step closer to the killer."

"Thank you, agents. That gives me hope." The captain stood. "I'll introduce you to the detectives on the case. Please join me in the conference room."

Chapter 5

Since Sam worked only three days a week and every other Saturday, he had plenty of time to scope out the best areas to find women. It wasn't the fact that they were women that mattered—blood was blood—but women were far easier to apprehend and control than men. Sam couldn't afford any problems along the way. Keeping his mother alive was too important.

He tucked the van into a spot at the far end of the parking lot. The paved trails weaved in and out, near busy streets, into the woods, and along a man-made lake. There were wide-open spaces, and that was usually where he'd find young ladies throwing balls for their dogs to fetch. That day, the parking lot was half full—just right. Too many people and he might be noticed by runners passing by. Too few and he wouldn't have enough options. Dogs were good icebreakers, but at times, they posed a threat too. He'd stay away from large dogs if at all possible. He sat in the van with the heater turned up high and stared out the windshield. People came and went, but he was patient and waited for the perfect opportunity. A lone woman running on the other side of the lake caught his eye. Fewer people jogged in that area since it was a distance away. Sam grabbed his binoculars and peered through them. It didn't look as though she had anything with her. He assumed she'd be grateful for a bottle of water. He slipped on his gloves, zipped a bottle into each side pocket of his lightweight jacket, and made sure his own bottle was on the left. He snugged his wool cap over his ears and exited the van.

It's time to get busy. Now to think of something to say that will cause her to stop.

Coming up from behind made the most sense. She'd have no idea how long he'd been running. It would give him time to chat and gauge how tired she was. Being a friendly, good-looking guy couldn't hurt.

He closed in on her as he rounded the farthest area from the parking lot. He glanced over his shoulder. All was clear. She was a hundred feet ahead—now fifty. When he saw the bench at the next bend, the location couldn't have been better. He'd pass her then cry out because of a leg injury. They'd sit for a minute, and he'd offer her some water as he drank his. The rest would be a cakewalk.

He called out that he was on her left as he passed by, then he stumbled near the bench and grabbed his leg. "Ouch. Damn that hurts."

She slowed to a stop. "What happened? Are you okay?"

"I don't know. I can't put any weight on my leg, and pain is shooting through it."

"Let me give you a hand." She motioned toward the

bench. "Here, sit down." She took a seat next to him. "What can I do to help? Did you twist your ankle?"

"No, I think it's a shin splint."

She nodded. "Those really hurt. Did you stretch and hydrate yourself before you started out?"

He grinned through the wince he had perfected. "No, but water is a smart idea and actually sounds good right now."

"It sure does."

Sam reached into his right pocket and pulled out the first bottle. He handed it to her.

"Oh, I can't take your water. You need it more than I do."

"I have two." He unzipped the left pocket and pulled out the second bottle. "I guess I had planned a long run." He chuckled and made sure she noticed the twinkle in his playful blue eyes.

She smiled. "It looks like your ambition may be cut short." She twisted the lid and took a deep gulp. Sam did the same.

"What's your name?" he asked.

"Molly Davis. What's yours?"

He did a quick scan of the area as he responded. "Sam—" He coughed into his hand to avoid saying his last name. He glanced at her shoes and laughed. "You'd be hard to miss with those lime-green runners."

"You like them?"

"Yeah, they're great. Do you come out here often, Molly?"

"About twice a week, yet I've never seen you before."

"Yeah, I'm a newbie at this location." He held up his plastic bottle to clink against hers. "To new friendships." He tapped bottles and took a drink. He watched as she did the same. Her bottle was nearly empty. "You must have been really thirsty. Want the rest of mine?"

"No, I'm good. Let me give you a hand back to your car," Molly said.

"Really, you'd do that?"

She pulled her cap down tighter. "What are friends for? It's getting colder outside, anyway. I'll probably just leave too." She stood and wobbled.

"What was that?"

She reached for the arm of the bench to steady herself. "I don't know. Maybe I stood up too fast. I'll be fine, but I'm going to sit in my car for a bit to make sure."

Sam pulled her tightly to him, his arm around her waist as they walked. Her legs were giving out. He had to get her to the van before somebody noticed them. There was one more bench before he reached the parking lot. With two people jogging toward them, he quickly sat down with Molly at his side. He leaned in and kissed her as the joggers passed. They had no idea she was unconscious.

Chapter 6

We took our seats around the oblong twelve-person conference room table along with the two detectives Captain Sullivan had introduced us to. Detectives Larry Andrews and Melanie Fitch were running the investigation on the blood-draining killer. I couldn't help smiling when I met them. The guy-girl detective team reminded me of my old partner Jack and myself, and even more recently, as an FBI agent partnered with J.T. The captain excused himself by saying he would let us get busy, but he asked us to meet with him before we left that afternoon for the medical examiner's office in Crown Point.

Melanie Fitch poured coffee for the four of us then took her seat. J.T. and I had received folders that were about half as thick as the ones in front of Melanie and Larry. That was a good sign. They obviously had plenty more to tell us.

"Where would you like us to begin, agents?" Melanie asked.

J.T. tapped the table with his pencil. "Let's go with the normal progression, one case at a time, starting with the first girl."

"That would be Corrine Lionel," Larry said.

I nodded and opened my folder to Corrine's pages. J.T. mirrored my movements and pulled out his notepad from the inner pocket of his jacket. I unzipped my purse and took out mine as well.

"Whenever you're ready," J.T. said.

Larry began by telling us Corrine's address and her parents' names. "Joe and Claire Lionel came into the station on October twenty-ninth and filled out a missing persons report. They said Corrine had left home the prior morning to go to work. Later that night when she didn't come home, they assumed she was at a friend's house. They called her phone a number of times, but it always went to voicemail. They realized something was wrong when they received a phone call from her employer on her scheduled Saturday to work. The company asked if she was sick because she had never returned to work after lunch on Friday, and she hadn't reported to work that next day."

I wrote as Larry talked. "Has anyone interviewed her employer?"

"Yes, we did, as a matter of fact. She worked at a lumberyard. Left for lunch at noon on Friday—nothing unusual there—but never returned. Nobody from Lang's Lumber has seen or talked to her since." Larry stole a glance at Melanie. "And you know the final outcome of that."

"And her body was discovered when?"

"December fourth, almost five weeks later," Melanie said, "at a quarry near the city limits. Kids messing around in the area literally stumbled over her frozen body."

"A horrible impression, for sure, that will likely linger in the minds of those kids. And because her body was frozen, there wasn't a way to know how long she had been dead?"

Melanie shook her head. "No, ma'am. She could have been lying outside the entire time or in a freezer for a month for all we know."

"How far away was her house from where she was found?"

Larry turned toward J.T. "Our notes say she was found nine miles from her home."

J.T. scratched his chin. "Yeah, that isn't any help. How old was Corrine again?"

Melanie checked her notes. "She was twenty-three, and yes, she still lived at home."

I added my two cents. "These days, many young adults live with their parents until they're in their late twenties. I guess doing that is easier on everyone financially. So you've interviewed her family and employer. How about close friends?"

"Give me just a second, please." Larry scooted out his chair and grabbed the pitcher from the shelf at our backs. Then he disappeared around the corner. He returned to the table a minute later with a handful of plastic cups and a pitcher of cold water. "Sorry about that. Talking a lot gives me a dry throat, and being a smoker doesn't help. Please, have some." He filled four cups and handed them out.

"Appreciate it." I took a deep gulp. It did help. "Okay, as far as friends?"

"Right." Larry picked up where he'd left off. "We

interviewed everyone in her close circle and came up with nothing out of the ordinary. I doubt if she would have confided with anyone at work about anything. The lumberyard employed mostly men. There was one other woman, quite a bit older than Corrine, though. Sorry, but we didn't find anyone or anything sinister going on in her life."

Melanie looked deep in thought.

"Melanie, is something bothering you?" J.T. asked.

"Not bothering me, really, it's just that Taylor's story is identical to Corrine's. Other than their physical differences and the places their bodies were found, the stories were the same. They had nothing unusual going on, no new boyfriend they spoke of, they both lived at home, and both disappeared after lunch. Her circle of friends and family said nothing unusual was happening in Taylor's life, either."

"So we'll hear the same story about Taylor that you just told us about Corrine?"

Larry nodded and looked at Melanie. "Yeah, wouldn't you agree, Mel?"

"Unfortunately, I would."

I checked the dates in Taylor's file and mentally calculated how long she'd been missing. "It looks like Taylor was found three and a half weeks after she was reported missing. She was discovered in an abandoned house in a rough neighborhood, and frozen, just like Corrine."

"That's right, and we don't think the dates the girls were discovered was important. We're assuming the only reason

Taylor was found sooner than Corrine was because that area was a known drug hangout. It had more foot traffic than the quarry did."

"The notes show Taylor was only nineteen. Did she work, or was she in school?"

"She went to Ivy Tech for their dental assistant program. According to her family, she was quiet and studious, hung out with friends now and then, and didn't date."

I took a deep breath. This case might be tougher than I had imagined. There didn't seem to be any leads or a person who stood out as someone questionable. The killer was smart. The girls weren't found near each other, they didn't have friends in common, and they didn't work together. This told us the killer didn't have a particular person in mind. It seemed that opportunity mattered more than anything else. Only one thing stood out to me—the women's age. All were relatively young, late teens to early twenties. That in and of itself could be a helpful clue. Our killer might be young as well, and the girls would likely feel more comfortable around somebody their own age. At that moment, it was all we had to go on. "Okay, let's move on to Heather Francis. She was discovered yesterday but last seen by her parents when she left for work Friday morning?"

"That's correct, Agent Monroe. Heather lived with her parents, who worked second shift. They had no idea she wasn't home Friday evening. When they came home from work, they assumed she was out with friends. They went to bed then realized the next morning her car was still gone. They called around, and nobody had seen her. So from

Friday after work until yesterday when she was found, plenty of time had passed."

"And according to St. Mary's Hospital, she was there for her entire shift?" J.T. asked.

Larry spoke up. "Yes, and they even showed us her work sheet. She left at six p.m."

"Her role there was?" I glanced up from my notepad.

"She worked in the lab as a helper to the technicians. She didn't have a degree, so she was more or less their gofer. Her parents said she was going to start school next semester but…"

I nodded. "We understand." I closed my notepad. "I guess that's it for the time being. We're going to head out to Crown Point. We have an appointment with the ME at two thirty. She's probably doing Heather's autopsy already, and I'm sure she'll have more to tell us when it's complete."

I handed the detectives my card. J.T. did the same.

"Let's coordinate our plans tomorrow morning," I said. "This afternoon we're going to do some knock and talks. Who knows, we might get lucky." We stood to leave the room. "The captain wants us to touch base with him before we leave. Would you mind making us a copy of your interview reports, Detective Fitch? We'd like to add them to our files."

"Of course, and I'll bring them to the captain's office when they're ready."

Chapter 7

J.T. took the surface streets over to State Road 53. From there it was a straight shot south, through Merrillville, until we reached East Ninety-Third Avenue, where we'd turn right. I pulled the map up on my phone to check the distance.

"The map shows it's only a half-hour drive. Hmm, this is interesting."

"What's that?" J.T. glanced my way.

"The Lake County Sheriff's Department is only a short distance from the coroner's office. Maybe we should introduce ourselves while we're in the area."

"It can't hurt. Even though the girls were all found within the city limits, I'm sure word gets around. There's a good chance some of those deputies and detectives live in Gary, anyway. Let's stop in after we talk to the medical examiner."

"Good plan. It'll be interesting to hear what the ME's take is on all of this. There might not be anything unique about Heather being found so quickly. It could be all about the location and have nothing to do with the killer's motivation. Marquette Park sounds like a popular place to go, and lucky for Heather, she was found sooner than the others."

"Yeah, you could be right."

I opened the folder again to Heather's information. "The report says she worked in the lab at St. Mary's Hospital." I gathered my thoughts for a few seconds. "The killer drained the girls' blood through the carotid and femoral arteries. Maybe the killer works at the hospital too and has medical training. They might have been coworkers." I closed the folder and set it back on my lap.

J.T. stopped at the red light and snickered. "Or the killer learned everything they needed to know online. These days there's a manual for every sick thing a person can think of. Did the interview report say who the detectives spoke with at the hospital?"

I opened the folder again and flipped to the last page. "Um, hang on." I ran my index finger down the sheet until I got to the part involving the hospital interviews. "Here we go. It looks like Larry and Melanie spoke with a few people in the lab yesterday afternoon, but the weekend employees aren't the same as the weekday employees. They got Heather's time sheet from the department head. The sheets get turned in to the payroll department on Monday mornings. The interviews aren't extensive, and certainly none were with her actual coworkers."

"Make a note of that so it doesn't get overlooked. We'll conduct a more thorough interview with the people she actually worked with."

Fifteen minutes later, J.T. turned right on East Ninety-Third Avenue. We had less than two miles to go. When he passed Main Street, I looked ahead and to our right. Then I checked the enlarged map on my phone.

"We're getting close. It looks like there's a huge government complex ahead on both sides of the street." I pointed at the sign in front of us. "Yep, the arrow shows the coroner's office is to our right." I checked the time. We had fifteen minutes before our appointment. "I hope she's finished with Heather's autopsy and can shed some light on a connection between the three girls."

"The coroner is a woman?"

"Yeah, she's the medical pathologist and the elected coroner. I guess she's been doing the job for quite a while."

J.T. parked, and we entered the building. We showed the receptionist our credentials and said the medical examiner was expecting us. We were led down a hallway to the office of Dr. Jane Felder. "Have a seat here," the receptionist said as she pointed at the small waiting area. It consisted of four guest chairs lined against the wall and a table full of magazines in the center of the room. "I'll see how soon the doctor will be available."

I nodded a thank-you, and she walked out and closed the door behind her. I grabbed the most recent gardening magazine off the table and took a seat.

J.T. glanced at the cover and did a double take. "That has to be from last summer. The ground is frozen solid right now."

I smiled. "Smart people live in warm climates year

round. I can wish, can't I?" I flipped the pages of the magazine and dreamed of summer's warmth and flower beds.

The door opened a few minutes later. A pleasant looking middle-aged blond woman entered the waiting area. She wore dress slacks and a burgundy sweater with an unbuttoned lab coat over her clothes. Embroidered above the breast pocket of her coat was her name, Dr. J. Felder, along with numerous medical abbreviations. We stood and shook hands.

"Please, agents, let's step into my office. I have an hour available to answer your questions, and I'll help as much as possible."

"We certainly appreciate that," J.T. said.

She tipped her head toward the chairs as she closed the door behind us. "Have a seat."

We sat in two matching guest chairs that faced her large Scandinavian-style desk. A half dozen framed diplomas hung on the wall behind her, likely there to reassure visitors of her credentials. To my right, several family photos, a blown glass vase, and dozens of medical books sat on a shelving unit.

I turned my attention back to the doctor. "Ma'am, have you completed the autopsy on Heather Francis?"

"Yes, I finished up about thirty minutes ago."

J.T. took over while I pulled my notepad from my purse. "We'll need to know your findings and how her autopsy compares to those of Corrine Lionel and Taylor Dorsey."

"I understand. When she was brought in, I drew enough

of Heather's remaining blood to do a toxicology screen. Unless a new liquid is introduced into the body as the blood is being drawn out, there will always be a certain amount of blood remaining. Obviously it was different in the earlier cases. They were in the elements for quite some time. Heather was found and brought to me quickly. Anyway, the tox report showed nothing unusual."

I raised my brows in question. "Nothing?"

"I'm afraid not, Agent Monroe."

"But if no drugs were found in her tox screen, how was she subdued? Nobody is going to lie still and let a person drain their blood. She had to put up a fight, didn't she? Were there marks anywhere else on her body like rope burns, tape residue, that sort of thing? Was she punched in the head and knocked out?"

"She did have light bruising across her chest, forearms, and ankles, which would lead me to think she was held down by something. It didn't cut into her skin, though."

"So would someone be lying down or suspended when blood is removed?" J.T. asked.

I grimaced at how morbid our questions had begun to sound.

"In a normal embalming situation, a person is lying down on a table. The blood is drained while the embalming fluid takes its place. But if this was some type of ritual killing, she could have been upright and suspended from something."

I took notes as Dr. Felder spoke. I looked up when she stopped talking. "But none of the bodies had embalming fluid in them, did they?"

She sighed deeply. "No, they didn't."

"What else can you tell us about Heather?" J.T. asked.

"Her stomach contents looked to be bologna, bread, and an apple."

"So possibly her lunch from Friday?"

"That sounds logical. As far as similarities to the other young ladies, Heather had bruising at her femoral and carotid arteries. There was no way for me to know when Corrine and Taylor were killed, though. Both of their bodies were frozen solid. If I had to guess by their condition when found, I'd say they were both dead for some time and out in the elements for several weeks."

"Other than obviously frozen, what was the condition of their bodies?"

She gave me a thoughtful smile. "I'm surprised you haven't asked to see the girls, Agent Monroe."

I raised my brows at J.T. "I haven't been in an autopsy room for a while, but it would definitely help us get a better understanding of the crimes. What do you say, partner?"

"I say absolutely." He stood. "Shall we?"

Dr. Felder led us down a short hallway to a closed door. Beyond that door, we continued down a flight of stairs to the bowels of the building. Every autopsy room I had ever visited had been in the basement. We walked through two sets of steel doors, each with a small window centered at eye level.

The doctor looked over her shoulder. "Just a heads-up, it's chilly in there."

I nodded. "Thank you, Doctor. We're aware."

A vacuum sounded when the doctor pressed a button on the wall, and the last door swung inward. We entered the cooled autopsy area, where two stainless steel tables stood dead center in the room. Each table had a supply cart at its side, filled with the medical examiner's tools of the trade. The walls were wrapped with stainless steel shelving and countertops. Built into the opposite wall were the refrigerated drawers containing at least three bodies—the latest victims. We followed Dr. Felder to that side of the tiled room. She lifted a metal plate that covered a list bolted to the wall. She ran her index finger down the names on the list.

"Okay, Corrine is in drawer fourteen, Taylor is in fifteen, and Heather is in seventeen. I'll pull the drawers out, then you can examine them side by side, so to speak, as I explain their injuries. Are you ready, agents?"

"Yes, Doctor. Go ahead."

We stood out of her way as she slid the drawers toward her. Corrine and Taylor's bodies were enclosed in body bags. Heather's was draped in a white sheet.

"Why the body bags?" J.T. asked.

"The first two young ladies' procedures were completed a while back. They've been stored in the morgue for some time. I had them brought in here to compare their injuries to Heather's. I'll return them to the morgue as soon as Heather's report is finished. Then she'll join them in there for the time being. We can't release the bodies to the family or a funeral home until the investigation is complete. Until then, they'll remain in cold storage. Mind you, the first two girls were frozen solid for who knows how long. In order to perform the autopsies, we had to keep them in a refrigerator for about a week to thaw slowly and evenly. I apologize if this is too much medical information, agents."

J.T. gave her the go-ahead nod.

"Well, if left out at room temperature to thaw, their skin and muscle tissue would have deteriorated before the organs thawed. It's purely science, but I needed all of the body to be the same temperature to perform an accurate autopsy. Heather's body, on the other hand, hadn't been exposed to the weather for very long. For her, two days in the refrigerator was sufficient. Hence, the reason her autopsy was performed today. Give me one moment to cover the girls properly, agents."

J.T. and I turned our backs and walked to the other side of the room.

"Okay, we're good."

We returned to the first drawer, where Corrine's body lay. Dr. Felder had already unzipped the body bag and had Corinne's private areas covered with white towels. The doctor pointed out the blackened area on the right side of Corrine's neck, where the blood had been drained.

"The same type of bruising is at her femoral artery, as is with the other girls too. What that tells me is the blood was drained while they were alive. Now, if you take a closer look, you can see pinching and light bruising on her forearms and across her upper chest. The same marks are found at her shins. The width of the marks leads me to think they're from straps."

I glanced at the autopsy tables.

Dr. Felder smiled. "And no, Agent Monroe, we don't strap down our deceased patients."

"Sorry, just natural curiosity kicking in. What kind of table would have straps on it?"

"No autopsy or embalming table would in its natural state. I'm sure the table has been altered to fit the needs of the killer unless the table's a gurney. They have straps built into them. Earlier, you asked about the condition of the bodies, Agent Monroe. When a body is found in the elements, temperature fluctuation wreaks havoc on skin, as do birds, foxes, coyotes, and feral animals. Corrine and Taylor's bodies were found in very poor condition, which is obvious. Luckily their faces were intact and in decent enough shape for the parents to make a positive identification. They weren't shown anything below the chins."

I thought back to all of the bodies that had been located outside during my years in law enforcement. I had seen it all. "At least during the winter the bodies are somewhat preserved."

The doctor agreed. "So you've obviously seen how bad summer discoveries look?"

I gave J.T. a sideways glance. "Unfortunately, we both have."

"Also, all of the girls were brought in nude, so I imagine that was the way they were disposed of. It could have been a way to lessen the chances of an ID from what the girls were last seen wearing or simply because the killer didn't want clothing in his way."

I asked if there were signs of sexual assault on any of the girls. The doctor assured us there weren't.

She continued. "As you can see, the pads of their fingers have been burned away."

"And that was done postmortem?" I asked.

She nodded. "Thankfully, yes. It looks like the killer might have dipped the fingers in acid and, excuse my bluntness, let them stew for a while."

"I can't even begin to understand that. All of the girls were identified, though, because of the missing persons reports filed on them, and their DNA."

Dr. Felder shook her head. "I can't help you understand the motivation of a crazy person. If I tried to get into the minds of every killer, I'd go insane myself."

"I agree, and that's our job, anyway. Are there any other similarities or differences between the girls?" J.T. moved on to the open drawer with Taylor, and the doctor showed us her similar wounds.

"Only that they were all young, Caucasian, and close to the same original weight. They lived in the metro Gary area, according to the police, and seem to be from the same economic and social backgrounds."

We approached a sheet-covered Heather. Her feet were exposed, and a toe tag hung from her right foot.

Dr. Felder lowered the sheet. "She looks better than the other two simply because the animals and weather conditions hadn't done a number on her yet. She does wear the same injuries, nonetheless."

I took in a deep breath. "I guess that's all we needed to

know and see. The police department has your findings on Corrine and Taylor, correct?"

"Yes they do, and I'll be forwarding my findings on Heather to them before the end of the day."

J.T. shook her hand. "We certainly appreciate the time you've given us." He pulled a card out of his inner pocket and handed it to her. "Please don't hesitate to call if anything else comes to mind. We'll show ourselves out."

We left the building having gained a short tutorial on autopsy protocol and an idea of what Heather had for lunch on the last day of her life.

Chapter 8

Sam thought twice about leaving Molly's car at the trailhead parking lot, but he didn't know which car was actually hers. He had taken the keys out of her pocket before rolling her in through the van's side door. Several miles from the trail, as he zigzagged through random neighborhoods, he pulled over and deposited the keys into a curbside garbage can. Then he continued toward home.

With a short grunt, he snugged the last strap over her body. "There, that should do it for now. I'll get back to you later." Sam turned off the light, crossed the garage, and went back into the house. The GHB would wear off in a few hours, but he wouldn't begin the blood draw until later that night. He wanted all of the drug out of Molly's system before he transfused her blood into his mother. He rapped on Adeline's bedroom door with his fist.

"Come in, honey."

The door creaked open, and he poked his head through. "How are you doing, Mom?"

"Good enough. The transfer is complete. Come on in and sit with me for a while."

He opened the door fully and walked through. "I'll get that IV bag disconnected. Did you watch your soaps?"

"Sure did, then I watched a crime show. I'm starting to get hungry, though. What time is it?"

"It's after four o'clock. I'm going to start dinner soon. How about hot dogs and macaroni and cheese?"

"We're running out of money, aren't we? I'm sorry I'm too weak to work."

Sam swatted the air as if to dismiss her comment. "Don't worry about it, Mom. I have other ideas of how to support us. It'll be fine." He turned toward the door. "I'm going to start dinner, but do you need help getting to the bathroom first?"

"Please, if you don't mind."

Five minutes later, and after Sam helped her out of the bathroom, Adeline sat at the kitchen table in her wheelchair. Sam made a cup of tea and placed it in front of her. He began making dinner.

"So what did you do this afternoon?" she asked.

"I needed to find a new person to bring home. She's sleeping it off in the workroom."

"Sam, you're going to get caught, and it just isn't right."

"As soon as the state health insurance accepts you, I'll stop. The killing will end, and nobody will be the wiser. We'll get back on our feet, I promise, even if it's in an apartment."

"What's your plan?"

Sam stood at the stove and stirred the milk into the drained noodles. With the cheese powder package open, he sprinkled it over the saucepan and began stirring. The water rolled to a boil in the pan to his right, and he dropped four hot dogs into it.

"Sam, I asked you a question."

"I'm still researching it but—"

"But what?"

"But there's no reason to let the women die. I'll keep them alive and sell their blood."

"Are you crazy?"

"No, Mom, I'm not." He tapped the spoon against the pan, turned the burner to low, and set the spoon on the counter. "I've researched this. There's actually an enormous market for blood, especially Type O Positive, which is a universal donor."

Adeline sipped her tea. "I imagine there is, but are you going to ask what blood type a person has before you snatch them? Plus, that's a black market enterprise. How would you get involved in that to begin with? And how do you know it wouldn't be a trap?"

"Like I said, I'm figuring it out, but I know one thing for sure. If there isn't a body for the cops to find, I'm less likely to get caught."

"So what are you saying? You'll keep live women here in the house and harvest their blood?"

He pulled two plates from the cupboard, scooped up a heaping spoonful of macaroni and cheese, and placed it on the first plate with two hot dogs. He carried the plate to the table and set it in front of his mom. "We'll see. I haven't made a firm decision yet. Do you want me to cut the hot dogs for you?"

"I'll cut them myself. I can still manage that."

After dinner, Sam stacked the dishwasher and wiped the table. He checked the time on the microwave as he passed by. Adeline sat comfortably on the couch, watching TV, so she was set for a while. Sam had been home for several hours. From his calculations of how much GHB Molly had ingested, she should be waking up by now. He was sure he'd hear her screams soon enough.

"I'm going to check on our guest, Mom. I'll be right back."

Sam exited the kitchen through the laundry room and took the cement steps into the garage. He hit the light switch and crossed the garage to the workroom. With the junk gone and the walls well insulated, that room was used almost entirely for draining his victims' blood, which would then be given to his mom.

The rusty hinges creaked as he opened the door and turned on the light. He stared at the table, where straps dangled near the floor on either side. It took a minute for Sam to compute what he was seeing. Had he really snatched a girl on the trails that day, or was he confused? What day of the week was it? There was no way in hell she could have escaped, yet she had. Molly was her name. He remembered that clearly now as he noticed two empty water bottles on the floor. Sam spun and looked at the chair in the corner. Her clothes and lime-green running shoes had been stacked there. Now they were gone. Only her underwear remained.

She had been there—he wasn't imagining it—but somehow she'd gotten away.

Chapter 9

We had spent the latter part of the afternoon speaking to the deputies and the lieutenant at the sheriff's department. Since we were in the vicinity, we wanted them aware of our involvement in the case. Nobody from the sheriff's department had been called in on the murders, but they were well aware of the three young victims that had been found. They didn't know any more about the murders than we already did. We left our contact information and took the lieutenant's card.

I glanced at the sky as we climbed back into the cruiser. "It's almost dark. Do you want to knock on a few doors before we call it a day?"

J.T. suggested we get the conversations with Corrine and Taylor's folks out of the way and worry about knock and talks tomorrow. "Why don't you call the numbers for the parents? Give them a heads-up that we'll be there soon. Let's begin with Corrine's mom and dad and tell them to expect us in a half hour. Call Taylor's folks too and set our appointment with them for six thirty. The families live how far apart?"

I opened the folder to double-check before I placed the first call. "The paperwork doesn't say the distance from house to house, only dump site to dump site. I'll check it on my phone." I typed in the addresses and hit Enter. "Give me just a second while it's thinking. Here we go. From Corrine's house to Taylor's is eleven miles. Looks like the best way to get there is on city streets. It's going to take a half hour between houses."

"Okay, set up Taylor's for seven o'clock instead. I hope you don't mind a late dinner."

"Nope, it's okay with me. Priorities first." I called the number for Corrine's mother. She answered on the third ring.

I heard her clear her throat before she spoke. "Hello."

"Hello, this is FBI Agent Jade Monroe calling. Is this Claire Lionel?"

"Yes, it is. Why would an FBI agent be calling me?"

"Ma'am, my partner and I would like to conduct an interview with you and your husband about Corrine's death. There seem to be similar murders in the Gary area, and we were brought in on the investigation. Were you aware of the other cases?"

"Nobody specifically told us about them. I did see something on the local news recently, but they didn't go into detail."

"Mrs. Lionel, it's imperative that we speak to you tonight. We'd like to come by in a half hour. Will your husband be home to join in on the conversation?"

"One second, please." I heard her blow her nose, then

she came back to the phone. "Yes, he's here. We'll be expecting you soon."

I stared at the blank screen on my phone.

J.T. turned his head. "What's wrong?"

"Nothing, I guess. She just hung up abruptly, and it kind of took me by surprise. Anyway, we're good to go. I'll call Taylor's family now."

I made the call, and they agreed to speak to us even though they said the detectives had already asked them plenty of questions. I assured Mrs. Dorsey there were always more questions that hadn't been considered.

We reached the Lionel home a bit after five thirty. They lived on a city street typical of an older neighborhood of Gary. The houses appeared to be from the 1920s or so. They were all two-story, average-sized residences, each with five cements steps that led to the stoops. Other than the different shades of gray, green, and tan, each house looked the same.

J.T. parked in the narrow driveway, behind what was probably the family car, and we got out. The uneven, cracked sidewalk took us to the steps and up to the stoop. I pressed the doorbell, and we waited. Footsteps sounded, and the porch light came on. A woman who appeared to be in her mid-forties pulled the curtain aside and peeked out.

From inside my coat, I pulled out the lanyard holding my badge. She nodded and came to the door.

"Mrs. Lionel, we're Agents Monroe and Harper. It's nice to meet you."

She opened the door wide enough for us to slip through.

"Please, come in, and you can call me Claire. My husband, Joe, is in the living room. Right this way."

We followed her past the dinette and kitchen to the back of the house, where we entered a room that looked to be an addition. A fawn-colored pug lay at the feet of a man seated on a corduroy recliner in the corner of the room.

I smiled as I approached him and shook his hand. "May I?"

Mr. Lionel nodded. I knelt and petted the adorable pup. I wanted everyone, including the family dog, to feel comfortable with our presence.

"That's Lucy," he said.

"Well, hi, Lucy. You sure are a cutie." I gave the dog a quick scratch behind the ear then pushed off my knee and stood.

"Please, agents, may I take your coats?"

I was happy to be wearing a blazer over my shoulder holster. I didn't want anyone distracted by the sight of our guns. We handed our coats to Claire.

"Thank you," I said as J.T. and I took seats on the couch. I waited for J.T.'s cue as I made small talk until Claire returned. When he pulled his notepad out from his inner pocket, I knew I would be asking the questions and he would be taking the notes. I was fine with that.

Claire picked up the dog and snuggled it against her side as she took a seat on an upholstered chair next to her husband.

I was sure the pup helped calm her nerves. "Shall we begin?"

Claire stole a glance at Joe. "Yes, I suppose."

"First, we'd like to establish what Corrine's daily routine was like, then we'll move on to her work environment and finally her friends. Sound good?"

Joe grunted with a nod.

"Thank you. Instead of me asking every question about Corrine's usual routine, why don't you just give me your best recollection of how she went about her day?"

"Joe, do you want to start?" Claire asked.

He shook his head then tipped his chin at his wife. "You'd know more about her day-to-day activities than I would, so go ahead."

Claire began. "Her normal workday at the lumberyard was from nine to five, Monday through Friday and two Saturdays a month. The hours were the same on Saturday except she was paid time and a half."

I glanced at J.T. He nodded for Claire to continue.

"She usually was up and dressed by eight o'clock, had a bowl of cereal, and left the house at eight thirty. Her routine never varied unless there was bad weather, then she'd leave a little earlier. After work, she usually came right home, gabbed on the phone until dinnertime, then watched TV until she went to bed. Sometimes she would go out with her best friend, Mia, maybe to the movies or the mall." Claire shrugged. "That was about it. She didn't have a huge social network."

J.T. flipped the page and continued writing.

"How far is the lumberyard from here?"

"Six miles, and it usually took her twenty minutes to get to work."

"Did Corrine ever mention anyone at work that she didn't like?"

"Sure, but we told all of this to the detectives."

I smiled. "Sorry, but it's important we know that too. All of the conversations aren't necessarily documented on paper. Sometimes things slip by that we haven't been told. Anyway, go ahead."

"She said Bobby Lang was a creep. He flirted with her nonstop, and she didn't feel comfortable around him."

"Did Corrine tell her boss about it?"

"Bobby was the son of the owner."

"I see. That had to be difficult. How long had she worked at the lumberyard?"

"Two years. There was only one other woman that worked there, the bookkeeper, and she was older. Corrine answered the phones. The only reason she stayed was because the job was easy, the location was convenient, and the pay was decent." Claire paused for a moment. "Agents, she didn't have a college degree. We couldn't afford that kind of expense."

"We understand, ma'am. So other than Bobby, she didn't mention anyone else that she had issues with?"

"Nope, she never said."

"Okay, let's move on. You said Mia was her closest friend?"

"That's right. They got together at least once a week. They were best friends in high school."

"Do you know if Mia was interviewed?"

Claire gave Joe a questioning look.

He responded as he repositioned himself on the recliner. "The detectives said they were going to."

"Sure. We'll check into that. Did either of them ever show an interest in the occult, any type of cult culture like vampirism, sacrifices, that sort of thing? Did you ever hear any of that mentioned?"

"Oh my God, no. Is that even a possibility?" Tears sprang to Claire's eyes.

"Nothing has been said, ma'am. We just need to cover all possibilities. Was Corrine on social media sites?"

"Yes, only Facebook, but we don't have her log-in information."

"Okay, we can investigate that. I think that's it for now." I looked at J.T. "Anything else you can think of?"

"That should do it."

We both stood, and Claire went to get our coats.

"We appreciate your time," I told Joe. I set two cards on the coffee table. "Please, if you think of anything else, give us a call. We'll show ourselves out."

We waited in the foyer as Claire gathered our coats. With our condolences and a handshake, J.T. and I walked out and took the sidewalk back to the car.

I clicked my seat belt as J.T. backed out of the driveway. "What do you make of the Bobby Lang thing? That wasn't in the police report. I wonder if the PD had the tech department check out Corrine's social media page. That wasn't noted, either."

"Don't know, but we'll find that out tomorrow. Let's move on to Taylor Dorsey's house."

Chapter 10

Sam was in a near panic. He had no idea how or when Molly had escaped, but it couldn't have been long ago. She would have been too groggy and unable to comprehend what was going on. She couldn't have gone far in that condition.

How in the hell did she get out of those restraints? They mustn't have been tight enough. I have to find her, and quick, before somebody else does.

He searched the garage in a frenzy, looking in and under the van, in the storage cabinets, and behind the stacked boxes along the wall. He raked his hair as he checked every nook and cranny. A cold breeze swirled in and engulfed the garage. He turned and noticed the door that led to the side yard was ajar. Sam smashed his fist against the wall and bloodied his knuckles. It was his fault he'd trusted the restraints while Molly slept off the GHB. He should have locked her in the workroom.

Sam slammed the garage door and stomped into the kitchen.

"What in the world?" Adeline called out. Sam glanced

quickly into the living room, where his mother craned her neck and looked at him.

He began pulling out kitchen drawers. "I need the flashlight, Mom. Where is it?"

"It's under the sink. Why? What happened?"

"The girl got away, and I have to find her fast. She couldn't have gotten too far."

Sam grabbed his jacket and ran out into the dark. From the side of the house where the door opened off the garage, Molly could have taken to the street or headed into the woods. Luckily, the five-acre parcel at the end of the cul-de-sac, with no neighbors nearby, afforded Sam some much-needed time. The home sat on the edge of Gary before the countryside took over. The closest neighbors in any direction lived five minutes away by car. Since Molly was impaired and stumbling through the dark, that could add another twenty minutes to her getaway time. Molly wasn't wearing a coat, either. She'd chill quickly in the nighttime temperature, which had dropped to twenty-two degrees.

Sam spun on his heels and ran back inside. He grabbed the van keys off the hook, climbed in the van, raised the overhead garage door, and backed down the driveway. Driving would make his search along the road that much faster. If he didn't find her wandering the street, he would head into the woods on foot. Frightened and unfamiliar with the area, she would probably try the street first, he assumed. Luckily for him, the night was pitch-black, and his road didn't have street lamps.

He drove slowly with the high beams illuminated. Sam

craned his neck to the left, then to the right, while he searched the shoulders and ditches along the quiet road. He drove west to the stop sign at the next intersection. He was more than a mile from his house, and he was certain she couldn't have gotten that far. He pounded the steering wheel and pulled a U-turn at the intersection. Then he headed in the other direction. By the time he reached his house, he hadn't seen any movement along the road. He continued on, this time driving east. At the half-mile mark, he spotted something ahead on his right. It could have been any type of nocturnal animal except this one was stumbling in the fresh snow cover and wearing a stretchy purple jogging suit. Sam slammed on the brakes and jammed the shifter into Park. He jumped out, rounded the van, and slid the door open on the passenger side. "Where the hell do you think you're going?"

The sight of him sent Molly scrambling into the woods. He went after her. They both knew she didn't stand a chance. She screamed for help while lumbering through the slippery snow. Sam was on Molly in seconds and grabbed her by the waist as she kicked and scratched, sending them both sliding into the ditch. As hard as she fought, getting her to the van was nearly impossible—he had to silence her. With a swift blow to the back of her head, he knocked her senseless and threw her into the van.

Within ten minutes, he had her nude body strapped down tightly this time. Sam shook with the chill of wet clothes and anger. Molly would learn her lesson this time— no mercy and no sedative. He'd drain her blood while she was fully awake.

Chapter 11

It was nearly eight thirty when we physically ended our workday. Our minds would continue on for several more hours. J.T. sat behind the wheel of our cruiser, his left fist jammed into his left eye as he tried to stay awake. We headed south on I-65, knowing our hotel was somewhere around Merrillville. Neither of us had eaten since noon on our drive to Gary, and my rumbling stomach reminded me of that. That morning, when we'd left Wisconsin, seemed like days ago. We still hadn't stopped to take a breath. Our packed bags remained in the trunk. I wasn't sure whether I needed to freshen up first or eat, but since I was with a man, I knew food was likely more important.

"Does this hotel have a restaurant?" I asked.

"I don't even remember the name of the place we're staying at."

We looked at each other and laughed.

"I'll check my text from Val again," I said. "It would help to know where we're going. Okay, that's right, it's the Fairfield Inn and Suites just off the freeway and Main

Street. It doesn't look like they have a restaurant, but there's plenty right in the area. Feel like Mexican food?"

"Sure, that sounds good."

"Okay, because there's a Mexican restaurant across the street from the hotel. Want to check in, or eat first?"

"If we check in now, I don't know if I'll have the energy to get back into the car."

"Yeah, let's eat."

J.T. turned right into the restaurant's parking lot instead of left at the hotel. We exited the car and entered the warm, cozy building. The tile floor and wall decor resembled an authentic Mexican restaurant, and the wait staff whispered in Spanish among themselves. We were seated near the fireplace.

I scanned the dining room as we got comfortable. "This place is really cute." I opened the menu and took a look. "The dinner choices look good too."

The waitress approached our table with two glasses of water. "May I get you something to drink while you browse the menu?"

"I'll have a Negra Modelo."

J.T. nodded. "Make that two."

I felt J.T.'s eyes drilling a hole through me. "What?"

"Your wheels are turning."

"Fine, they are, but I figured you'd want to eat in peace."

"No time for peace. Go ahead."

"Taylor's folks didn't tell us much more than Corrine's. Of course there are a few things we need to check out for ourselves, but I'm wondering why there was no mention in the police reports or from the parents as to what happened to the girls' cars."

"There wasn't anything in the folders about that?"

"Nope, not a word."

J.T. scratched his chin. "They've been missing for months. Where the hell can their cars be?"

"Good question, and why didn't anyone check into it?"

J.T. sighed. "And the parents didn't get them back?"

I shook my head then put my index finger to my lips. The waitress was returning with our beers.

"Have you decided on dinner?"

I gave her a smile. "Yes, I'll have the enchilada plate with black beans."

"And I'll have the tamales with refried beans and rice." J.T. handed the menus to the waitress, and we continued our conversation after she walked away.

I leaned across the table and spoke in a quiet voice. "Should I call the families and double-check before they go to bed?"

"Yeah, it's important to know."

I made the quick call to Corrine and Taylor's parents before our food came. Both families gave me the same answer. The cars were never mentioned as being located, and they were never returned.

"That's another thing we need to check on. What the hell happened to the cars? The vehicle description, if there is one, normally goes out with the missing persons reports, right?"

"Absolutely, and that's how the patrol cops usually

locate vehicles in some random apartment or mall parking lot." J.T. pulled his notepad out of his inner pocket and jotted that down. He chewed on the end of his pen. "We need to talk to Bobby Lang, find out about the cars, and what else?"

"Tomorrow morning we'll regroup with the detectives and ask why locating the missing cars was overlooked. I want to read the original missing persons reports myself and see if the cars were listed by description and plate number. Then, we have to find out exactly who they spoke to in depth, if anyone. We need to know if they've checked out social media pages, looked into the cult culture idea, and even find out if that type of activity is prevalent around here. Shit, we haven't even started with Heather Francis yet. We should also see if there's any connection between her job in the lab and the fact that the killer was draining blood through the major arteries. I want to know if the detectives have interviewed all of Heather's coworkers yet and if anyone seems suspicious."

J.T. jotted that down too then closed his notepad. He tipped his head to the left. "Our food is coming."

He spread the cloth napkin over his lap as the waitress set our steaming meals in front of us. I did the same and dug in.

Chapter 12

Sam stared at Molly, his face scrunched. He could feel the heat burning through his cheeks, and his heart was still racing. He couldn't believe she'd tried to pull that trick. She was regaining consciousness, and she'd get what she deserved after trying to escape like that. Sam had no intentions of getting caught. That one mistake would be his last.

He strapped her head down with a short rubber cord that stretched over her forehead and hooked on either side of the gurney. Her chest, hands, and legs were already secure. She couldn't thrash around, even if she tried.

Once again he considered the idea of selling blood, especially after that close call. Maybe he wouldn't kill her just yet. She would be of more use to him as a living donor. The work area had enough room for two more tables if he moved equipment around. He couldn't afford gurneys, but he'd rig up something else, maybe even chairs nailed to the floor, if he had to.

That new plan would give him plenty of blood for his

mom and extra to sell. He could quit his menial hospital job, lie low, and draw blood every day from the women he had captured. Nobody would be the wiser, and the search for the killer would dwindle. Within a month, it would be considered a cold case. The news channels wouldn't broadcast it anymore. The only time he'd go out would be to buy groceries and to sell the blood. As soon as the state-funded health care for his mom was approved, he'd stop killing, Adeline's health would improve, and life would be good again. Sam was sure of it.

Molly squinted and saw him standing over her. She opened her mouth as if to scream. Sam balled up his fist and cocked his arm.

"Do you want me to hurt you?"

"No. Why are you doing this? Why am I here?" she sobbed. Tears rolled down the sides of her face, pooling in her ears.

"Not your concern." Sam tossed a blanket over her body. "You're going to be lying there for a while. You might get cold."

He held her clothing and walked to the door. Her clothes would stay with him. He looked over his shoulder at her before leaving the room. The straps were as secure as possible without cutting into her skin. There would be no escaping a second time. Sam closed the door and locked it at his back before entering the house. He had more research to do. He had to know how much blood he could safely draw from any one body on a daily basis. He already knew the shelf life of blood when it was refrigerated and kept at a constant temperature. That part wouldn't be a problem. His most important task was to find a reliable source to sell it to.

Sam entered his mother's bedroom and unplugged the laptop on the side table. He carried it into the living room, where he noticed Adeline had fallen asleep on the couch. He carefully lifted the TV remote from her hand and turned the volume down, then he took a seat on the recliner. He watched as his mom slept peacefully.

Sam typed some key words into the search bar and began scrolling the page. He clicked on numerous websites and read for hours. He caught his head bobbing more than once as the night went on. He finally closed the laptop and set it on the coffee table next to his chair. He'd continue the research tomorrow and plan to find two more women. Sam checked the time. It was late, and Adeline still had to be helped to bed. He'd begin with Molly in the morning, then buy two used tables or chairs at a secondhand shop and figure out how to make them suit his needs.

Chapter 13

Our plan was to meet in the police department conference room with Detectives Andrews and Fitch at nine a.m. tomorrow. That would give us time to enjoy breakfast at a real restaurant as opposed to the inside of the cruiser with the console as our table. With the list J.T. had started over dinner tucked safely in my purse so it wouldn't get misplaced, we said good night to each other at my hotel room. J.T.'s room was two doors down.

"What time do you want to head out in the morning?" he asked.

I calculated how long breakfast would take and the distance from the hotel to the police department. "How about seven thirty?"

"Sure thing. I'll bang on your door then. Good night, Jade."

"Good night." I closed the door and looked through the peephole. Suddenly, a finger blocked the glass, and I heard a chuckle.

I called out from behind the closed door. "Go to your room, J.T., and you aren't funny."

"Yeah I am, and admit it, you think so too."

I heard him laugh as he walked away. I ducked into the bathroom and turned on the shower faucet. I hoped the hot, relaxing water would send me off to dreamland quickly.

Out of the bathroom fifteen minutes later and propped up in bed with pillows behind my back, I checked my emails and sent a short text to Amber to see whether she was still awake. If she responded, I'd call her and chat for a bit. If not, I'd try her at some point tomorrow. I turned on the TV as I waited and caught the tail end of the news. After five minutes of useless commercials, the anchorman began the final segment with breaking news.

"Channel 4 at Night has received word that yet another local woman has gone missing. Twenty-three-year-old Molly Davis is still unaccounted for after being absent from a party that was given in her honor. Family members say numerous calls to her phone went unanswered. The young woman's car was located several hours ago at the public trails along James Street, where she often ran. But after an extensive search of the area, Molly remains missing. At this point," the newscaster said, "foul play is highly suspected."

I sat up in bed and clicked the volume higher. Right then, I hoped Amber was asleep and wouldn't return my text. I needed to hear more about this latest missing woman. A photograph of Molly Davis came across the screen with her height, weight, and hair and eye color listed next to it. I paused the TV, took a picture of the screen with my phone, and continued with the broadcast.

"If anyone has seen this young woman, you are asked to

contact the downtown police headquarters immediately at the eight hundred number shown across the bottom of the screen."

"What the hell?" I dialed J.T.'s phone, hoping he hadn't fallen asleep yet.

He picked up on the third ring and groaned. "Miss me already? Don't you ever sleep?"

"J.T., I just watched the news, and they said another woman went missing today."

"No shit? Why didn't anyone tell us?"

"I don't know. It sounded like she was supposed to be somewhere tonight and didn't show up. Maybe it was only called in a little while ago. The news broadcast said her car was located at some public running trail, but she wasn't with it. Sounds like the family may have searched for her on their own without luck and finally called the cops. The police must have taken her absence seriously enough, given the circumstances, to allow the news to broadcast it already."

"I'll be right over." J.T. abruptly clicked off.

"Damn it." I dove out of bed and threw on my bathrobe. I didn't need J.T. laughing at my sheep-patterned flannel pajamas.

Within five minutes a knock sounded on my door. I squinted through the peephole just in case. J.T. stood on the other side, wearing plaid flannel pajama bottoms and a white T-shirt. I opened the door, and he marched through. He stared at me with threatening eyes. "Don't even."

I grinned and felt relieved. We sat at the table together.

"Here, take a look at this. I paused the TV and took this picture during the segment." I handed him my phone.

"Smart thinking, Jade. Tell me word for word what the newscaster said."

I went over everything I could remember with J.T.

"So, what do you want to do? Should we leave tonight's legwork for the locals, then address this new situation and everything else on our list, in the morning?"

"Yeah, I suppose so. Other than interviewing the family, there probably isn't much the cops are doing tonight, anyway. They may tow her car to the evidence garage, and that will give us a good opportunity to mention the other cars too."

J.T. stood and filled a glass of water for each of us then took his seat again. He passed a glass across the table to me.

"Thanks. You know there's a chance of finding this girl before he kills her, if she was actually abducted by the same guy who drains their blood. As of right now we don't have evidence that he's killed any of the women right away."

"True. I think we need to dig into the cult world tomorrow. We have to find out who in the area has a fascination for human blood. The cops can handle everything else on our list." J.T. guzzled the water. "Get some sleep, Jade. I have a feeling tomorrow is going to be a long day." He pointed across the room. "Turn that boob tube off, or you'll never go to sleep."

I closed the door behind J.T. and climbed back into bed. I clicked off the television. With a quick glance at my phone, I checked to see whether there was a return text from

Amber, but there wasn't. I reached for the lamp, turned the switch, and hoped to power down the gerbil wheel for the night and get some sleep. I closed my eyes and felt myself drift off.

My phone alarm buzzed on the nightstand. Instinctively, I turned toward the window to see if it was really morning, but the blackout curtains made it impossible to know. I hoped my phone was playing tricks on me. I rolled to that side of the bed, climbed out, then remembered that at six thirty in the morning, it was dark, anyway. I found my reading glasses on the credenza, put them on, and crawled back into bed. Squinting, with my phone cupped in my hand, I read the time—6:30. "Damn mornings. Why can't nights last a little longer?"

I scrolled through my emails, deleted the spam, and checked for texts. There wasn't anything from Amber yet. She was probably just waking up too. With a deep sigh, I threw back the blankets, started the four-cup coffeemaker, and hit the shower.

My phone rang as I applied the light makeup I wore every day. J.T. was calling.

"Do you like pancake houses?" he asked.

"Yeah, sure, as long as they have bacon too."

He chuckled. "I'm pretty confident most of them do. I'll be banging on your door in about three seconds." He clicked off and pounded on my door.

I peeked out, knowing I wouldn't see anything but a fleshy-colored finger over the hole. I pulled the door open, anyway.

"That wasn't very safe. I could have been a bad guy."

I laughed. "Then I would have shot you, so quit putting your finger over the peephole. I swear, you're just like a kid."

"Are you ready?"

"Give me five minutes to brush my teeth." I closed the bathroom door behind me and heard the television go on. I brushed, rinsed, applied lip balm, then dropped the tube into my front pants pocket and came out. The channel was turned to the morning news. "Anything on the girl?"

"Nah, but I'm sure we'll find out something at the precinct. Let's go eat."

We didn't linger too long at the pancake house. After two cups of rich coffee, a four-pancake stack, and four strips of crisp bacon, I was ready to go. I was thankful the staff was quick and efficient and brought our check as soon as we finished our meal. We needed updates on this new case as well as more answers on the existing ones. We were in the cruiser and heading toward downtown Gary by eight fifteen.

J.T. had received a parking pass yesterday when we arrived. All he had to do was swipe the card and the gate would lift. We pulled into the parking garage. The guard recognized us and waved us through. Parked on the fourth level, we took the footbridge to the building and entered. We checked in at the counter, grabbed two coffees, and made our way down the hall. We were intercepted by Captain Sullivan, who had apparently arrived just ahead of us.

"Agents, got a minute?"

I nodded. "Sure thing."

We were fifteen minutes early, so we joined him in his office. I took the inside guest chair, and J.T. took the one nearest the door.

"Have you been briefed on the latest abduction?"

"Not yet, sir. All we know is what I caught on the ten o'clock news last night. We haven't seen Andrews and Fitch yet this morning." I checked the time. "They're meeting us in the conference room at nine o'clock."

"I'll be sitting in on that too. We had patrol officers searching along that stretch of trails last night and canvassing the area. Nobody had anything useful to tell them. Fitch and Andrews were out there for an hour or so. The patrol units briefed them on what they knew. That's likely what we'll hear this morning. Go ahead"—he jerked his chin toward the door—"I'll grab some coffee and meet you in there."

"Yes, sir." J.T. and I left his office then reconvened with our coffees in the conference room down the hall. We took the same seats we'd had yesterday and waited for the others to arrive.

"Got the notes?" J.T. asked.

"Sure do." I opened my purse and removed the folded slip of paper along with my notepad. J.T. placed his notepad and pen on the table.

"Here they come." I tipped my head at the three of them on the other side of the glass wall. Detective Fitch opened the door and said good morning. She took a seat across from

J.T. Andrews sat next to me, and Captain Sullivan sat at the head of the table.

The captain leaned back in his chair and stretched. Then he locked his fingers behind his head. "Okay, let's hear the latest."

Andrews spoke up. "We walked the trails on foot until two a.m., sir. Four patrol units joined us with two canines, and three units in squad cars drove along James Street and around to the back of the lake. We didn't find a body, a piece of clothing, or anything that appeared disturbed. Everything will be checked again now that it's daylight. But up to the point where we called it a night, we didn't find a thing."

"What about her vehicle?" I asked.

"The forensics team has it in the evidence garage and went over it throughout the night. There's no sign of a struggle or unidentified prints inside."

"What was the position of the seat?"

Detective Fitch responded. "It was in the correct position for a woman who's five foot three, Agent Monroe."

I wrote that down then remembered from the newscast that Molly Davis was indeed five foot three. "I watched the segment on the news last night. What was the event that was supposed to take place in her honor?"

"According to the officer who took the statement from her parents, she was promoted at her workplace to assistant manager. Her folks were throwing a party for her."

J.T. wrote that down. "Where did she work?"

Fitch checked her notes. "At First Federal Bank on Sixth and Montclair."

"Did her folks say anything about the frequency of her running at those trails?" J.T. asked.

"Actually they did. They said she went there often."

"So maybe somebody had been watching her. Any CCTV cameras in the area?"

"Unfortunately not, Agent Harper."

Captain Sullivan spoke up. "So what's the plan for today on this newest abduction?"

"May I bring something up, sir?"

"Go ahead, Agent Monroe."

I took a sip of coffee to wet my throat. "First off, we have to keep in mind that this person isn't holding these ladies for ransom. Their lives are in danger every second he has them. That much is obvious from the bodies that were found. Because of the weather, we don't know how long they were dead prior to being dumped. He could have kept them alive for minutes, days, or weeks, except for Heather, but we just don't know. What I do know is there's no time to waste. We could actually find this girl before he kills her and drains her blood, if it is the same man. Does your department have anything at all on this guy, even one tiny clue to go on?"

The room fell silent.

"I guess I'll take that as a no. Has anyone checked into cults?"

"Cults? Suggesting what?"

"I'm suggesting that somebody has a reason to drain these women of their blood, sir. If these abductions were only about murder, the girls could be killed in any manner of ways and dumped. Chances are they wouldn't necessarily be nude, either. The ME said none of them were sexually assaulted. And what about their cars? What happened to them? Has anyone even looked for them? Corrine and Taylor's cars were never located, or at least they were never documented as being located. They could have been parked at the killer's home for all we know. Was there ever a BOLO put out for the vehicles?"

J.T. nudged me under the table with his foot. I felt my face getting hot, and he probably saw it.

I took a slow, deep breath. "I'm sorry, but these have been open cases since Corrine went missing in October. The police department isn't any closer to solving these crimes than they were on day one. And since Corrine went missing, two more young ladies have died. Just yesterday another woman disappeared under suspicious circumstances. I asked for one tiny clue, so I'll ask again. Does anybody know anything?"

Andrews responded with a touch of sarcasm. "In our own defense, Agent Monroe, Corrine and her car were missing. She could have been a runaway. Anyone at her age legally has the right to disappear."

I shook my head in impatience. "And nobody thought it odd that three weeks later, it happened again with Taylor?"

Detective Fitch replied that they didn't. "It wasn't until the bodies were found that we knew it was an abduction, and that was a good time later. The cars didn't seem important by then."

"You do realize it's only Fitch and me on the case full

time, Agent Monroe? You have to cut us some slack."

"I'd hate to have the families of the dead girls hear you say that, Detective Andrews. Anyway, we're here now, and we intend to make progress in days, not months." I looked at the captain, who hadn't said much during the meeting. "Captain Sullivan, if you're serious about catching this guy, I'd suggest putting more officers on the case." I glanced from Fitch to Andrews. "Who interviewed the department coworkers at the hospital where Heather worked?"

"They don't work the weekend shifts," Fitch said.

"And they don't have houses where you could have gone to conduct the interview?"

She gave me a blank stare.

"See where I'm going with this? Now back to my second question. Do any of you know anything about cults in the area?"

Captain Sullivan rubbed his temples. "There's a local group of troublemakers that go by the moniker Crimson Clan. You can take that name any way you want. I don't know if it's just what they call themselves or if it's an indication of some type of cult."

"Who runs it?"

"A punk by the name of Alex Everly. He's someone to start with, and he has an extensive jacket."

I wrote down the name. "Good, now what about people claiming to drink blood, vampires, that sort of thing? Are there vampire raves in Gary?"

Andrews laughed as he slapped the table with his open hand. "This is Indiana, not Transylvania."

"So you don't actually know?"

Andrews stared at me without speaking.

"Okay, Agent Harper and I are going to spend the day checking on those types of places. We'll conduct the interviews with Heather's coworkers at the hospital too. I hope when we reconvene later, you'll have found out something new with the Molly Davis situation. I'd suggest calling private tow companies and junkyards about the cars too, but that's just my opinion. The killer may have left his DNA behind." I stood and jerked my chin at J.T. "Come on. We have work to do."

J.T. and I left the building and headed to the parking garage.

"You know you're going to get a call from Spelling soon," he said.

"Why, because the captain is going to tattle on me for being too harsh?"

"Yeah, that's exactly why. You were out of line in there, Jade."

"J.T., we're here to help find the criminal, not babysit and do all the work for the police department. These are grown-up law enforcement officers. They're supposed to know how this works. It's been more than three months since Corrine went missing, and they don't have any leads at all? That doesn't sit well with me." I stopped in my tracks just before we reached the car.

"What's wrong?" J.T. asked.

"We have to go back inside. We need computers to work with and a location for Alex Everly. Let's head to the tech department. They can let us use their extra computers for a while."

Chapter 14

Sam had to work that day from noon until five. He rose early to get Adeline squared away with breakfast. He helped her to the living room and started the coffee. With her sheets changed and her freshly washed clothes in the bathroom along with the shower chair, Sam returned to the kitchen to start breakfast.

"Have you checked on your guest this morning?" Adeline asked.

"Yeah, she's asleep or pretending she is. After breakfast, I'll get her situated. Tonight, I'll start the gradual blood draw and rearrange the room. I need a few more tables or armchairs to actually set this up as an enterprise that will support us for a while. I'll see what's available at the secondhand shops."

"How can you handle three girls at once, Sam? They'll need to eat and use the restroom."

He smiled. "Have some faith in me. I can do it. Even if I only sell two pints a week, that's six hundred bucks, and I'd be staying way under the radar. We'd do okay on that much money, Mom. The girls will be given a lot of electrolytes and iron. I've researched this, and it'll be fine. But first I have to set up the room and find a couple more women." Sam pulled the skillet out of the lower cabinet. "I'm making fried eggs, bacon, and toast"—he looked over his shoulder—"your favorite."

Sam carried a cup of coffee to the couch where Adeline sat and placed it on a coaster on the side table to her left. He snugged an afghan around her exposed legs.

"Sorry it's cold in here, Mom, but the electric bill is too expensive. I have to keep the thermostat set below seventy degrees. I can get you another blanket."

"No worries. I'm fine."

"Want the TV on?" He handed her the remote and went back to the kitchen to flip the bacon.

"What's her name?"

Sam responded from the kitchen. "The girl in the room?"

"Yeah, her."

"Molly Davis, why?"

"They're showing her picture on the news. You didn't touch her car, did you?"

Sam came around the corner with the dish towel in his hand. "No, I had no idea which car in the lot was hers."

"Good, because the cops took it to the evidence garage at the police department."

He waved away the comment and returned to the kitchen to start the eggs. "They aren't going to find a body this time, Mom. That ought to confuse the hell out of them.

They'll think her disappearance is linked to someone else. It's better that way, and it'll earn us some much-needed cash. Want breakfast out there or in the kitchen?"

"Here is good, then you don't have to mess with the wheelchair."

"Sure thing. I'll sit out there with you." Sam carried two plates into the living room and placed Adeline's on a TV tray. He refilled her coffee and put a juice box next to her cup. "After breakfast I'm going to bring Molly in here to use the bathroom, but I'll blindfold her first. She doesn't need to see you. Are you all right with that?"

"I suppose for now. I can't wait until this is over with, Sam. I don't like other people in our house, and I don't like what you're doing to them."

"I know, Mom, I know."

Chapter 15

We reentered the building and read the directory panel on the wall. The tech and forensics departments were on the fourth floor but down a different corridor on the west side of the building. We headed that way.

"We've never met anyone in tech or forensics, Jade. We should have cleared it with the captain first so he doesn't feel like we're stepping on his toes."

I sighed and put away my irritation with the department for a minute. J.T. was right. We'd have more help if we played nice, at least on my part.

"Okay, I'll call him. I'm the one who was out of line. We don't even know the person's name that runs the show in there." I dialed the captain's office phone, and he picked up immediately. "Sir, it's Agent Monroe calling. I'm sorry for my attitude earlier and wanted to let you know we're standing outside the tech department. We're going to need to use a few computers in order to track down some of these questionable people." I paused and paced while the captain spoke. "Yes, sir, and we'd really appreciate that too." I clicked off.

"So, what did he say?"

I grinned and gave J.T. a poke to the arm. "You're a smart guy, John Thomas Harper."

He chuckled. "So you kissed and made up?"

"Yeah, pretty much. He's heading over here to make the introductions, and he's bringing along Alex Everly's file."

Captain Sullivan rounded the corner a few minutes later with a folder in his hand. I gave him an appreciative smile.

"Let's start over as a team. What do you say, Agent Monroe?"

"I say yes. Thank you, sir." I reached out and accepted Alex Everly's file.

"Come on." He tipped his head and pulled the door handle. "I'll make the introductions."

Captain Sullivan led us into the tech department. Inside, we found three long rows of tables, each with a half dozen computers filling the space and the same number of people sitting behind them. One shelf, built into the wall at waist level, held five additional computers with chairs in front of them.

The captain pointed in that direction. "Those are the extras in case anything goes on the fritz. Help yourself to them, but let me make the introductions first." Captain Sullivan tipped his head to the left, and we followed. "Charlie, can you break for a minute?"

A man who appeared to be in his thirties stopped the conversation he was having with a female at a computer station. He popped his head up and walked toward us. Captain Sullivan put his hand on my shoulder. "Charlie

Eustis, these are FBI Agents Jade Monroe and J.T. Harper. They're here to lend a hand in these abductions and murders. Charlie is in charge of this department."

Charlie stuck out his hand, and we shook it. "What can we do to help, agents?"

I smiled. "Glad you asked. First, we'll need to use two computers for maybe an hour or so."

"Done. What else?"

"How would you go about getting into somebody's social media account without knowing their password?"

He chuckled. "Yeah, we deal with that more than you'd realize. We can do it. All we need is a bit of information about the person."

I looked at Captain Sullivan. "I forgot to ask if we could pull up the name Bobby or Robert Lang to see if he has a criminal record. He's the son of the owner of the lumberyard Corrine worked at, and according to her parents, she thought he was creepy."

"We can do that while we're here. Shall we get started?"

"That would be great."

J.T. spoke up. "I'll take care of that while you give Charlie everything you know about Corrine so we can get into her social media account." He handed me his notepad that contained the information he had taken down at the Lionel house the night before.

I sat with Charlie and read everything we'd been told about Corrine. He wrote as I read off her birthdate, parents' names, dog's name, best friend's name, street address, mother's maiden name, high school she attended, and so on.

"Okay, I'll get started with this, Agent Monroe, and see if anything pops."

"Thanks." I walked to the counter where J.T. and Captain Sullivan sat. I pulled up a chair and took a seat to J.T.'s left. "Find anything on Bobby Lang?"

"Nah," J.T. said, "he's clean, just a creep, which isn't illegal."

"So now what?"

"We're going to pay Alex Everly a visit today. But right now I want to see if there's any information about Crimson Clan or other groups in the area who consider themselves vampires."

"I'll admit, I never thought my department would be digging in to something like that," the captain said.

I heaved a deep sigh. "Welcome to our world, sir."

J.T. leaned in closer to the screen. "What's this?"

"What?" I scooted my chair a few inches to the right. The captain did the same on the other side of J.T.

"Check this out. There's actually a vampire rave website, and it shows members, what state they're from, and the gatherings they hold. This could prove to be very useful information. Let's print out the names and addresses for members in this area and see how many people we're dealing with. I'm curious to see if Alex Everly is on that list." J.T. clicked on Indiana and narrowed the search to a twenty-mile radius of Gary, then he hit Print next to the member roster. "We have to start with something manageable and go from there. I don't want to spend too much time barking up the wrong tree." J.T. stood and retrieved the printout from the machine. He glanced down at the list. "There aren't many names in a twenty-mile radius, but it looks like they all identify themselves by aliases."

I waved off his concern. "We'll track them down. What's most important to know is if they're really drinking blood, and it they are, if it's human."

The captain clicked through the photographs posted on the website. "That's him."

I leaned over his shoulder. "Who are you pointing at?"

"Right there, that's Alex Everly. I know that face, but it looks like he's going by the name Massimo on this site."

I smirked. "Seriously? He must think highly of himself."

J.T. raised his right brow. "So Massimo isn't just a name, it has a meaning?"

"Sure, most names mean something. Massimo is a variation of the Italian name Maximus. It means *the greatest*."

J.T. chuckled. "We'll see about that."

Captain Sullivan continued reading. "He posted online about a ritual at eleven o'clock tonight at Dasher Point."

"Do you know the place?" I asked.

"Absolutely. It's an abandoned steel mill on the outskirts of the city toward the southeast."

"Okay, find out everything you can on Alex Everly and his known associates, especially the local people that belong to this group. We'll plan a coordinated surveillance on their activity tonight. If any blood shows up during their powwow, they're all getting arrested until it's tested to see if it's human or not. Let's meet back here later. We'll hold off with Alex's interview for now. We don't want to spook him." I gathered my things. "J.T. and I are heading to the hospital to interview Heather's coworkers. Have Charlie keep you informed about Corrine's social media site and if he was able to access it. Your detectives should follow up on the cars and Molly Davis."

The captain said he'd get more officers working the case. We agreed to reconvene in the conference room at six o'clock. We'd go over everything we'd found out during the day and plan our approach for later that night.

Back in the car, I pulled up the address for St. Mary's Hospital in Gary. "Okay, from here the hospital is about a twenty-minute drive. We need to get on Grant Street and go south to West Twenty-Fifth Avenue. You'll turn right there and go about ten blocks. Sounds like a piece of cake."

"Speaking of cake, when do you want to break for lunch?"

"Is it that late?" I glanced at the clock on the radio panel and saw it was eleven forty-five. "Damn, where did the morning go?"

"Okay, let's make a quick stop before the lunch traffic begins. I'm fine with a drive-through restaurant, so I'll keep my eyes peeled."

Thirty minutes later as J.T. pulled back into traffic on West Twenty-Fifth Avenue, we each had a chicken sandwich and fries on our laps. Our sodas sat in the cup holders.

"I hope dining in a car doesn't become my new normal," I said around a mouthful of roasted chicken and a swallow of soda.

J.T. nodded. His mouth was too full to talk. I pointed when I saw a six-story brick building coming up on my right.

"That may be the hospital. Slow down a bit and get in the right lane." I looked over my shoulder. "You're good."

He clicked his blinker and slipped between two cars.

"Yep, that's the place. I can see the sign from here."

J.T. turned in and followed the arrows for the visitor parking lot. We finished our meal before we got out. I balled up our wrappers then pulled the visor down to check my mouth and teeth. "Good to go." I grabbed the folder from my door pocket, and we headed to the main entrance.

We entered through the automatic glass doors and stood behind an elderly couple at the registration counter.

"May I help the next in line?"

I already had my unclipped badge cupped in my hand. J.T. pulled the FBI ID wallet from his jacket pocket. We quietly announced who we were, showed our badges, and explained that we needed to be directed to the lab.

The receptionist suddenly looked anxious.

"Is there a problem?" I asked.

"Well, yes, ma'am. We can't let you wander the hospital on your own."

"Sure, I understand." I panned the room and saw a friendly looking face at a desk near the waiting area. It belonged to the hospital guest volunteer lady. "How about her?" I pointed in that direction. "She can walk with us."

"I suppose so. Give me a minute." The registration woman came around the counter and approached the lady at the desk.

J.T. and I stood to the side and watched as they spoke with each other and pointed in our direction.

I chuckled. "Not very discreet, are they?"

"Nope."

After a brief conversation, the registration woman returned to the counter. "Go with her. She'll guide you to the lab."

"Thanks for the help," I said as she called the next person in line.

J.T. and I joined the volunteer, Nancy, and followed her to the elevator. She pressed the button to the fourth floor.

"Here to visit someone in the lab?" she asked.

I smiled. "Sort of."

The doors parted, and she exited ahead of us. "Right this way. The lab is two doors down on the left. Here you go," Nancy said. "Is there anything else?"

"That should do it," J.T. said. "Thanks for your help."

I opened the glass door. A tiny area with two chairs against the wall was to our right. Straight ahead, we saw a sliding glass window with a woman sitting in a cubicle on the other side. She glanced up when we entered.

"What can I do for you?" She pushed the glass to the side and snapped her gum.

We pulled out our badges again and held them up. "We need to speak to everyone that worked directly with Heather Francis."

She huffed. "That's impossible, they're working."

I smiled. "Nothing is impossible, dear. We need to speak to everyone, one at a time, starting now. We also need a private area to conduct our interviews in."

She rolled back in her chair and stood. "Just a minute." She disappeared around the door behind her.

"I guess we'll wait." J.T. took a seat, and I remained where I was.

She returned within a few minutes and spoke to us through the opened window. "We have nine people staffed today. Do you intend to speak to all of them?"

"We sure do, one at a time, like I said earlier."

"There's a small room where the employees keep their personal belongings"—she craned her neck out the window and pointed to her left—"right there. It's the best we can do."

"That ought to work. You can send the first person in, and we'll try to keep each interview under ten minutes."

J.T. opened the door to a room barely larger than a bathroom. Three folding chairs were stacked against the wall. We set up all three and waited. Minutes later, a young woman stuck her head in the half-opened door.

"Deb said I'm supposed to talk to you?"

"Sure." I motioned to the last available chair. "Have a seat."

"What's this about?"

"Heather Francis, but we'll get to that in a minute. We'll begin with the typical questions like your name, how long you've worked here, where you live, that sort of thing. May as well get that out of the way first, right?"

"Sure, okay." The girl fidgeted with her hair, twisting the ends one way and then the other.

I stared at her with my notepad and pen ready. "You can go ahead and start."

"I'm Sara Brady, I've worked here three years, I'm twenty-six, and I live at 142 Jackson Street."

J.T. stuck out his hand. "It's nice to meet you, Sara. Did you work last Friday with Heather?"

"Um, Friday? Yeah, I was here."

"Until when?"

"I worked the early shift from seven in the morning until three p.m."

"So you left before Heather?"

"I don't know. I guess so."

I wrote that down. "Did you share your Friday night plans with each other?"

"Not really. Heather and I weren't friends, and I went out with my fiancé Friday night."

I tapped my notepad. "Uh-huh. Any reason why you and Heather weren't close?"

"No, we didn't hang in the same circles, that's all."

"Okay, is there anyone in particular she hung out with?"

"Not that I noticed. She was the gofer, and nobody really paid attention to her. You know, kind of invisible."

"Right. That should do it, Sara. Will you send in the next person, please?"

"Yeah, sure." She stood and walked out.

I watched her leave the room then turned to J.T. "Nice girl, huh?"

The door opened again, and a woman older than Sara entered and took a seat. "Hi, I'm Joan. It's really sad about

Heather." She folded her hands in her lap. "I saw the segment on the Sunday news."

J.T. took over. "Thanks, Joan. Your last name is?"

"Miller. I'm married and have two teenage daughters."

"Did you and Heather talk much at lunchtime or during work?"

"No, we rotated lunch breaks so half of the staff was always working. Heather was kind of quiet, but her eyes sure lit up whenever she saw Adam."

"Adam? Adam who?"

She chuckled. "Adam Drake, our blood storage and distribution tech."

I shot a glance at J.T. and wrote down the name.

Joan noticed and waved her comment away as if to erase what she had just said. "It was one of those 'young girl with a crush on a married guy' sort of things. I'm sure it lasted all of five minutes."

"Is Adam working today?"

"Yeah, I saw him this morning, but he comes and goes throughout the day."

I sighed. "Okay, thanks. Please send in the next person." I scratched out a note to myself to find and interview Adam Drake too. I watched as Joan walked out and closed the door behind her. "I hope Andrews and Fitch are having luck on their end. These interviews all sound the same."

The door opened, and a young man entered and took a seat. "Hi. I hear you're FBI agents." He smoothed the wayward strands of blond hair from his eyes and smiled.

I returned the smile and relaxed for a minute. He seemed

pleasant and sincere. I pointed at his head. "What's your role here? I see you aren't wearing a hairnet like the others."

He touched his hair as if by instinct then tucked the ends behind his left ear. "I file the blood samples in alphabetical order before they're tested. I don't actually work in the lab with everyone else. I guess you'd say I'm the guy nobody sees."

"Were you and Heather friends?"

"Nah, I barely knew her. I was usually in the back while she ran around doing menial chores for the techs. We only spoke a handful of times." He paused and stared at his shoes. "But what they showed on the news about her was heartbreaking. Nobody deserves that fate."

"True enough. Did you work last Friday?" J.T. asked.

"Nope, I only work part-time. I had Friday off."

"And nobody in the lab was close to Heather?"

"I couldn't say for sure. She talked to the other employees because of her job, but I don't know if she was actually close to any of them outside of work. Like I said, we didn't hang out, so I don't know what went on in her social life."

I looked over my notes. "And you live where?"

"Just off of Second Street, about a half hour west of here."

"Okay, that should do it, thanks. Wait, hang on." I chuckled when he stood. "I completely forgot to ask your name."

He laughed. "Yeah, I get that often. I guess I'm easy to forget." His eyes twinkled playfully as he looked from me to J.T. and back to me. He stuck out his hand to shake mine. "The name is Sam—Sam Reed."

Chapter 16

Sam maintained his composure as he returned to the blood labeling room behind the lab. He closed the door at his back and felt the heat spread upward from his neck to his face.

Now the FBI is involved? This is such crap. The government and big pharma are to blame, along with the bureaucracy bullshit. They're the reason I have to resort to this madness. I was a normal guy before Mom got sick.

He paced the room as he talked to himself in a low whisper. "Okay, keep your cool. FBI agents or not, they aren't going to find out anything. Keeping the girls at home, safely tucked away in the back of the garage, is the answer. Nobody dies and no bodies are found. News of the deaths will eventually fade, and life will go on. People forget these things in time."

Sam spent the afternoon planning and plotting his next move. He had to be more than careful. Luckily, Heather was the only girl he had an actual link to, and he had played that well. Pretending he barely knew her seemed to work. The agents didn't question his story.

He took a deep breath, shook his strained shoulder muscles, and jotted notes to himself as he thought of his next tasks. He'd buy used chairs from now on and figure out a way to strap the girls still as he drew their blood. He envisioned the process like the one used at blood donation centers. The girls would have to sleep in the chairs, but that was a far better option than death.

Yeah, I'll make it work, and I'll stop at a secondhand store on my way home. They're bound to have what I need.

At five o'clock, Sam stood in line with the rest of the hospital employees leaving for the day. When he reached the time clock, he took his card from the slotted holder on the wall, slid it into the machine, and waited for the sound of the punch. Blue ink indicated the time he clocked out. With his time card back in the wall slot, he walked through the lunchroom, turned at a short hallway, and exited the employees' door to the parking lot. He repeated that same process each and every day he was scheduled to work.

He sat behind the steering wheel of the van and watched as everyone drove away, happy to be heading home, going somewhere normal, somewhere they could unwind and relax.

Not me. I'm going home to my own personal hell, but first I have to buy two chairs and have them ready to go. Later, I'll prowl the streets and grab an unsuspecting victim or two. They'll accompany me home and find out for themselves what hell is really like.

Chapter 17

J.T. and I finished our interviews with all of Heather's coworkers and acquaintances. We tracked down Adam Drake before we left, and he said he was surprised to learn of the short-lived crush Heather had on him. He laughed it off but admitted he felt flattered that a young woman like Heather would have a crush on someone forty-five years old.

"I didn't know her well, but we'd rib each other now and then when we passed in the hallway or ate at the same time in the lunchroom. She seemed like a good kid. I mean, my own kids are nearly her age. I was sad to hear of her death, and I sure feel bad for her family."

I handed Adam my card. "If there's anything else you can think of."

He tipped his head. "Sure thing, agents, and I wish I could have been more helpful."

I rubbed my forehead as we crossed the parking lot to the cruiser.

"Got a headache?" J.T. asked.

"No, I just wish that those interviews didn't feel like a waste of a full day of work."

"Yeah, I understand, but it's all part of narrowing down the suspect list."

I jerked my head toward J.T. and faked shock. "We have a suspect list?"

"Very funny, but actually I wish we did. At least I'd feel like we were making progress." J.T. pushed up his coat sleeve and glanced at his wristwatch. "We have fifty minutes before we're expected back in the conference room. Do you think that's enough time to actually sit at a table to eat dinner?"

"I don't know, but I'm willing to try. Worst-case scenario, they start the meeting without us."

Several blocks from the hospital, we found a small diner with a near empty parking lot. That told me one of two things was true—the food was bad, or we were sitting down to eat earlier than most people. I hoped for the latter. Inside, we found a dated restaurant with booth seating against the inner wall and a long dining counter near the kitchen. The place was definitely stuck in the sixties, but it looked clean, and the waitress wore a big smile. She called out for us to sit anywhere we liked. I guess I understood why. Only two people were at the counter, and all of the booths were empty.

We sat at the booth nearest the kitchen. The waitress would have a short distance to walk, and we could possibly get back to the police department on time. With the menus standing between the napkin holder and the condiments, we had already chosen our meals by the time the waitress walked over.

"Hi, folks. What can I get you to drink?"

"I'll have coffee, but I'm ready to order too. We have somewhere to be."

"Sure, go ahead, and I'll tell the cook to put a rush on the meals."

I almost laughed since there wasn't a backlog of orders waiting to be filled. There weren't any orders at all. "I'll have a bowl of clam chowder and an order of fries, and a cup of coffee too."

J.T. spoke up. "Make that two coffees, and I'll have the cheeseburger with fries."

She reached for the menus and placed them back against the napkin holder. "Thanks, I'll have him start your dinners right away."

I grinned at J.T. "She's cute."

He looked at her as she walked toward the kitchen. "Yeah, she is. So, did anything stand out to you during the interviews?"

"You mean like a gut instinct?"

"Yeah, like that."

"Not as far as the people we interviewed, but it seems weird that Heather didn't hang out with any other employees."

"I thought the same thing." J.T. pulled out his notepad and flipped through the pages.

"Something ring a bell?"

"Odd how Corrine's folks said she didn't have many friends, just Mia."

I tore the paper seal that covered my napkin, removed the silverware and placed the napkin on my lap. "I think it's because of their jobs. Corrine was employed at a predominantly male lumberyard, and only one other female worked there. As far as Heather goes, I think it's because a hospital lab is an intense place to work, and you can't afford to screw up. I doubt if anybody socialized during work hours. Plus, like they all reminded us, she was *only* a gofer. I hate it when people think they're better than others."

J.T. caught my attention. "Heads-up, the waitress is bringing our food."

I stopped talking for the moment as she set our meals on the table then walked away. "At least they're quick here. Let's continue this conversation after dinner."

We ate in silence, and to my surprise, the food was delicious. We were finished eating and settled up in less than a half hour.

As J.T. drove the twenty minutes to the police department, I thought about the case. We had three dead girls that we knew of and another missing. "We have to tighten up this investigation. Hopefully, the detectives will have some news on Molly Davis, the cars, and something that might be of interest on Corrine's social media page. That's if the tech department figured out the password. Did we scratch Bobby Lang off the list?"

"Yep, he isn't on our radar anymore. We can't arrest him for being creepy."

"That's true. Let's not overlook Taylor Dorsey. We haven't learned much about her. There's the surveillance later tonight too," I said. "We're going to find out more about the cult world than we probably want to know. I'll admit, that's a lifestyle I'm not familiar with."

"I hear you, partner, and we'll have plenty of time to go over everything before we leave."

Chapter 18

Sam pulled up a list of secondhand stores on his phone. The nearest one was only four miles from the hospital and in the same direction as home. Their website showed the store was open until nine o'clock that night. Sam made the call. He couldn't afford to waste time at a store that didn't have what he needed. The night was going to be busy as it was. He listened as the phone rang.

"Hello, Second Life Resale, Emma speaking. How can I help you?"

Sam smiled as he listened. The store name was more than ironic. "Hello, I'm wondering if you have any armchairs for sale."

"We do, but do they need to match?"

"Not at all."

"Then yes, we have five armchairs in various conditions for sale. I'm afraid the upholstery is stained on all of them, though."

"No worries, they sound perfect. I'm practicing the craft of reupholstering furniture. They're probably exactly what

I'm looking for. I'll be there in fifteen minutes." Sam clicked off and followed the directions on his GPS.

He found parking along the curb several stores down from Second Life. He scanned the street for anything or anyone who looked suspicious before getting out of his van. The area was sketchy at best. He noticed that most buildings had barred doors and windows, and he was thankful that the occasional ambient store lights helped illuminate the sidewalk. He'd make this quick, buy the chairs, and get out of the area to places he was more familiar with. Even South Chicago looked more inviting than that neighborhood.

Sam exited the van and clicked the fob to lock the doors. The sun had already dipped beneath the horizon, and the early evening air had a definite bite to it. He pulled his hoodie over his head and tightened the drawstrings to keep the wind out. Then he zipped his jacket and walked quickly to the front door. Inside the store, he scanned the area for the large upholstered chairs. He hoped to find some that were sturdy, with high backs and wide arms. They had to meet his needs. Sam browsed the selections as he envisioned how he'd keep the women still while drawing their blood. Several chairs that could work caught his eye.

"Hi. Can I help you find something?"

Sam jumped. He didn't realize someone had come up behind him.

She chuckled through the hand she had put to her mouth. "Sorry, I didn't mean to scare you—or laugh."

Sam sized her up as he began the conversation. She

could be a future prospect. "Yeah, no problem. I guess I zoned out for a minute. It's that artistic thing. I was picturing the fabric I would cover these chairs with."

"Are you the guy that called earlier about the armchairs?"

"Guilty. So, what do you have?"

She pointed. "Well, there's the two that you were fawning over"—she grinned—"and three more back here." She led the way to the rear of the store as Sam followed.

He imagined how the chairs would function as he gave them the once-over. "Ah, yes, these are nice too. I'm looking for the heaviest chairs with wide arms."

"Sure, and the condition and fabric don't matter, right?"

Sam gave her a long smile. "Not at all."

She tipped each chair back to feel the weight then patted the one on the left. "I'd say this one is the heaviest of the three here"—she walked back to the first two—"and this one is the heaviest of these."

"Yeah, and the arms are wide enough."

"Wide enough for what?"

"For comfort. I'll take those two."

"Okay, I'll get Jerry from the back and have him give you a hand loading them. Where is your vehicle parked?"

"Out front a few buildings down."

"Sure, but pulling around the back to our loading dock will work better. The front door isn't particularly wide."

Sam nodded and left. Ten minutes later, with the chairs secured in the van, he went back inside and paid thirty-seven dollars for the two of them. The clerk passed the receipt across the counter, and Sam shoved it into his jacket pocket.

"Thanks. It was nice doing business with you, and I hope you enjoy the chairs."

He looked over his shoulder as he left. "I'm sure we'll see each other again."

The buzzer sounded as Sam pushed through the rear service door and exited Second Life. His mind was a flurry of thoughts as he climbed into the van, turned the key, and pulled out of the alley.

Now to get home, secure the chairs against the wall, make dinner, draw blood from Molly, then leave to prowl for women. Thank God I'm not scheduled to work tomorrow.

He had plenty to do and still no idea who he'd sell the blood to.

Chapter 19

We congregated around the table, this time with four additional officers that Captain Sullivan brought in on the case. We had several hours to review what each of us had discovered that day. Then we'd switch our focus to the gathering Alex Everly had arranged to take place later at Dasher Point. We'd surveil them from a distance, but if anything looked off, we'd bust up their vampire party. As it stood, they'd be trespassing on private property, which would give us the legal right to move in.

Captain Sullivan began by introducing the additional officers. All four were men—Bill Stone, Clark Mills, Peter Jeffries, and Joe Christopher. Sullivan explained that they would be in charge of conducting in-depth interviews. The notes from each interview would be forwarded to us. That would free up time for J.T., me, and the detectives to really dig in and do everything in our power to apprehend the killer.

Sullivan put a fist to his mouth and cleared his throat. "So, Andrews and Fitch, let's hear what you discovered today."

Andrews began. "Well, the tech department did get into Corrine's social media site. There are a few more friends she had contact with, which we'll pass off"—he nodded to his left—"to you guys to interview. No mention of a boyfriend or anybody she had recently met."

Sullivan tipped his head toward Fitch. "Mel, have anything?"

"Yes, sir, and it isn't actually a new development but something we found odd."

J.T. spoke up. "We're good with odd."

She gave him a quick smile. "Anyway, we pulled up every garage, tow service, junkyard, chop shop, and statewide police department that could have come across, or had in their possession, Corrine, Taylor, or Heather's vehicles. Not one facility in Indiana had their plate numbers or VINs on file. Of course, a chop shop wouldn't admit it, anyway."

"Humph," J.T. said. He gave his cheek a thorough scratch. Yesterday's stubble was popping through. "That is odd, especially with Heather's vehicle. You'd think it would be sitting somewhere with a half dozen tickets on it, or the city would have had it towed. And with Heather's case being a recent investigation, why hasn't a BOLO hit on the car?"

I added my thoughts. "Unfortunately, it takes months before cars are reported as parked where they don't belong. That's especially true in large apartment complexes. Nobody notices an extra car sitting around as long as it isn't parked in somebody's assigned spot. We all know it could take time to find those cars, but it's time we don't have."

"Nothing turned up on Molly's car, but hers wasn't moved. You'd definitely think since the cars weren't located where the bodies were found, the obvious explanation would be that the killer drove them away," Fitch said.

"Exactly, but that would also tell us he had to leave a trail behind. Either someone picked him up, meaning an accomplice, or—"

Sullivan interrupted with a moan. "Please don't say that word."

"Sorry, sir, but I had to throw it out there. So, either somebody picked him up, he walked back home from the spot he left the vehicles at, or he took some type of public transportation."

"Maybe you're on to something, Jade," Sullivan said as he sat upright.

"Possibly, but the trail has likely gone cold on Corrine and Taylor's cars. It's been months."

Andrews and Fitch looked down at the table and fidgeted. It took a moment before Andrews spoke up. "That was our oversight. We messed up and let valuable information get by us."

"Well, we still have Heather's vehicle to look for. Chances are, since the others weren't found, the killer may have taken her car to the same place he dumped the first two. Why change something if it has worked to perfection?"

Captain Sullivan wrote that down. "Mills and Stone, follow up with that. Triple-check to make sure Heather Francis's car isn't anywhere in Indiana, then move on to

Illinois. I-90 runs through both states and they each use tollbooth cameras and plate readers."

Sullivan turned his focus to J.T. and me. I began. "We interviewed every coworker that had direct access to Heather. Not one person seemed any more suspicious than the next. As with Taylor and Corrine, Heather's personality came across in the interviews as someone who had few friends and seemed somewhat introverted. The killer may be preying on that type of victim, but how he would know that without being an acquaintance baffles me."

"It could be luck, nothing more," Stone said. "He could have been watching any one of the girls for some time from a distance. It's possible he overheard conversations, watched their mannerisms, and so on. You can generally tell if someone is demure and approachable before too long."

"Good point, Stone. Okay, in the morning I want you and you"—Sullivan pointed at Peter Jeffries and Joe Christopher—"to keep conducting interviews. Hit the neighborhoods of all the girls, see if the parents of Heather and Taylor know social media sites their daughters had accounts for, pull the phone records for each girl, and so on. You get my drift? Mills and Stone, find out where those cars went. How well did we search Marquette Park, where Heather was found, and the trail system where Molly Davis ran?"

Andrews answered, "Pretty well, sir."

"Not good enough. Do it again."

I took another turn. "Tomorrow, J.T. and I are going to talk to Molly Davis's parents and workmates ourselves. If new information comes in from everyone else, we'll address that by need and urgency. I'd suggest since Heather and Molly are both very new cases, we keep their profiles and pictures running on the news. Has anything come in on the tip lines?"

"As of before this meeting began, nothing with substance, even though our officers are following up on every lead," Sullivan said.

I drummed my fingers on the table as I thought. "Did Molly's parents know what she was wearing when she left home?"

"They said they didn't see her leave."

"But they acknowledged Molly ran often, correct?"

"Yes," Andrews said, "according to the statement they gave."

"Then they should know what she normally wears to run. Most people who are real runners have several outfits they rotate. They could go through her clothes and see what's missing."

"Not a bad idea. Fitch and Andrews, follow up on that tomorrow." Sullivan leaned back and stretched, then he slapped the table with his open hands. "Take a ten-minute break, then we'll move on to our surveillance plan for Dasher Point and Alex Everly."

We stood and stretched too, then everyone headed for the door. J.T. followed at my back.

"Want a coffee?" he asked as we entered the hallway.

"Yeah, I'm going to need a pick-me-up. We still have a long night ahead of us." We turned right at the first corridor. The break room was straight ahead. Several vending machines lined the wall, and a half pot of coffee sat on the warming tray of the turned-off coffeemaker.

I looked at the coffee suspiciously. "I'm going with the vending machine coffee. That stuff in the pot was probably from this morning, and it's cold, anyway. Want a candy bar or chips?" I opened the zipper on my coin purse and dumped all the change out onto the table. Quarters spun and pennies rolled and fell to the floor. "Damn coins are weighing my purse down."

"So it's necessary to get rid of them?"

"Yeah, kind of."

"Okay, I'll take a bag of chips, then. You know, all of those coins dumped into a sock and tied would make a pretty good weapon."

"Hmm, but so does my Glock 22, and I have a lot more range with that." I pulled my coffee from the door at the bottom of the machine, handed J.T. three quarters for his, and moved on to the snack machine.

Five minutes later, everyone was back in their seat with a cup of coffee in front of them. I tossed six bags of chips onto the table and told the group to help themselves.

Captain Sullivan slid color photos of the abandoned steel mill across the table. "Have any of you officers ever been out to Dasher Point?" Grumbling and headshakes confirmed that nobody had. "Well, like most abandoned steel mills, Dasher Point is large and has many areas where a gathering can take place, inside or out. The mill has been closed for thirty years, and the structure is dangerous and rickety. My best guess would be the gathering, or ritual, as they call it—" He stopped and looked across the table at Andrews. "How many people were going to be at this hoedown according to that site Alex posted on?"

"Between twenty and thirty, sir."

Sullivan rolled his neck. "Okay, with that many people, they'll be hard to miss. I'm sure they'll either be outside near the structure where they can build a bonfire or on the lower level where the floors have succumbed to the dirt. We'll watch for fire and listen for chanting, or whatever those weirdos do. I've done a little research, but since this is just a theory, I don't want to spend too much time on it. Anyway, they either feed on each other's blood or have safe donated blood they share. Apparently, they believe they need to drink blood for energy. Most of the time they dress the part, especially when they go to the vampire dance raves. I think—but don't quote me on it—the rituals done outside are mostly chanting their beliefs and sharing blood, usually with a bonfire for warmth or ambience."

I shook my head, and Sullivan turned to me.

"Jade, what are you thinking?"

"If they're just drinking each other's blood, with permission, then the MO wouldn't fit. They aren't killing random people to drain and drink their blood."

"Maybe or maybe not. The larger these covens get and the more popular that vampire lifestyle becomes, the more blood they'll want. Some so-called vampires drink blood daily, others less often. No matter what, they're trespassing, and that will give us the right to investigate into their activities. If they have extra blood, it could be animal or human, and if it is human, we're going to find out where it came from." He jabbed one of the photos with his index finger. "There are several ways to get into this place. I'm guessing they'll take the most well-known, easy route in, and that's what used to be the main entrance. It's overgrown but drivable. We'll go in through the back. It's a road the big trucks used to go in and out of to the loading docks. They probably don't know that road exists. We'll park and walk in, so make sure you're dressed for the weather. Wear sturdy shoes, gloves, and a warm hat if you have one. We've got plenty of binoculars to pass around. We'll watch their activity and see what shakes loose. No matter what, Alex Everly, or as he likes to call himself, *Massimo*, has some explaining to do."

Chapter 20

We moved in, and other than the occasional crunch of a rock under tires, our approach was smooth and silent. Each cruiser followed the one before it, apparently unnoticed by the group farther ahead that would soon be under surveillance. We parked and exited our cars several football field lengths from the twenty to thirty people we saw through our binoculars. We crept in closer on foot. Nine of us had positioned ourselves about a hundred yards back from the deserted mill. Crouched behind stacks of rusted metal that had been thrown in a waste heap, we had been surveilling the group for twenty minutes. With binoculars pressed against our eyes, we watched as they piled old boards and two-by-fours ten feet high to start their bonfire. One person was clearly in charge. I whispered to Sullivan and asked if that was Alex. He gave me a nod.

They dressed in similar fashion, each wearing black pants, a coat, and shoes that resembled combat boots. Through the binoculars, they looked like any other person under thirty and weren't donning the white skin, fangs, or capes seen at Halloween. Maybe they chose to look more exotic only when out in public at dance clubs. They circled the now ten-foot-tall flames with their hands locked. From our position, we heard the sounds of chanting, or possibly prayers, but we couldn't make out the words. For all I knew, they could be reciting something in Latin or Romanian.

I kept my binoculars focused on Alex. If anyone were to call out commands or start the blood ritual, it would likely be him. As they completed their chant, they lifted their heads and split into several groups.

"It looks like something is about to go down," J.T. whispered.

Several men approached a group of antique looking wooden boxes trimmed with brass nail heads. The boxes sat ten feet to their backs. Four other men went to the double rear doors of an extended van and lifted out a long wooden table. With two men at each end, they carried it to within ten feet of the fire and set it on the ground. Two chairs were lifted out of the van and placed at either end of the table.

I adjusted the focus to get the best clarity. Bonfire smoke clouded their actions at times, but now Alex was back in view. He was seated on the far right end of the table, and another man sat on the left.

"Who the hell is that—his underboss?" I turned to look at J.T., who was shoulder to shoulder with me. He shrugged.

Several of Alex's minions placed the wooden boxes in the center of the table. We had a clear view of their movements.

Alex stood and, with his right hand, drew a symbol in the air. The group mirrored what he had just done, and they waited as Alex approached the first box to his left. He removed eight knives that looked to be about six inches long. The man who had been seated on the left end of the table rose and approached Alex. He stood at his side and removed eight hand towels from a bag slung over his shoulder. He placed them on the table next to the knives. One by one, a line of people approached the table, took a knife and towel, and knelt beside another person sitting on the ground.

"Here we go. Those people sitting must be the donors," Sullivan said. "The ones with the knives are going to cut them and drink their blood."

I was glued to my binoculars. "Humph…this stuff actually takes place in our modern world. This is the first time I've ever witnessed such an act."

"That holds true for all of us, I expect," Sullivan said.

I wiped the lenses of my binoculars with the thumb of my glove. The damp cold air had fogged them over. "That's so messed up. What I want to know is what's inside that big box."

After more chanting, that particular ritual began. We couldn't see the actual cutting, but I did get a glimpse of people pushing back their sleeves. Moments later, the group that performed the ceremony wiped their mouths with the towels they held then returned to the table. Each person reached into the box farthest to Alex's left. The largest box, in the center of the table, remained unopened. They pulled out gauze pads and tape, then they walked back and bandaged each donor's bleeding arm.

"Anytime now," I said as we waited to learn what was in the middle box.

Alex finally opened the lid of the largest box. He reached in and pulled out a dozen or so small glass bottles and a tray. Each was filled with what appeared to be blood.

"Bingo, there it is," I said. I was ready to leap from my spot when J.T. grabbed my arm.

"Hold your horses. We have to see what they're going to do with them first. Just because they're oddballs doesn't mean they're doing anything illegal other than trespassing."

"Sorry, you're right."

We continued watching as, one by one, Alex placed the bottles on the tray and walked to the last group of people and handed them out.

Andrews spoke up. "I guess those are for the people that would rather not cut and drink right from the source."

I added. "We have to get down there before all the evidence is consumed."

"Not a problem," Sullivan said. "There will be plenty of residue left in the bottles. We have to see them actually drink it first. For all we know, it could be tomato juice."

"Doubtful."

"Yeah, but let's give them five minutes, anyway, then we'll move in."

We waited and watched until the tray was passed from one person to the next and the empty bottles were collected.

With a wave to get everyone's attention, Sullivan gave

us the okay to move in. We had no intentions of drawing our weapons as we approached unless they gave us a reason to. I kept in mind the lengthy rap sheet Sullivan said Alex had. Having dealt with Alex in the past, Sullivan approached him first, and J.T. and I followed. We ran down the hill, completely taking the group by surprise. In speedy fashion, the officers gathered the twenty-five or so stunned people into one area, where they were told to sit and wait. J.T., Sullivan, and I laser beamed our sights on Alex before he could slip away unnoticed.

"Alex Everly," Sullivan shouted, "we need a word with you."

Alex spun toward us with a surprised look that quickly turned into anger. He resembled a rabbit ready to bolt. With a quick charge, I grabbed his arm before he had too much time to think of an escape plan. I bent his arm high behind his back and held him in place.

"What the hell do you want? Is this some sort of religious harassment?"

"Last time I looked, being a vampire, or vampire poser, as you call them, wasn't a religion. Turn around and put your other hand behind your back." I spread his legs with my foot and snapped the cuffs over his wrists.

He laughed in my face. "What grounds do you have to arrest me?"

"Actually, I'm under no obligation to tell you anything yet, but for now, we'll go with trespassing on private property. How's that? Tell your friends to go home unless every one of them would like to be fitted with cuffs tonight too."

He snickered at me. "Tell them yourself, pig."

I yanked on his cuffs, and he stumbled backward and fell to the ground. I leaned in next to his ear. "That's Ms. Pig to you. Last chance, *Massimo*," I chuckled. "Tell them now, or you all go to jail."

He jerked his body away from me. "Everyone, go home. You'll hear from me tomorrow."

I patted the top of his head. "Good boy. Let's go."

J.T. grabbed one arm and Sullivan the other and lifted Alex from the ground. "This way," J.T. said as he tipped his head in the direction we had come from.

Sullivan yelled out to the officers. "Squelch that fire and make sure all those trespassers have left before you return to the station. Andrews, Fitch, gather all of this evidence and get it to the forensics lab immediately."

"Yes, sir," Fitch said.

Alex sat in interrogation box number one a half hour later. I could almost see the steam coming out of his ears. We watched him for a while through the one-way mirror. I wanted a sense of his personality other than the already noted smart-ass attitude. According to Alex's rap sheet, he was a jack-of-all-trades whose skill set included B&E, assault, and burglary. Now we could add the misdemeanor trespassing and maybe more to the list.

With the residue from the bottles being tested in the forensics lab, we had plenty of time to hold and question the head honcho of this so-called vampire clan. We needed to know whether the source of the blood was human or animal. There was a chance Alex would be turned back out onto the streets with a stern warning, or he could cozy up to a nice roommate and become a new tenant downstairs in the city jail.

I tossed my cardboard coffee cup into the trash can. "You guys ready?"

J.T. and Sullivan nodded, and we entered the cold, steel-gray room.

Alex sat on the other side of the table, his cuffed hands in his lap. "Does somebody want to tell me why I'm here?" He spewed the words at us as if he'd done this dance before. "I've put in my time for every offense I've been convicted of."

Sullivan pulled up a chair and plopped down next to him. "We know that, and you're only here because we're looking for information."

"Ha! Why the hell would I help you? You're the pig that threw me in jail on four separate occasions." He turned toward me and snickered. "And who are you two wannabe cops? Don't believe I've ever come across you newbies before."

I raised a brow at J.T. "This guy is a rocket scientist." I looked back at Alex. "We aren't from your neck of the woods, smart boy. We're FBI agents, and I'm sure if we dug deep enough we could find some type of federal charge to pin on you."

"Whatever."

I jerked my head and chuckled. "Now he shuts up—funny how that works." I stood and gave J.T. the other vacant chair. I leaned against the wall and locked eyes with Alex.

J.T. took over. "We need information about the recent murders. I'm sure you've seen something about that on the news. You do watch the news now and then, don't you?"

"Yeah, sure. So what about the murders? Don't even think you're going to pin them on me." Alex leaned back in the chair and flicked his long, greasy hair as he stared at the ceiling.

"Feeling guilty about something?" J.T. asked.

"Hell no."

"We want to know what the talk on the street is. Women's bodies are turning up nearly drained of blood, and that's far from normal. You know, run-of-the-mill murderers just go ahead and kill people. This guy has a reason. He's using the blood for something, maybe even drinking it."

"I don't know shit about that."

"We'll see. We're testing the blood residue left behind in those bottles from your little party. I'd be sweating my ass off if I were you, especially if the test results come back as human blood," J.T. said.

"That doesn't mean anything. We donate our own blood and store it."

"So it will come back as human blood. Is that what you're saying?"

"Maybe."

"We certainly can test the blood residue against your followers and see if their DNA matches. If there isn't a match, you may be going away for human blood trafficking. That's black market illegal stuff, Alex, and a big no-no. We need you to start talking. If we have to match all of your groupies to the blood left in the bottles, you know how long we'll have to hold you here until we have the results? Hell, it could be weeks, even months," J.T. said.

"Fine. I used to buy blood, but I don't trust it anymore. There are too many diseases and drug addicts out there."

"So you're a responsible vampire now, is that the story you're going with? Who did you buy it from?" I asked.

"That was years ago, and from a guy that worked at a blood bank. He would skim from the top, so to speak."

Sullivan nodded. "It's true. Paul Olsen, the son-in-law of the director of the blood center, is serving six years in the state pen for selling blood. It was quite a scandal."

I walked over to the table and took a seat on its edge. "So, who currently sells blood, and who buys it?"

"I don't know who supplies it, but cults, like witches and warlocks, buy any blood they can get their hands on. They don't care where it comes from because they aren't drinking it. They may smear it over their bodies and do crazy-ass blood dances while bathed in it, but for a sacrifice, they'd want the actual body."

I crossed my arms over my chest and heaved a sigh. "They wouldn't drain the blood from the body, would they?"

"Probably not. They'd slice it open and dip their hands into the cavity, but I've never heard of anyone locally doing an actual human sacrifice."

"So that takes us back to you and your clan. Maybe you screen the blood better now."

A knock sounded on the door, and Sullivan rose. He exited the room, then he came back a few minutes later and peeked in. He signaled for J.T. and me to join him.

I looked over my shoulder as I crossed the room. "Don't go anywhere, Alex."

"Yeah, real funny."

With the door closed behind us, Sullivan announced that the blood results were in. "Here's what the lab said. A few of the bottles had traces of human blood, but the majority was pig blood."

"That's pretty disgusting but understandable. Pig blood is relatively similar to that of humans. So what do you want to do about Alex?" I asked.

"We'll turn him loose but with conditions. He has to let us know if anyone contacts him about buying blood. Just in case he opts not to reveal any intel he may get, we'll put a tracker on his phone and monitor the websites he visits," Sullivan said.

"Maybe we can go one step better. He has to imply on those sites that he's interested in buying blood. We'll see if anyone bites." When J.T. chuckled, I realized what I'd said.

"Nice play on words, Monroe."

Sullivan rolled his eyes then dug his fists deep into his pockets. He jiggled his change. "Yeah, I like it. Let's go tell him."

It was one thirty in the morning when we finally cut Alex loose. He rubbed the redness on his wrists as he listened to our conditions.

I cocked my head and gave him a smile. "Cuffs too tight?"

"Hell yeah."

"Good, and here's how you can keep those tight cuffs off."

Sullivan explained that Alex had to inform us if he was contacted by anyone wanting to sell human blood. His face contorted. He said he didn't like the idea of setting anyone up, but he was told in no uncertain terms that if he didn't work with us, we'd find a reason to throw him into county lockup. With his criminal record, it wouldn't be difficult to find something that had previously been missed.

We showed him to the door, where that same van from earlier waited at the curb.

Chapter 21

Sam yawned as he checked the time—1:40 a.m. The house was quiet, and everyone was tucked in for the night. Adeline and Molly had eaten dinner separately hours earlier. A fresh pint of blood had been drawn from Molly's arm and given to Adeline just before bed. Now they were both asleep.

The two upholstered chairs from the secondhand store had been secured to the wall and floorboards with five-inch nails. Nobody, once bound in those chairs, would break free. Sam would escort them to the restroom several times a day, and that would be their exercise. He had never kept anyone prisoner and was sure there would be a learning curve. As long as it didn't involve another escape, he'd deal with it.

Now, as tired as he was, Sam had to find at least one girl to take home that night. Bars closed in Gary at three a.m.— there was still time—and that night happened to be ladies' night. With half-priced drinks for women throughout the evening, he was sure to find somebody on the verge of passing out. A little Rohypnol would go a long way in helping him get a woman home without a fuss. Several places he had frequented in the past came to mind. Paul's Tap was the closest, about a twenty-minute drive. Not too far and not close enough to his house to connect him to anything. In the bathroom, with cold water cupped in his hands, he splashed his face, combed his hair, and changed clothes. It was time to leave and introduce himself to a lady or two. He grabbed the baggie of quartered Rohypnol tablets and left the house.

Paul's Tap was still packed when Sam arrived. He pulled into the pea-gravel parking lot and found the only available space just as someone else left. He had forty minutes to pull out his bag of tricks and put on the charm.

Patrons huddled near the entrance as they smoked cigarettes. The night was cold and brisk, and snow was forecasted by morning. With his collar pulled a little higher and his shoulders involuntarily stiffened, Sam quickly crossed the parking lot and entered the building. Plenty of bodies, neck to neck and shoulder to shoulder, warmed the bar space. The standing-room-only crowd and loud music made his job that much tougher. Getting the attention of a bartender could take some time.

Sam scanned the room and saw two young women sitting together at a bar table fifteen feet away. He'd play the accidental-bump ruse, as if somebody had pushed him into their table. He'd apologize and offer to buy them a drink before the *last call* lights came on and everyone was funneled to the door. The free-drink approach was a guaranteed icebreaker, especially when it was well into the night and everyone had their guard down. Hopefully, the girls didn't ride together. If they were in an impaired state, it could be difficult, but not impossible, to overtake both of them.

Pushing through the crowd and calling out apologies, Sam inched closer to their table. He noticed they were drinking bottled beer. That could make his task of slipping the Rohypnol into their drinks a bit harder. He'd play up his charm and offer them a more sophisticated cocktail, something in a rocks glass.

As if someone had pushed him forward, Sam bumped the blonde on his right. Her beer bottle teetered, and he grabbed it before it tipped over.

"Nice save!" She grinned, clearly admiring his attractive looks.

"I guess I'm good at something—I have a quick hand." Sam shook back his blond hair and smoothed it with his left hand while sticking out his right. "I'm Sam, and I'm really sorry about that." He glanced over his shoulder at the imaginary person who had bumped him. "Man, it's packed in here." He extended his hand to the second woman. "You two look like you invented the word *mischief*."

The brunette laughed as if taken aback. "Who, us?" She hiccupped and reached out to grasp his hand. "I'm Bethany"—she pointed at the blonde—"and she's Kristen."

"Looks like your beers are almost empty. How about I buy you another drink, something fitting for classy ladies such as yourselves?"

Kristen smirked. "Damn, nobody has ever called me

classy. Okay, sure. What do you have in mind, Sam?"

He scratched his chin as if in thought. *I don't care what you drink as long as I can slip the roofies into it.*

"You ladies look like the single malt scotch type—something nice and smoky."

Bethany's eyes widened. "Ooh, that sounds delicious."

"Then it's settled. Don't go anywhere. Those are expensive drinks, and if I have to down them myself, I'll fall flat on my ass. I'll be right back."

Sam heard them giggle as he walked away. Luckily, the cash he'd pulled out of Heather's wallet Friday night would help pay for the frivolous drinks he would never have purchased otherwise. It was the cost of doing business.

He reached into his jacket pocket and thumbed the zipper seal of the baggie as he walked toward the bar. The pills needed to be dropped into the drinks as soon as he got them. It would take several seconds for the chunks to dissolve, but with a few swishes of the stirring sticks, nobody would be the wiser. Especially the two women who had no idea what the drinks were supposed to look like, anyway. Sam called out and waved to get the bartender's attention. "Two Laphroaigs, neat, in rocks glasses, please."

"Coming right up. Don't often have requests for that—nice choice."

Sam watched as the bartender was generous with a decent pour in each glass.

"Here you go. That'll be eighteen dollars."

Sam handed him a twenty. "Keep it and drop a stirring stick in each. My friends like to chew on the ends."

The bartender nodded his thanks and put a red plastic stick into each glass. With the pill pieces wedged between his fingers, Sam dropped two chunks into each glass as he walked slowly to the table. He kept a watchful eye on the drinks and tried his best to mix the dissolving roofies into the alcohol. By the time he pushed his way through the crowd and reached the table, the Rohypnol had dissolved.

Now it's just a waiting game. Hopefully, by the time the bar closes, they're going to need my help getting to their cars.

"Wow, I'm in luck," he joked as he set the glasses on the table. "You ladies stuck around."

"Well," Bethany said, "I was curious about this classy drink you mentioned. I've never had scotch before. I hope it's good."

"Scotch is something you learn to love over time, but the smoky taste is the real attraction. I think you'll enjoy it. Anyway, cheers." Sam held up an imaginary glass and toasted the ladies. "Sip it and swish it in your mouth. You'll get the full flavor that way."

He watched as Bethany and Kristen sipped the Laphroaig.

"Whoa, this is different but good. Yeah, I'm a fan," Kristen said. "Thanks, Sam. You're a real gentleman."

He smiled. "You aren't sisters, are you?"

Bethany rolled her eyes. "No. Do you actually think we look alike?"

"Nah, just making conversation. Did you drive here together tonight?"

"Nope," Kristen said. "I came here from work. Bethany

got here earlier to save a table. Can't you tell? She's already three sheets to the wind."

Bethany flipped her hair smugly with the back of her hand. "I am not. I'm only two sheets in. I have a full sheet to go."

"How are you doing with the drinks?" Sam glanced at his watch. "There's still time for one more."

"I'm good, but I'm suddenly really warm," Bethany said. "I feel flushed."

"Yeah, it's the booze, and your face is bright red," Kristen said.

Bethany pushed back her stool and almost fell off. "Maybe I should go."

Sam frowned as he steadied her. "It doesn't seem like you're in the best shape to drive. I'll give you a lift home."

"You'd do that for me?"

"Sure, what are friends for?"

"I have an idea," Kristen said. "You drive Bethany to her house in her car, and I'll follow you. Then I'll drive you back here to your car. We'll all get home safely that way."

"That's a great idea. Are you ladies ready to go?" Sam asked.

"Yeah, but can you help me walk?" Bethany cradled her head between her hands. "The room is suddenly spinning."

"Don't worry," Sam said. "I've got you."

Chapter 22

With Sam on one side of Bethany and Kristen on the other, they helped her across the parking lot to the passenger side of her car. The cold night air hit them all in the face. By now, Kristen wasn't much help. The Rohypnol had begun to affect her too. Sam scanned his surroundings as they neared Bethany's car. The parking lot, packed with vehicles, was dead quiet. The bar's patrons were still inside chugging down their last drinks of the night. Maybe it wouldn't be hard grabbing both girls after all.

They propped Bethany against the car door as Kristen dug through Bethany's purse to locate her keys. Sam's mind was in overdrive. He'd unlock the car, Kristen would help Bethany in, and then he would strike. He'd knock Kristen out, toss her in the backseat, and quickly leave, but he wouldn't go far. His van and Kristen's car couldn't be left behind. The last thing he wanted was to raise suspicion. He needed to act before people began spilling out of the bar.

With Bethany's car keys in hand, Kristen clicked the

fob. The door locks popped up. Sam pulled the door open, and Bethany nearly fell inside.

"Get that seat belt around her," he said as he kept a watchful eye on the front door of Paul's Tap.

Kristen fumbled far too long. Sam grasped the back of her neck and smashed her head against the doorframe, knocking her out cold. With his arm around her waist, he opened the back door and tossed her in. He had to move the van and her car several blocks away so they couldn't be seen from the Paul's Tap parking lot. It would take only a minute. With both girls fastened in with seat belts and unconscious, he rummaged through Kristen's purse and found her keys. He clicked the fob twice and saw headlights blink four cars away.

Not too bad. This is doable.

After a double-check of both girls, still lying silently, Sam ran to Kristen's car and climbed in behind the wheel. He sped out of the parking lot and drove three blocks south, turned left, and parked along the curb near the next intersection. Instead of returning along the street, he realized that cutting across lawns was faster. At that time of night, most homeowners were asleep, anyway. Sam climbed into his van, drove to the same street, but turned right that time. He parked the van halfway up the street. The cold air he sucked in made him ache, and his lungs burned like fire as he ran for the last time back to Paul's Tap. People had just begun exiting the building. The timing couldn't have been better. He opened the driver's side door of Bethany's car and drove away with two girls added to his donor list.

He calculated the driving distance and time it would take to make several back-and-forth trips from car to house, along with the time he needed in order to secure both women. It would be daybreak before he'd be able to sleep for a few hours.

When he pulled into his driveway a half hour later, Sam slammed his open hand against the steering wheel. The garage door remote was in the van. Just one more delay before he could get everything accomplished. He shifted into Park and looked over his shoulder at Kristen. He killed the engine. With Bethany's car keys tucked in his left hand, he pulled his own keys out of his pants pocket and ran up the sidewalk. He slid the key into the front doorknob and turned it to his right. Quietly, he tiptoed through the house so he wouldn't wake Adeline and entered the garage. He slapped at the wall until he made contact with the button. He pressed it, and the overhead lifted. Back in the driver's seat, Sam pulled Bethany's car in, got out, and closed the garage door. He didn't have time for finesse. As long as the girls were secure for the moment, he'd worry about the details tomorrow. He dragged Kristen to the back room, unlocked the door, and continued on to one of the chairs. He propped her up in it. Molly woke and began crying.

"Shut up or I'll shut you up permanently," he yelled.

She went quiet. Sam secured a length of rope around the right chair leg, then five times around Kristen's body and, finally, around the opposite chair leg before he knotted the ends together. He noticed a cut on Kristen's head that must have come when he smashed her into the doorframe of

Bethany's car. He shrugged it off—she'd have other things to worry about once she regained consciousness. Sam tore duct tape off the roll and placed it over Kristen's mouth. He wound a length of tape around each of her hands and legs. He ran back and heaved Bethany out of the car. He dragged her to the back room and repeated the process. Now he'd return Bethany's car to the area where he'd abducted the girls, but he'd leave it on a different block. He was careful to wear gloves at all times except when in his own house. That was one less thing to worry about—wiping prints off the cars.

Thirty minutes later, with Bethany's car parked against a random street curb and her wallet emptied of cash, Sam ran to Kristen's car. He moved it several blocks farther from Paul's Tap, emptied the contents of her wallet too, and threw both sets of keys in a gutter drain. He returned to his van. After he climbed in, he took a deep breath. He sat and thought for a minute, not wanting to overlook anything. With a clear head and cash in his pocket, he checked his surroundings then pulled out onto the street. The clock showed it was four forty-five a.m.

Chapter 23

I texted an update to Amber as J.T. drove to our new favorite breakfast restaurant—Flapjacks, the pancake house down the street from our hotel. That morning I again ordered the four-stack breakfast, which included bacon, but this time the cakes were buckwheat with pecans. As always, real maple syrup sat on the table.

I asked for the carafe of coffee to be left with us and filled both our cups as J.T. read over his notes. "What's on our agenda today?" I took a sip of the rich coffee as he spoke.

"We need to interview Molly's family ourselves. Remember, we wanted to find out if they knew what she was wearing when she went running, using the process of eliminating what was missing from her room."

"That's right, I remember now. We also need to go over any promising calls that might have come in on the tip line and see what the officers found out about Heather's car, if anything. They were supposed to do more knock and talks too, right?"

"Yeah, but I think the majority of that was going to

happen today," J.T. said. He took a bite of his pancakes and rolled his eyes.

"What's wrong?"

"Nothing. It tastes like heaven, and all these years, I've settled for a bagel every morning."

I grinned and stuck a piece of bacon in his face. "Here, eat this and see what heaven is really like. Keep hanging with me, and I promise you, you'll be enjoying deliriously good breakfasts a lot more often."

He patted his stomach. "True, but I don't want this to expand. I've seen what heavy meals can do to a guy's midsection, and it's disgusting."

"Well, speaking as a woman, I love pancakes and bacon, and Amber is a spectacular cook, yet I remain svelte."

"Yeah, yeah, high metabolism, that's all. Anyway, chow down. We have a busy day ahead of us."

We reached the police department at eight thirty. Sullivan sat in the conference room alone and looked to be reviewing his stack of notes. From the sagging bags under his eyes, it was obvious he hadn't gotten much sleep. I was sure these deaths, as well as Molly Davis going missing, weighed heavily on his mind.

"Captain," I said with a nod as J.T. and I entered the room. "Anything new since last night?"

"I sure as hell hope not. Stone is collecting the tip line updates, and we'll give those a look when he gets in." He checked his watch and glanced at the hallway beyond the glass wall. "The group should be here any minute."

J.T. and I took seats facing the hallway and waited. I

jotted down what we'd be doing that day in order of importance. Footsteps sounded, and we looked up through the glass wall. Fitch and Andrews led the group, and Stone, Mills, Jeffries, and Christopher took up the rear. Fitch pushed the half-open door and entered. One by one, they said good morning and took a seat.

Sullivan pressed his fist against his mouth and cleared his throat. He poured water into a plastic cup from the pitcher on the table. "Okay, people, are you ready to get this day started?"

Papers shuffled as we prepared to take notes. We all said yes.

"Anything on the tip line, Stone?" Sullivan tapped his pen against the table, clearly ready to write.

"The usual, sir. Fourteen calls came in through the night, but most were after the ten o'clock news. I guess Molly has one of those faces, you know? Nothing very distinctive about her features, and she doesn't have any obvious tattoos that someone would notice. You'd think the red hair would definitely ring a bell, but the leads were all over the board. One person saw her at a house party in Indianapolis. Another swore they saw her shopping on Michigan Avenue yesterday."

I spoke up. "Yeah, those types of leads will spread your workforce too thin. We need something specific. If she disappeared from the trails, which it seems she did since her car was left behind, wouldn't she still be wearing her running outfit, or would the kidnapper have her put in something different?" I glanced at J.T. "Maybe we could save time with just a phone call since Molly's parents were already interviewed in person."

"I'd say go for it. We could put our legwork to better use."

"Do you guys mind if I do that right now?" I looked from face to face.

Sullivan swiped the air. "Not at all, go ahead."

"Okay, here we go. I'll put the call on speakerphone."

We listened as the phone at the Davis home rang several times. A click sounded and then a voice. It was Mrs. Davis answering.

"Hello."

"Mrs. Davis, this is FBI Agent Jade Monroe calling, ma'am. I know we haven't been formally introduced, but time is of the essence in your daughter's case." I placed my phone in the center of the table and set it to the highest volume. "Oh, and by the way, I have you on speakerphone. I'm at the police station with my partner, Captain Sullivan, and the detectives and officers you and your husband spoke with Monday evening."

"Yes, of course. Do you have news about Molly?"

"I'm sorry, ma'am, but not yet. The reason I'm calling may sound unusual to you, but it's actually very important." I paused for a moment.

"Yes, go ahead."

"I know you mentioned that you didn't see Molly leave the house on Monday, but knowing what she was wearing could ring a bell with someone. Since we don't have the exact time she was at the trails and we don't know who else was in the area at that time, her outfit could be very helpful to us. We'll include that information with the news broadcasts that air several times a day. It could produce leads, ma'am."

"But I—"

I interrupted. It sounded as though she was becoming upset. "I realize you don't know what she wore that day, but you could see what's not in her bedroom anymore, correct?"

"Yes, I could do that. It just didn't occur to me before. Oh no, we've wasted precious time." She trailed off, but I needed her to focus.

"That's okay, Mrs. Davis. It isn't your job to think like a cop. What I want you to do is go into Molly's room. Look through her running clothes in the drawers, closet, or wherever she kept that type of stuff. Think hard and call me back in fifteen minutes at this same number. Do your best to remember her outfits. Whatever isn't there is likely what she wore on Monday."

"Okay, I'll do that immediately and get right back to you."

I hung up and checked that off my to-do list. "Hopefully that will help stir somebody's memory. What else do we have?"

"We made additional calls yesterday about Heather's car," Stone said. "This time we contacted every precinct and sheriff's department in the state. Nobody has received a report about an abandoned car fitting that description."

Sullivan spoke up. "That means it's time to hit the freeway plate readers and the tollbooth cameras. Let's start with Illinois first and then Michigan just because they're the nearest states. Get that done today and go back to Friday after five p.m."

Stone wrote that down. "Yes, Captain."

"Is the tracker set up on Alex's phone?"

Fitch responded. "We should have the okay by noon, sir."

"Good enough. Okay, today is about revisiting the parks and expanding our neighborhood knock and talks."

"We'll pitch in on that, Captain," J.T. said. "It doesn't sound like Molly's employer has been interviewed yet. Is that correct?"

"Not yet," Andrews said. "That was on the list for today as well."

"We'll take care of it. I think the neighbors of the girls need to be spoken to again. Taylor Dorsey was in college. There should be a faculty person that can shed some light on her activities or school friends. Parents don't know everyone their children hang out with, especially if they're only acquaintances are from work or school."

"But it's been months in Taylor's case," Fitch said.

"That's true, but expand your horizons a bit beyond the school personnel. The college must be near food joints or coffee shops where students hang out. Take her picture along to the neighborhood eateries. See if anyone recognizes her," J.T. said. "If she was a regular at any place like that, there's a good chance they'll remember her and anyone that joined her there."

My phone, still sitting in the center of the table, rang. I

pulled it toward me. "It's Mrs. Davis. I hope she has something for us." I answered and tapped the speakerphone icon. "Hello, Mrs. Davis. Did you come up with anything?"

"I did, and I know if anyone saw Molly, it will ring a bell. Her purple running suit is missing. The zipper jacket and stretchy pants matched, and they're both gone."

I took a deep breath and tipped my head at J.T. We were getting somewhere. Captain Sullivan wrote as she spoke.

"We need a good description of that running suit, ma'am," J.T. said.

"She just bought it three months ago. Like I said, it was purple, and it had a lime-green-and-black stripe that ran down the sleeves of the jacket and the sides of the pant legs. I teased her about the mismatched colors, but she liked the lime-green stripe because it went with her favorite running shoes."

"Her shoes?"

"Oh my God, those shoes were so bright. Hang on a second. I didn't check her closet floor."

We heard footsteps and then what sounded like a door opening.

"Agent Monroe, I just opened her closet and looked down. Her lime-green running shoes are gone."

"Okay, that's a huge help, Mrs. Davis. Do you know if there are pictures of those items anywhere?"

"I don't think so, Agent Monroe."

"Sure, not a problem. Was the running suit light purple or deep purple?"

"Definitely a deep purple."

"Okay, we're going to get that information on the noon news. I hope it sparks new leads. Thank you, ma'am, and if you think of anything else, please call me back." I hung up. "That information could be the help we need. I'm calling the news stations right away."

"Okay"—Sullivan pushed back his chair and stood— "let's get to work."

Chapter 24

A noise sounded against the wall opposite his bed. It came from his mother's room.

"Sam, are you awake?"

He stirred, rolled over, and lifted his head and checked the time—9:10 a.m. "Shit, I didn't plan to sleep this long." He yelled out, "I'm awake now. Give me ten minutes, Mom."

Sam threw the blankets back, slipped quietly out of his room while pulling a T-shirt over his head, and took the hall to the bathroom two doors down. He'd shower later. A quick splash of cold water to wake up would have to do.

He knocked on Adeline's bedroom door. "Sorry, Mom. I had a late night. Can I come in?"

"Sure, it's okay."

He entered her room and turned the wand on the blinds. "The sun is out today. Let me help you up."

Sam pushed the wheelchair to the side of the bed as Adeline slid over the best she could. He reached under her armpits and lifted her to the chair. Then he knelt and opened the footrests. He noticed how she felt lighter every time he lifted her. "Comfortable?"

"Thanks, honey, I'm good."

With a hand on each grip, he pushed the wheelchair to the kitchen table and locked the brakes. "I'll start the coffee, then I have to check on our newest guests. I won't be long, though. Want the TV remote?"

"Sure."

Sam noticed the worried expression on his mother's face.

"Don't you think you're getting in over your head?"

Sam shrugged. "Not sure yet. I've never kept anyone alive before. If it doesn't work, I'll go back to the way it was. Let me do the worrying, Mom. I'll figure it out."

He poured a cup of coffee for Adeline and kissed her cheek. "I'll be back in a half hour, then I'll start breakfast." He turned on the TV and set the remote on the table in front of her. "Your morning soap is about to begin." He went back to his room and grabbed Molly's clothes. Then he crossed the kitchen and entered the garage.

The muffled sounds from the back room only got louder as he turned the key in the knob. Sam walked in and closed the door at his back. Panic-stricken faces stared at him. He hated that part of the process, but with three girls as donors, he might not need to bring home any more women.

"I have to use the bathroom, Sam, and who are those girls?" Molly said.

"Don't worry about it." He slipped the T-shirt over Molly's head. "I'm going to unstrap you so you can put your arms in the sleeves. Don't try anything you'll regret."

She lay still as he unbuckled her.

"Sit up and put your arms in the shirt."

She did as told.

"Now lie back down."

"But I have to go to the bathroom."

"You can wait for a few minutes. Now lay down."

Molly did, and he buckled the strap tightly across her chest and arms. "Here are your jogging pants."

"Are you letting me go?"

He snickered. "Hardly, but I only need your arm from now on. I'm going to release your legs for a minute. You kick me and you die, understand?"

"Yes, I understand."

He put a foot in each pant leg then loosened the strap across her calves. He slid the pants up to her waist then snugged the strap again. He looked over his shoulder at Kristen and Bethany. "I'm going to bring a bucket out here for you three to use. I don't want any of you in my house. I'll be back soon."

"But wait—"

Sam didn't stop. He closed the door and locked it behind him.

"What do you feel like eating for breakfast, Mom?" Sam had just entered the kitchen and glanced at the table across the room. Adeline's head lay slumped on her chest, and the remote had fallen to the floor. "Mom!" He raced across the kitchen and lifted her out of the wheelchair. He placed her on the living room rug. "Can you hear me?" He put his ear against her chest and heard her heart beating. Thankfully, she was alive. He checked her pulse—it was weak. Sam ran to the bathroom and wet a washcloth. He placed it across her head. "Mom, wake up. Please wake up."

She moaned and opened her eyes. Sam let out a deep breath and rushed to the kitchen. He filled a glass with orange juice and placed it on the coffee table. "Let me scoot you back against the couch. I want you to drink this juice."

"What happened?"

"I don't know. I'm guessing your blood sugar is low or your anemia is getting worse. I'll be right back." Sam returned to the kitchen and pulled the refrigerator handle. He stuck his head in the door and saw that only two pints of blood were left on the shelf. In her weakened state, Adeline would need a pint that day. He pulled one out of the refrigerator.

I need to keep four pints on hand at all times. I'll be drawing blood after Mom gets her transfusion.

He returned to the living room and took a seat next to her. "Are you feeling better? Did the juice help?"

"Sort of, but I'm still a little dizzy."

"You need to get back in bed so I can give you a transfusion. You're getting weaker, Mom. I'm going back to the way I was doing it before."

"Sam, I'm dying. Just admit it and let me go."

He wiped his eyes. "You aren't dying yet. The insurance will come through. Until then, I'll do the best I can." With the wheelchair at her side, Sam helped Adeline into it and rolled her back to her room. "I'll get everything set up, but first, let's get you in bed." He lifted her onto the bed, slid the pillows behind her, and then pulled the blankets up to her chest. "I'll get you some water. You need to stay hydrated."

Sam returned a few minutes later with a pint of blood and a tall plastic cup of water. A straw poked out of the lid. "Here you go." He handed her the cup and moved the roller table over the bed. He hooked the bag onto the IV stand and inserted the tube into the port taped to the back of her wrist. He opened the valve. "Do you need anything else, Mom? Want the TV on in here?"

"Yes, that would be nice."

"You got it." He clicked the remote and placed it on the roller table. "I'll leave the door open. I don't want anyone upsetting you, so they aren't coming in to use the bathroom anymore. I'll take a bucket out there."

"Sam."

"It's okay. They'll get used to it. I'm going to get them squared away with food, then I'll start their blood draws. Call my cell if you need anything."

He took three bottles of water with straws and six chocolate chip cookies out to the workroom. He placed them on the counter and left. A moment later he was back with a large blue bucket.

"Here's your toilet, Molly. It's either that or piss yourself, your choice." He glanced at the other women. "Guess you'll need buckets too."

Molly began sobbing. "Just let us go."

"Don't start with me. I have enough problems without listening to your whining." Sam walked around the room and looked for something that would restrain her but still give her the movement she needed. "Damn it, I can't think of anything. You're getting taped. It's the easiest way to do this." He released the chest straps. "Sit up so I can tape your hands behind your back. Your legs are getting taped together too. I'll help you off the table, then you can figure out the rest on your own."

Chapter 25

J.T. read the directions as I drove. I had missed being behind the wheel and needed to let off a little steam. We were into our third day with nothing more than interviews that led nowhere. The color of Molly's running suit was the most helpful lead we had gotten since arriving on Monday.

"Okay, First Federal Bank is two blocks ahead on your right, according to the GPS."

"Who do we ask for?"

J.T. pulled his notepad from his inner jacket pocket. He flipped to the last page of notes. "It says her boss was Angela Farrow. I guess she's the one that suggested the promotion for Molly."

"Good, that means they had a nice working relationship. Maybe Molly confided in her too."

"Maybe." J.T. pointed. "Here we are."

I turned in to the designated lot for the single-story brick building that looked like any typical neighborhood bank. Double glass doors were positioned in the center of the facade facing the parking lot, and the drive-through banking with three lanes was directly to our right. I parked, and we exited the cruiser. J.T. held the door open. I entered first.

"Guess chivalry isn't dead yet." I gave him a thoughtful smile. "Thanks, partner."

A branch assistant, almost like a banking concierge, greeted us. "Hello, how may I help you with your banking needs today?"

"Thank you, but we're here to see Angela Farrow."

"Certainly. One moment, please." She stood from her desk near the door and disappeared down a hallway.

J.T. tipped his head. "There's one of those fancy coffee machines with the flavor pods. Want one?"

"Sure, I'll have a macchiato."

J.T. busied himself at the coffee machine while I flipped through banking brochures. He carried over two foamy coffees and stood at my side. "See anything interesting?"

"You mean an account that will pay me interest on my hard-earned money?"

"No such thing, right?"

"These days, not so much."

I saw the woman we had talked to a few minutes earlier exit the hallway with a woman at her side. She tried to be discreet as she pointed at us before returning to her desk. The new woman, presumably Angela Farrow, headed in our direction.

"Hello, is there something I can help you with?" She extended her hand.

I introduced J.T. and myself as FBI agents, which seemed to surprise her.

"I understand Molly is missing, but bringing in the FBI? I'm kind of shocked."

"Ma'am"—I looked around at the customers coming and going— "is there a private place we can talk? We have a few questions for you."

"Oh, of course, my office is right this way." She led us to a group of offices at the back of the bank. "In here, please." The plaque attached to the door had Bank Manager stamped across it in gold lettering. Angela opened the door and motioned for us to take a seat. J.T. thanked her for both of us. She rounded the oversized, ornate walnut desk and sat down facing us. "Now, what can I help you with, agents?"

I pulled a pen and notepad out of my purse and flipped the pages to a clean one. J.T. asked the questions.

"Ma'am, how close were you and Molly?"

She seemed to be thinking that over. "Close coworkers, I'd say. We had lunch together twice a week."

"Did you share personal information and have private conversations, things you'd keep between yourselves? You know—best-friend secrets, rants about coworkers. Situations you discussed between the two of you but nobody else?"

"I was Molly's superior, Agent Harper. That would be inappropriate, and I wouldn't go so far as saying we were best friends."

I wished she would get off her high horse and just be honest with us. We weren't interested in her 'bank manager persona' responses.

"Ma'am." I forced a smile. She was giving us generic answers, and I wondered why. "Were you close friends with Molly or not? I doubt if you went to lunch twice a week and only discussed the rising interest rates." I felt J.T.'s leg bump mine under the desk. I flashed him a "knock it off" frown.

"We did talk about other things now and then."

"Such as?" Getting answers from her was like pulling teeth, and I was about to grab my pliers.

"Our relationships, or lack of."

We stared across the desk and watched her fidget.

"Okay, we both had relationship concerns." She rearranged herself in the chair several times, clearly uncomfortable with where the conversation was going. "My husband is cheating, and I'm considering a divorce. I told Molly that. She said she had recently met a guy named Mitchell and was very intrigued by him, but something seemed off."

"In what way?"

"I don't know, like he was too good to be true and kind of rushing things. She even said he asked her to go away with him for a few days. She hadn't made up her mind yet since she didn't know him that well, and—"

"And what?"

I wrote as J.T. continued in my place.

"And she had just gotten the promotion at my suggestion. She didn't know if the timing was right to leave for a few days."

I raised my brows in question. "Why wouldn't they just go for the weekend? She wouldn't miss any workdays, then."

Angela shrugged. "I don't know, Agent Monroe. This guy sent up red flags in my opinion, and frankly I was surprised she didn't show up for work on Monday."

"So Molly didn't have Mondays off?"

"No, but we have late hours on Mondays and Fridays. Molly was scheduled to work that afternoon for three hours before her promotion party."

"I doubt if disappearing without telling anyone is Molly's MO, then. Am I right?"

She pressed her forehead then rubbed her temples. "No, it isn't her MO—it's not even close."

"Did she tell you Mitchell's last name?" I waited with my pen suspended above the notepad.

"Yes, um, I remember it was a president's last name. I teased her about that. It wasn't Clinton, but it began with a C."

"Cleveland?" J.T. asked.

"No. Carter, it was Carter."

I wrote that down. "Is there anything else, even if you aren't sure of its importance?"

"Only that she wanted him to meet her parents before she gave him an answer." She looked at me with concern. "That was something I liked about Molly—she was old-fashioned and kind. You think something bad has happened, don't you? Why would the FBI be involved otherwise?"

"Sorry, ma'am, but it's an ongoing investigation. We aren't at liberty to discuss it with you. We appreciate your help, though." J.T. pulled his card out of his pocket. "We're only a phone call away if you think of anything else."

Angela stood and rounded the desk then escorted us to the lobby. "Thank you, agents. I hope you find her soon."

After we got to the car and J.T. clicked the door locks, I climbed into the passenger seat. I fastened my seat belt and pulled my phone out of my purse. "I'm calling Sullivan. He can get someone to do a background check on Mitchell Carter, and I think we need to pay the Davis family a visit." I made the call to the precinct and told Sullivan about our interview. Next I scrolled through my contact list and found the phone number for Mrs. Davis, I hit Call.

She picked up quickly. "Hello."

"Mrs. Davis, it's Agent Monroe calling. New information has surfaced, and my partner and I would like to stop by and discuss it with you as soon as possible. Would twenty minutes from now be okay?"

"Certainly. My husband and I are both home. Agent Monroe, is it bad news?"

"No, it isn't. Just a few more questions, that's all." I heard her take in a deep breath and let it out. "I'll need your address, ma'am." She rattled it off and said goodbye. With the address programmed into my phone, I guided J.T. to their house.

I watched the house numbers as J.T. drove slowly down Emerson Street. "Even numbers are on my side, so theirs should be that blue one." I pointed at a two-story Colonial two houses ahead. J.T. slowed the car to a crawl. The house number was prominently displayed above their garage door. "Yep, that's it. Pull into the driveway."

He parked, and we got out and followed the freshly cleared sidewalk. Mr. Davis must have shoveled the one-inch snow cover that had fallen overnight. I appreciated it. J.T. rang the bell. The door swung open, and Mrs. Davis stood on the other side. I made sure my badge was exposed.

"Agents?"

"Yes, ma'am, Jade Monroe and J.T. Harper."

"Please come in out of the cold."

I pointed down as I wiped my shoes on the porch mat. "Sorry, but our shoes are wet."

She swatted the air. "We've got tile floors, so just don't slip and fall. Let's sit in the kitchen. I'm brewing a fresh pot of coffee."

We followed her out of the foyer, past the family room, and into the kitchen that faced the deck at the back of the house.

"Please, have a seat. I'll get my husband. He's in his office."

A moment later they entered the kitchen. Mr. Davis shook our hands and took a seat across from us. Mrs. Davis brought four cups to the table along with the coffeepot then sat down.

"You said something new has surfaced?"

"Yes, ma'am. Have either of you ever heard of Mitchell Carter?"

Mr. and Mrs. Davis gave each other questioning looks. Both shook their heads.

"That name doesn't ring a bell with either of us, Agent Monroe. Who is he?" Mr. Davis asked.

"Were you aware that Molly was seeing someone?"

"You mean as a boyfriend? Was it this Mitchell guy?"

J.T. faced Mrs. Davis. "We've just learned from one of her coworkers that Molly mentioned Mr. Carter as somebody she was seeing. He actually asked her to go away with him for a few days."

Mrs. Davis wrung her hands. "That doesn't sound like something Molly would do. Do you think this man has abducted her?"

I responded as I poured coffee for all of us. "Ma'am, it's too early to know. The police department is running a background check on him as we speak. I'm sure we'll track him down before the day's end and find out more. Has Molly acted different lately, secretive, maybe, or distant?"

Mrs. Davis wiped her eyes. She looked as if she hadn't slept in days. "We both work"—she looked at her husband—"normally, I mean."

"Understood, ma'am."

"To be honest, she was excited about her upcoming promotion and the party that night. It seemed like she was on top of the world."

"She never mentioned anyone having a beef with her?" J.T. asked.

"Not at all. She was her normal self, upbeat and positive. She enjoyed running, she went out now and then, and she liked her job."

I took a sip of coffee and jotted down the comments. "You said she went out now and then?"

"Yes, with Maddie, a friend from college. They'd go to

Penelope's Café, which is a pretty happening place with the millennials. It's a strange venue, but the kids like it. They have a small organic restaurant, a bar, and a coffee shop. The only alcohol they serve is beer—all from microbreweries in the Midwest. Live music plays every Wednesday and Saturday night."

"What is Maddie's last name?"

"Trapp."

J.T. and I stood.

"Okay, thanks," I said. I'll double-check to see if anyone from the PD has spoken with her yet. May we see Molly's room, just to get an idea of who she is?"

Mrs. Davis pushed back her chair. "Of course, it can't hurt. Right this way."

J.T. added, "We'll also need her hairbrush and toothbrush sealed in a plastic bag."

Mr. Davis took it upon himself to gather those items.

Chapter 26

We left the Davis home with a better sense of who Molly was. She didn't seem to have planned to disappear, and from the condition of her room, she hadn't planned on leaving for good. Clothes lay scattered about, and a nice outfit—likely what she'd chosen to wear to the party that night—hung over the top of the closet door.

I checked for any incoming calls or texts once we drove away. "Here we go. Stone checked out Mitchell Carter. Uh-huh, now I understand."

J.T. backtracked the way we had come and got on Central Avenue heading northwest. "What's that? Is the guy dirty?"

"Nope, his record is clean. He's just married."

"Dirtbag."

I smirked. "You're quick with the clever comebacks, but either way, he still needs a talking-to. Okay, let's get back to the police station. The noon news is going out soon with the description of Molly's running suit and shoes. Hopefully the tip line will begin lighting up like a

Christmas tree. Also, I want to know if we're monitoring Alex's incoming and outgoing calls. We need to get things checked off our list."

We entered the station at twelve fifteen and dropped off the bag containing Molly's hairbrush and toothbrush at the forensics lab. At that time of day, many of the officers were either out on patrol or eating their lunch in the break room. We headed to Sullivan's office to let him know we were back. We saw him through the glass, elbows on his desk and staring at the computer screen with his sandwich suspended in his hand. I knocked on the half-opened door. "Sir?"

"Come on in, guys. Take a load off."

We entered and sat in the two guest chairs that faced him.

He wiped his mouth with a paper napkin. "Stone tell you the news?"

"About Mitchell Carter?" I asked.

He nodded and took another bite.

"Yeah, we know he's married with no priors. That doesn't make him innocent, but it doesn't make him guilty of a crime, either. We're going to check on a few things, grab a bite to eat at the vending machine, and pay Mr. Carter a visit later. What's the status on Alex's phone?"

"We're good. Charlie has a couple of his guys listening in on the calls."

"So it's in real time?" J.T. asked.

Sullivan grinned and took a swig of his soda. "Is there any other way to go?"

"Anything on Heather's car?" I asked.

"Mills is on that. He's looking through the CCTV camera footage at the toll plaza in Indiana on I-90 going toward Chicago. The problem is, Heather had an E-ZPass, and even if the plate reader caught her car passing through at sixty miles an hour, it's unlikely they could tell who's behind the wheel. Paying at the booth would be much more helpful, but there are a lot of variables."

I groaned. "Enlighten us."

"Her car hasn't hit on a plate reader at all. That means either it wasn't driven on an interstate or freeway or the license plates were removed or swapped out. If Heather's car was driven into Illinois, we sure as hell haven't found it yet. He probably took back roads."

"What about Michigan?" J.T. asked.

"Let's put it this way, J.T. None of the interstates between Indiana, Illinois, and Michigan have had a plate reader hit on her car."

"Then that leads me to think it's either parked in the killer's garage or it was chopped and sold off already."

Melanie Fitch rushed into Sullivan's office.

"Where's the fire, Fitch?"

"Sorry, boss, but we just received a very interesting tip that came in on the noon segment of the news. I think this one is legit."

I spun in my chair. "Who took the call?"

"I did, and the conversation is taped. Come and listen to it."

We gathered around Melanie's desk in the bull pen. Several other officers in the room stopped what they were doing and listened in too. We heard the female voice begin by saying she saw the noon news and thought she might have seen the woman in question. Mel's voice took over for a minute and asked the caller's name and what time she thought she saw the woman at the trails. The caller, Erin McNare, said she and her boyfriend were finishing up their jog around two o'clock. They were doing a short cooldown lap when they passed a man and woman sitting on a bench near the parking lot. She said they were kissing.

"Pause that tape for a second." I turned and gave J.T. a frown. "That can't be right unless Mitchell Carter was with her. What makes this Erin so sure it was Molly?"

"Here's where it gets good." Melanie clicked the button on the phone, and the message continued. Mel asked the caller that very question.

Erin continued talking. "The description of the woman never rang a bell with me until today when her outfit was described on the news. I remember chuckling at the running suit because the purple with the green stripe clashed so badly. But when I saw the lime-green shoes, I understood and continued on. I even mentioned the crazy color combination to my boyfriend. I'm positive it's the lady that disappeared."

Mel clicked the button again. "That's the gist of it. She gave me her phone number and address, which I have right here." Mel held up a piece of paper where she had written down the information.

"That whole kissing part doesn't feel right," I said. "What we need is a good description of the man Molly was with. Then we have to locate Mitchell Carter and see if he resembles that description. Call her back, Mel. I want to know everything she can remember."

Mel sat at her desk and dialed Erin's number.

I jerked my head toward the door. "We'll be right back."

J.T. and I headed for the lunchroom. We hadn't eaten anything since that morning and needed a little something to hold us over until dinner. We returned to the bull pen in less than five minutes, each with a can of soda and a club sandwich.

Sullivan suggested we go into the conference room, where it was more comfortable. He led the way as J.T., Mel, Larry, and I followed. We took our seats and waited as Mel got situated. She placed the paper with her notes on the table and looked at each of us.

I held up my hand before she got started. "Give us a second here." I tore open my sandwich wrapper and popped my soda can tab. J.T. did the same, then I gave Mel a nod. We didn't want to cause a distraction while she talked.

"Okay, I got Erin back on the phone, and here's what she said. The guy and girl were on the bench nearest the parking lot. That would be the west bench. The woman was on the right, the man on the left. Erin and her boyfriend were heading toward them."

"So the man would be facing them?"

"That's correct. She admitted she was looking at the woman's clothing more than anything else, and the fact that they were kissing distracted her too. From the twenty seconds it took for them to pass, she said the man didn't appear much taller than Molly because they were face to face. He wasn't leaning down to kiss her."

"Molly is—"

"Five foot seven," Mel said.

"Then the guy could be anywhere from five seven to five ten without looking much taller. What else?"

"She said they both had on stocking hats, and she thought she saw blond hair sticking out from beneath the man's cap."

"Molly's hair was auburn, right?" J.T. said.

"Yes, and Erin confirmed that the woman's hair was red."

I bit into my sandwich as Mel continued. I was glad everyone was taking notes. That gave J.T. and me time to wolf down our lunches. I swallowed a long gulp of soda. "What about body size?"

"Average build. He was sitting and wearing a jacket, but she didn't think he looked heavy. She estimated from her own boyfriend's size and weight that the man on the bench was somewhere around one hundred eighty pounds."

I opened my mouth to speak then closed it.

Sullivan noticed. "Jade?"

I waved it off. "I was about to ask his eye color, but if they were kissing, I assume their eyes were closed. Anything else that could help, Mel?"

"Only that he was wearing a windbreaker type of jacket, and it was black."

"That should do it. Now the fun begins." I elbowed J.T., grabbed our food wrappers, and pushed back my chair. "Come on. Let's go find Mitchell Carter. His wife is in for quite a surprise."

Chapter 27

He released the girls one by one that morning and allowed them to do their business. Now back from the store, he carried two new buckets into the workroom and placed them next to the chairs occupied by Kristen and Bethany. Earlier, they'd had fits of hysteria, but now they sat quietly, their heads lowered. Their faces wore red welts from being slapped. He reminded them they would be punished every time they acted up. He needed to keep them under control. The girls were only there to act as donors and if they behaved, they would remain unharmed.

Sam disappeared into the garage for a moment and returned with a folding chair. He pulled it open in front of Kristen and Bethany and took a seat. Molly already knew the drill. With a deep sigh, he looked from one girl to the next and began.

"I'm going to tell you why you're here, and you're going to listen closely—your life depends on it. I'm not a horrible monster, and my intentions aren't to cause you harm. Simply put, I'm going to take blood from you ladies every three days. Now, there's a huge difference between taking blood and draining blood. Taking blood means you live, and draining blood means you die. As a matter of fact, you can die in twenty minutes if I drain your blood, and the choice is yours. Your roles are to do everything I say, and we'll get along fine. Understand?"

They both nodded.

"Good, then it's time to begin." Sam moved the folding chair close to Kristen. Then he crossed the room beyond Molly's gurney and rummaged through the old desk. He returned with everything he needed and sat down. He placed the sterile blood bag on Kristen's lap. The long slender tube attached to the bag held a port on the opposite end. "Okay, here's how this works. I'll find a healthy vein and insert the needle. It's going to be taped in place so you can't dislodge it. The tube is also going to be taped to your arm, and your blood is going to flow into the bag as soon as I flip the valve. When the bag is full, you're done. Easy peasy, right? I'll do the same thing with Bethany as soon as we get you started. All you have to do is relax and act like you're donating blood, which is exactly what you're doing."

"We're going to die."

Sam looked over his shoulder at Molly and glared. "Shut the hell up."

"But we will. Nobody can give whole blood that often. I've donated blood before, and that's what they told me. You've already taken plenty from me, and I can tell I'm getting weaker."

"Too bad. It's once every three days, like I said. You're

on a rotation, so deal with it, and you aren't going to die. Eat the food and drink the juice I give you, and you'll be fine."

He tapped the vein on the inside of Kristen's elbow and noticed how it popped up. "Good, you're hydrated. Ready? I'm putting the needle in." He pricked her vein and pushed the needle in deeper.

She moaned.

"There we go. Now I'll tape it down and connect the tube to it. We're almost set." Sam held the roll of white medical tape and tore off a strip with his teeth. After making sure the needle was positioned properly, he taped it to Kristen's arm. He inserted the port at the needle's end to the clear plastic tube and taped it near her wrist. "Okay, no kinks. Everything looks good." He flipped the valve. Deep red blood flowed from her arm to the bag.

Tears ran down Kristen's cheeks as she stared at the bag that would soon be filled with her blood.

"Suck it up. The whole thing is only going to take fifteen minutes, max." Sam stood and picked up the folding chair then moved on to Bethany. "Have an arm preference?"

She looked away.

"No? Okay, then it will be the same for everyone—the right arm."

Chapter 28

My cell rang as J.T. and I climbed into the cruiser. I fished it out of my coat pocket and answered. Melanie was calling, hopefully with the update on Mitchell Carter.

"Hey, Mel. What did you find?" I put her on speakerphone.

"I found out where Mitchell Carter works. He runs the computer department at Synasys, Inc. He does travel now and then, which would make sense if he asked Molly to go out of town with him during the week. Obviously, he couldn't do that on the weekends when he's not working and supposed to be home with the family."

"Does he have kids too or just the wife?" I asked.

"Two boys, ages nine and six."

I glanced at J.T.

He shook his head. "Double dirtbag."

"Okay, did you confirm he's at work?"

"I did, and he is. Here's the address."

I set my notepad on the console and wrote down the address. "Great, we're on our way. Mr. Carter isn't expecting us, is he?"

"Nope, I only confirmed that he was on site."

"Even better. He won't have time to make up an alibi. Thanks, Mel." I clicked off, programmed the address into my GPS, and led the way. Twenty minutes later, J.T. turned in to the parking lot of a large four-story brick office building.

"What actually is Synasys?" J.T. asked.

"I have no idea. Data storage, maybe? Let's go find Mr. Carter and let him explain it."

The marble foyer led to the reception counter directly in front of us. Three women, each with a phone and computer, sat in the space. We approached and asked to speak with Mitchell Carter.

"Certainly. May I ask what this concerns?" a blond-haired woman asked.

I took the lead and enjoyed the wide-eyed expression people usually wore when I pulled out my badge and told them it was an FBI matter. I'd explain, clearly but tactfully, that it was none of their concern. That day was like all the others.

"Ma'am," I said as I pulled out my badge from beneath my buttoned coat, "we have a private matter to discuss with Mr. Carter. Would you please page him?"

Her face went bright red. "Oh, of course. One moment."

J.T. and I waited at the end of the counter for several minutes. A bank of elevators and what appeared to be a main hallway were within eyeshot. When a bell dinged, we looked toward the elevators. The doors of the second elevator parted, and a man stepped out and turned in our direction.

I whispered to J.T. that it must be Mitchell Carter. The tall man wore a suit, had a thick head of black hair, and was relatively attractive. He appeared to be in his late thirties or early forties. I sighed, knowing we were back to square one. "Don't think he's our guy." I immediately sized up the bewildered man walking toward us. Clearly he wasn't our suspect.

He extended his hand as he got closer. "I'm Mitchell Carter. Is there something I can help you with?"

We shook his hand, and I scanned the area. "FBI Agents Jade Monroe and J.T. Harper here, sir. Is there a private place we can talk?"

"Um, sure. What is this about?"

J.T. spoke up. "Please, Mr. Carter, I'm sure you'd rather keep our conversation private."

"Yeah, okay." Mitchell dragged his hand through his hair. His face was already turning pale. He pointed at a grouping of four chairs at the far end of the lobby. Two chairs faced two others, with a low, magazine-covered table separating them. I assumed he didn't have a private office where we could go. "How's this?"

"Sure, that area will be fine."

I led the way across the lobby and took a seat. J.T. sat next to me, and Mr. Carter faced us on a chair from the other side of the table. I pulled out my notepad from my purse.

"Why do you agents want to speak with me? Have I done something wrong?"

"That depends on you, sir. We've been told you're close to Molly Davis." I made sure to note his initial expression when I said Molly's name. As I expected, his face went white, and he seemed as if he was about to get ill.

"Molly Davis? That name does sound somewhat familiar."

I smiled. This wasn't our first rodeo. We'd been through these types of interrogation sessions plenty of times. They were always the same. The person questioned initially played dumb, then they got a severe case of amnesia, and finally, when the jig was up, they'd backpedal, claiming they hadn't heard the name correctly and thought we were asking about someone else.

"Yes," J.T. said, "Molly Davis. We heard you two were seeing each other. Seems she confided in a coworker of hers at First Federal Bank. That's how we knew who you were."

Sweat droplets formed on Mitchell's forehead. He pulled the pocket square from his suit coat and dabbed his face. "Agents, I'm a married man and have two sons."

"We're well aware of that too," J.T. said.

I heard the disdain in J.T.'s voice. My partner was a man of high moral integrity, which I admired about him.

"When was the last time you spoke to or saw Molly?" I asked. The pages of my notepad were rolled back and folded under the clean sheet I was about to write on. I waited as Mitchell feigned the amnesia part of the session.

"Um—I think it was last week."

"Last week since you saw her or last week since you spoke to her?"

"Uh, what? Can you excuse me for a minute? I need some water."

"Sure, go ahead." I normally wouldn't let anyone get up and disrupt the questioning, but since a water fountain with cups was only thirty feet away, I waved him on. I whispered to J.T. "What do you think? I swear he's about to faint."

"He's probably only guilty of being a cheating husband, but in his mind, that's plenty. I'm sure he needed a few seconds to get his timeline right too."

Mitchell returned and took his seat.

"So?" I asked.

"What was the question again?"

"When was the last time you saw or spoke to Molly? Exact dates, please." I stared him down.

"I spoke to her on the phone Friday as I was driving home from work. I wanted to meet with her, but she said she was going out to dinner with a friend. I wanted an answer about going out of town with me next week. She said she'd think about it and let me know, but I haven't been able to get through to her. Maybe she found out I was married."

I wrote down what he said. "So, you're saying Friday was the last time you spoke to her? Nothing since?"

"That's correct. My wife doesn't need to find out about Molly, does she?"

"Molly is missing, Mr. Carter. Did she threaten to expose you to your wife?"

"What? Missing? No, nothing like that happened. She didn't even know I was married."

"Have you ever been to the running trails with her?"

"Never. I made sure to keep our meeting places discreet."

"And she never asked why?"

"She probably had her suspicions since I felt her pulling away."

"And that pissed you off?" I asked.

"No, it didn't piss me off. I really like Molly. How long has she been missing?"

I ignored his question. If he wasn't involved, as he claimed, nothing about the case was his concern.

"How tall are you, and how much do you weigh, Mitchell?" J.T. asked.

"Why?"

J.T. held his stare and waited.

"I'm six foot two and weight two hundred pounds."

"Were you at work all day Monday?"

He glared at me. "Of course I was."

"Can somebody corroborate that?"

"Everyone that works here can."

"How about after work?" J.T. leaned forward, his elbows resting on his knees. "Where did you go?"

Mitchell dabbed his forehead again. Sweat rolled down his hairline and settled in his sideburns. "Straight home, I swear."

"We're going to ask your wife when you arrived home, and you better hope your stories match. Your extracurricular activities aren't our concern, so if you need to explain something to her, that's on you. What's her cell number?" I asked.

After a moment of hesitation, defeat written across his face, Mitchell rattled off the number.

"Your wife's name?"

"Jody. Do you have to say why you're asking?"

"No, but don't you think a wife would want to know why an FBI agent is asking where her husband was after work on Monday?"

Mitchell buried his face in his hands and moaned.

I stood. "I'll be right back. Stay put."

J.T. gave me a nod. He wasn't going to let Mitchell out of his sight.

I pushed through the double glass doors and dialed Jody's number as I stood in the vestibule. I was within eyeshot of Mitchell, who was facing my way. Jody and I spoke for two minutes. It wasn't my responsibility to explain her husband's infidelity. She confirmed that Mitchell was home by six p.m. on Monday, as he was most of the time except during overnight business trips. She said she remembered that time specifically because they watched the news together as they ate. I hung up from the call and reentered the lobby. Then I took my seat. "You're off the hook for now, at least with us."

He responded sarcastically. "Gee, thanks."

"No problem." I passed my card across the coffee table to him. "Don't go far. We may want to speak to you again." I closed my notepad and tucked it into the side pocket of my purse. "That should do it for now." I tipped my head toward the door, and J.T. stood. We gave Mitchell a nod goodbye and left the building.

Buckled in the car and heading back to the precinct, J.T. spoke up. "I guess Mitchell can go to the bottom of the suspect list. He's guilty of being a cheater but probably nothing else."

I agreed.

"Let's have a quick dinner as long as we have the time," J.T. said.

"Pull in there." I pointed at a nondescript diner at the corner of Williams and Drexel. "Soup and fries are enough for me."

J.T. parked in the ten-car lot, and we went inside. It wasn't quite the dinner hour yet, so we had the place to ourselves. I figured soup and fries couldn't take too long. I ordered a cup of coffee too.

"I'll have a BLT and fries," J.T. said to the motherly looking waitress who stood at the end of our booth. She wore an apron tied around her midsection and a pencil wedged above her ear. A pair of teal glasses was perched on the bridge of her nose. Thanks to our easy-to-remember orders, she didn't need to write them down.

"Want me to bring out the coffees right away?" she asked.

Her mannerisms reminded me of my own mom, and I smiled. "Yes, please."

It took only a half hour before we were back in the car and with full bellies. That dinner would likely hold us over until morning. I climbed in on the passenger side and pulled out my phone. The vibration signaled a call or text had recently come in. I tapped my password on the home screen and checked. Sullivan had sent me a text ten minutes ago. "Shit."

J.T. raised his right eyebrow as he pulled out of the parking lot and turned right. "That sounds daunting."

"It is. Two girls went out together last night, and neither has returned home or made contact with their families. We need to get back to the station and see what's up."

Chapter 29

"Are you comfortable, Mom?" Sam tucked the blanket around Adeline's feet as she lay on the couch and watched TV. Concern for his mother filled his mind, but he tried not to show it. He turned his back and wiped his eyes with his sleeve. Adeline's color was off, and she appeared weaker each day. He didn't understand why the transfusions hadn't improved her anemia. A sallow color took over her face, and dark rings circled her eyes. Her infections were getting worse as time went on. Sam tried not to appear shocked when he noticed new problems—red sores erupting from her arms and legs.

"I'm okay, honey, just a little weak today."

"Let me see your veins." Sam held his mother's frail arm. Her skin was paper thin, but her veins were barely noticeable. "You need more fluids. How about vitamin water or a bottle of that electrolyte drink?"

"I'll take the raspberry vitamin water."

"Sure thing." Sam pushed off the couch and entered the kitchen. He opened the refrigerator door, moved the three pints of new blood to the side, and grabbed a bottle of vitamin water. He cracked open the lid and stuck a straw in then returned to the living room. "Let me prop you up a little so you can drink this."

She groaned with every movement as he placed pillows behind her back. The cancer was spreading throughout her body. She was deteriorating fast.

All she needs is more blood. Two transfusions a day will keep her alive. I'm taking another pint from each girl tomorrow.

"Tonight you're getting another transfusion. I need to dial in the right amount to keep you healthy, Mom. I don't think you're getting enough new blood."

"Are you sure, Sam? Taking too much from them and giving me more than you should doesn't sound like a good idea. We may all die."

"Give me a little time to research this. Why not take a nap? I'm going to be on the computer for a bit, anyway."

"I will if you stay in the living room with me."

"Not a problem. I'll bring the laptop out here."

Sam took notes as he searched the Internet. Two hours had passed, and the clock let out six deep chimes. Sam glanced at his mom, still fast asleep. He'd wake her soon and give her dinner and plenty of fluids. The Internet search did little to soothe his anxiety, but he really hadn't expected it to. His mother needed more blood, that was all there was to it. And to support the household and the girls in the workroom with healthy food and drinks, he'd have to sell at least half the blood he was drawing from them. He couldn't bring more women home. Three was already too many. One might have to die after all.

Sam rubbed his pounding head. Worry had overtaken his mind, and his headaches occurred more frequently. He tipped the aspirin bottle and shook out four tablets. He washed them down with the glass of tepid water that had been sitting on the end table for two hours.

His thoughts turned to Molly. She had been with him the longest and had said she felt weaker. Since Monday, he had drawn three pints of blood from her, and her veins were collapsing. Pretty soon they would be all but gone. Molly had to die.

Sam rose from the recliner and walked quietly out of the living room. A linen closet stood at the end of the hallway. He opened the louvered door and pulled out one queen-sized blue sheet and a white full-sized sheet. He'd drape them between Molly and the other girls so they couldn't see what he was about to do. He remembered that a bucket of clothespins always sat on a shelf by the back door of the garage. Months ago, when Adeline was still healthy, she'd hang the wet laundry on the clothesline behind the house. Sam smiled at the memories of better days. Adeline had always loved the fresh scent of air-dried sheets.

With the linens draped over his arm, he tiptoed through the laundry room and into the garage. He closed the door at his back. With the bucket of clothespins in hand, Sam unlocked the workroom and went inside. He flipped on the light, waking the women.

Molly squinted. "What are you doing with that stuff?"

"I'm sectioning off the room."

"Why?"

"Don't worry about it." Sam took a length of rope and wove it through an eye hook against the wall. He stretched the rope across the room and threaded it through another eye hook. He pulled it tight then knotted it. With each sheet folded over the rope and secured with clothespins, he'd sectioned off the room perfectly. Molly couldn't see Kristen and Bethany, and they couldn't see her.

Sam walked out and locked the door behind him then went back into the house to start dinner. He peeked around the living room corner, Adeline's eyes were still closed.

He opened the cabinet above the stove and pulled out the bottle of succinylcholine and a clean syringe. After dinner, Molly would get the needle, and he'd take her blood for the last time.

Chapter 30

When he saw us enter the hallway, Captain Sullivan waved to get our attention.

J.T. opened the captain's office door, and we stood against the framework. "Two more girls have gone missing?"

The captain pushed back his heavy desk chair and got up. He jerked his head to the right when he reached us. "Meeting in the bull pen." He jiggled his change in his pocket as he gave us a brief explanation while we walked. "Stone took the call from a Mrs. Kelly, and Mills took the call from a Mrs. Henry. They have the details."

We entered the bull pen and pulled a few vacant chairs into the aisle between Mills's and Stone's desks. Sullivan sat on the corner of Andrews's desk and crossed his arms and legs. He pointed at Stone. "You go first."

"Yes, sir, I have the notes from the caller right here. A Mrs. Kelly called about a half hour ago. She said her daughter, Bethany, went to Paul's Tap on the east side of town last night for ladies' night and never returned home."

I nodded. "That makes sense. Tuesdays are ladies' night at most bars."

Stone continued. "Anyway, I told the mom we couldn't consider her daughter a missing person until twenty-four hours had passed. Under the circumstances, though, I got her contact number and said I'd call her back in an hour. That's about the time Mills got a similar call. Turns out these girls are best friends and went out together last night for half-priced drinks. That's when we informed Sullivan."

"Did the mothers do the usual? Call all the closest friends, check their daughters' social media pages, their jobs, and so on? Didn't the girls work?"

"We didn't ask all the details yet, Agent Monroe. I wanted to run this by you two and the captain before we alarm the parents any more than we already have."

"You did the right thing, Stone. Not a problem," J.T. said. "Did either mom say if they went to Paul's Tap and asked questions?"

"We didn't get that far."

I looked at Sullivan. "We're ready to pursue this, Captain. What's your take?"

He stared at the ceiling as if he were counting tiles. "I agree. We need to move on this while it's fresh."

"Oh, by the way"—I turned to Fitch—"Mitchell Carter isn't our guy." I saw the disappointment on her face. "He has black hair, and he stands six two and two hundred pounds. He said he hadn't talked to Molly since last Friday. Let's put him on the back burner for now and keep looking."

Captain Sullivan spoke up. "Okay, Andrews and Fitch, keep working the Molly Davis leads. Stone and Mills, follow up with the parents of the most recent missing girls."

I grabbed my jacket from the chair and put it on. "We'll go to Paul's Tap and ask questions. Text us the vehicle information for both girls. They did drive to the bar individually, correct?"

"According to the initial notes we took, yes," Stone said.

J.T. and I were back in the cruiser minutes later with the directions to Paul's Tap displayed across my cell phone screen. "From here it looks like a fifteen-minute drive." I watched out the passenger window as we passed block after block of the most depressed areas of Gary. "This investigation is going nowhere, J.T. We need more details."

"We do have a description of sorts. A medium-sized guy that possibly has blond hair was seen kissing Molly at the trails. That much, we're certain of. He has to be our number one suspect. With her car still on site, we know she didn't leave there alone."

"Right, but we still need more than that. I'm thinking he's in the same general age range as the girls. So far, we have Taylor Dorsey as the youngest, at nineteen, and Corrine Lionel and Molly Davis, the oldest, both at twenty-three. Other than these latest girls, has anyone checked to see if the ladies had any common friends, hobbies, clubs they belonged to, that sort of thing?"

"Not sure, but call Sullivan and ask. With Corrine, Taylor, and Heather going missing months apart, they probably had no reason to connect them to each other.

We'll definitely start putting a profile together to work with, though. We need to know if there's any current chatter going across the phone lines with Alex too. At this point, anything will help."

I dialed the captain's office phone. He picked up right away. "Captain Sullivan, Jade here. We never asked if anyone had made a connection between the girls."

"We were working that angle with officers Jeffries and Christopher. They were checking the coffee shops around the university Taylor was a student at."

"Has anything popped? Did any employees recognize her picture?"

"I'll get back to you on that. It's a long shot, Jade. Taylor went missing months ago."

"I know, sir, but there has to be a common thread somewhere. I'll touch base after we talk to the employees at Paul's Tap."

J.T. pulled into the pea-gravel parking lot and killed the engine. Three cars sat side by side, and two of them probably belonged to employees. We got out and scanned the area.

"Wow—this place is dead."

"Nah, it's just early, that's all. The younger generation doesn't go out until ten or later. That way they don't have to spend so much money on drinks. They get started at home then enjoy the buzz once they're at the bars."

"How do you know so much about the drinking habits of youth?"

I shot J.T. a sideways grin. "Amber used to bartend, plus she's young. I learned everything I know from her."

"That's scary."

"Actually, it's very helpful. I just taught you something new, didn't I?"

"Humph, I guess so, but still, wouldn't kids worry about getting a DUI before they even get to the bar?"

"Do kids worry about anything? That job belongs to their parents."

We took the four cement steps up to the front door. Inside, one person sat cozied up to the bar, drinking a glass of beer. The bartender looked to be in his mid-twenties and wore a long brown ponytail and a goatee. He busied himself stocking the refrigerator with canned and bottled beer. He looked up and gave us a nod. J.T. and I seated ourselves at the opposite end of the bar.

The bartender wiped his hands on a rag and walked over. "What can I get for you two?"

"How about a couple of coffees and a side of information?" J.T. asked.

I chuckled. He was clever and a fast thinker.

"Sure, coming right up."

I watched as the bartender poured two cups from what looked to be a fresh pot of coffee. I was thankful for that. He set them in front of us with a couple of packaged sugars and creamers.

"So what can I help you with?" He wiped the bar with his damp rag, probably out of habit. It looked perfectly clean the way it was.

I thought it best to introduce ourselves and hoped he'd feel more obliged to be as truthful as possible. "My name is

Jade Monroe, and this is my partner, J.T. Harper. We're FBI agents, and we have a few questions we hope you can help us with."

He raised his brows. "I've never met FBI agents. You look like regular people."

I smiled. "We are regular people. Your name is?"

"Jackson Clark."

"Nice name. My old commander at the Washburn County Sheriff's Department in Wisconsin was a man by the name of Chuck Clark. Anyway, Jackson, were you tending bar last night?"

"Tuesday night, most definitely. Actually, there were three of us tending bar. Ladies' night, you know. This place really gets hopping after ten. What's funny is, Tuesday brings in the masses, but come Wednesday night, it's pretty dead here. Everyone stays home because they're still nursing a major hangover. It's like clockwork every week."

"So last night was packed?"

"Jam-packed."

"Do you have regulars?"

"Sure do. They're the people we depend on most." He topped off our coffees and placed a few more creamers on the bar.

"Do you know Bethany Kelly and Kristen Henry?"

He grinned. "Who doesn't? They're here every Tuesday night. Bethany comes first and holds down the fort until Kristen gets off work."

"Kristen works nights?" J.T. pulled his notepad out of his inner pocket and wrote that down. "Do you know where?"

"Yeah, at the movie theater by the mall."

I had no idea where that was, but it didn't matter. Getting vital information from Jackson was more important. "Were they here last night?"

"Yeah, I'm pretty sure I saw them from a distance, but I didn't wait on them. Jen worked the bar tables. I worked the bar along with Abe."

"Do you have any idea what they drive?"

"Nah, never asked."

I looked around. "No cameras?"

"Nope. The owner is still stuck in the seventies, when he used to frequent this place on his way home from work every night. He eventually bought the joint. He says there's no crime in the area, so we don't need that expensive crap." He smiled. "His words, not mine." Jackson knocked on the bar surface. "So far he's been right. This is a local hangout, mostly kids in their twenties. Haven't had any real problems, probably because it's a low-key type of place. We're kind of invisible to the outside world."

"Did you happen to see anyone sitting with Kristen and Bethany?"

"Can't say that I did, but Jen would be the person to ask." He looked over his shoulder at the clock. "She gets in at nine."

"Thanks." We had over an hour wait before Jen started her shift. "What do you want to do, J.T.?"

He tossed six bucks on the bar for our coffees. "Check your phone and see if you got a message about those cars. Then let's walk the neighborhood. Maybe somebody saw or heard something unusual last night."

We left the bar and crossed the lot to our cruiser. Inside, with the car on and the heater blowing, I checked my phone calls. A new message had come in twenty minutes earlier. I nodded at J.T., and he pulled out his notepad.

"Stone says Kristen has a late-model white Honda Civic, and the plate number is 429-FNP. Bethany has an older blue four-door Subaru wagon, and the plate number is YYK-604. He and Mills are still conducting the interviews with the parents."

"Okay, ready to go out and do some knock and talks?"

"Sure, I just wish it wasn't twenty-five degrees outside." I slipped my hands into what was the only thing in the cruiser that might help a little—a pair of latex gloves pulled from the box in the backseat. I pulled up my coat collar and zipped it as high as it would go. "Okay, I guess I'm as ready as I'll ever be."

Chapter 31

Sam filled the dishwasher with the dinner plates and closed it. He couldn't put off the inevitable any longer. It was time to tend to Molly. He leaned over the couch back and patted his mother's shoulder. "I'll be back in a half hour, Mom. I have to check on the ladies."

He pushed the coffee table closer to the couch so Adeline wouldn't have to reach for anything. With his mother temporarily situated, Sam passed through the laundry room and entered the garage, where he loaded the syringe with succinylcholine. The sterile jugs, needles, and tubes used for blood draining sat to his right. He'd take them into the workroom after he injected Molly. By that time it would be too late for her to tense up. She'd be paralyzed long enough for him to get the job done. With Molly unable to react, his job would go much smoother.

Sam fished the key to the workroom out of his front pants pocket and unlocked the door. He crossed the room and stood next to her.

"I have to go to the bathroom," she said. "Can I get up?"

"Sure, I'll give you a hand." Sam released the straps across her chest. "Sit up and get your bearings for a minute so you won't be dizzy." He thumbed the syringe in his pocket, popped off the cover, then walked around to her left side. "I'll hold you upright."

"Thank you." She sat up slowly.

With the syringe cupped in his right hand, Sam jammed it into the back of her neck and pressed the plunger until it wouldn't go any farther. The succinylcholine was released into her muscle and began to take effect within seconds. He pushed her back down and ran out to get the equipment he needed. He'd have to drain her blood fast before she died of asphyxia. With a needle and drain tube placed in her carotid artery and one in her femoral artery, the blood flowed into the jugs beneath the gurney.

"Sorry, Molly, but this is something I have to do. It isn't personal. I promise it will be over soon." Sam heard moaning from the other side of the draped sheets. He was certain Kristen and Bethany had heard what he'd said. He checked the jugs to make sure they were still filling then walked around the makeshift room divider. "Is there something you ladies need?"

When Kristen nodded, Sam pulled the tape off her mouth.

She screamed Molly's name and was quickly silenced with a violent slap across the face.

"We use our indoor voices here. The sooner you realize that, the sooner I may let you go without the tape. Got it? That goes for both of you." He gave Bethany a threatening glare.

"What did you do to her? Why isn't she responding?" Kristen asked.

"That isn't your concern." He placed the tape back over Kristen's mouth and dipped under the wall of sheets. "I'll get your dinners." Sam checked his watch. Ten minutes had passed, and Molly was likely nearing death. Quickly glancing at the jugs before exiting the room, he saw they were almost half full. He'd bring food back for the girls and, afterward, remove Molly's tubes. He needed to think of a place to dump her—somewhere remote where she wouldn't be found.

Chapter 32

J.T. pulled the cruiser out of Paul's parking lot and turned onto the first street to our left. He parked against the curb at the beginning of the street, and we got out.

"Have a preference, left side or right?" he asked.

I tipped my head. "I'll take the right. I like the houses over here better."

"It's dark outside. How can you see them?"

"Okay, you busted me. I'm right brained, right handed, and I sat in the passenger seat, which is on the right side of the car. I just like the right side of things."

"Good enough. If anyone has something to tell you, call me over. I'll do the same."

We parted ways. I headed up the sidewalk to the houses on the right, and J.T. crossed the street to the houses on the left.

I knew that each of us would begin the process in the same way. We'd introduce ourselves, show our badges, and cut to the chase. We wanted to cover a few blocks as quickly as possible. The night was cold, and we wanted to speak with the bartender named Jen as soon as her shift began.

The first few residents offered nothing. They neither heard nor saw anything. At that time of night, they were sound asleep. The owner at house number two said his dog was barking like crazy in the middle of the night.

I pulled out my notepad. "Sir, do you remember exactly what time that was?"

He scratched the top of his head as if that would ring a bell. "Well, Pearl normally sleeps soundly, so when she did bark, it startled me. I sat up in bed and listened, just to make sure nobody had broken into the house. The clock showed it was after three a.m."

"Then what?"

"Then I got up and double-checked every door lock. I even peered out the window but didn't see anything. I chalked it up to the bar being around the corner. Pearl curled up and went back to sleep, and I went back to bed."

I wrote down his statement, name, and house number and thanked him for his time. I gave him my card and continued on.

J.T. yelled from across the street. "Anything?"

I followed the driveway down to the sidewalk. "Nothing that will matter, only a dog barking at bar time. How about you?"

"Nothing yet."

The street we were on was laid out in an east-to-west fashion and had six houses on each side before it intersected with a north-to-south street. It was a simple grid of square blocks, nothing complicated other than the amount of time it would take and how far we wanted to expand our knock and talks. We reached the end of that block and met on my side of the street.

"Now what?" I asked as I jammed my nearly frozen fingers deep into my pockets.

J.T. panned the area. "Let's go up one more block and head west. By the time we finish there, Jen will probably be at the bar."

"Yeah, makes sense. Same sides?"

"Sure." He gave me an eye roll. "Don't want to screw with your right-side OCD issues."

I could do six more houses. If nothing popped, we'd have patrol expand the search tomorrow. By the time we finished the next six houses—probably nine thirty or so—people would be less likely to answer their doors, anyway. We continued on.

I walked up the sidewalk of house number three. The house was well lit. Through the picture window, I saw the reflection of the television playing. At least somebody was near the front door and would hopefully answer quickly. Other homeowners had peeked out the side window, then again through the sidelights, and finally turned on the porch light before asking who was there. My badge was already positioned between my stiffened fingers and held at eye level. I rang the bell. A gray-haired gentleman pulled the curtains to the side. I turned toward him, flashed my badge, and smiled through my shivers.

He immediately pulled the wooden door open and pushed the screen door forward. He wore only jeans and a white T-shirt. I was sure the conversation would last about ten seconds before he felt the night chill too.

"Please, come in. It's way too cold to be standing out on my porch, plus I don't want the heat to escape. What can I do for you?"

I introduced myself and told him why J.T. and I were canvassing the neighborhood.

"Please, Agent Monroe, have a seat. I may have something helpful."

"Would you mind if I call my partner in to join me first?"

"Nope, go ahead."

I dialed J.T. and told him I was in the well-lit house and the homeowner might have information for us. He said he was two houses ahead of me but would be there in less than a minute. I hung up. "Thank you, sir. He'll be right here. Your name is?"

"Jeff Simmons. I used to be a dispatch officer at the Merrillville Police Department, but I retired last year. Enough is enough, you know? I put in nineteen years with that department."

"We certainly appreciate your service, and I'm sure the state of Indiana did too."

A knock sounded at the door. Jeff pushed off the chair he sat on and crossed the room. "I guess your partner found the place." He pulled the door open after a quick peek through the peephole. "Can never be too careful."

"Absolutely."

I introduced J.T., and with a hearty handshake between the men, J.T. took a seat next to me.

"Now, what can you tell us, Jeff?" I asked.

"Well, you said you were looking for anything that seemed off about last night."

"That's correct." I noticed J.T. had already pulled out his notepad. I appreciated it since my fingers weren't quite thawed yet.

"This was around bar time, definitely after three a.m. I'm sure you notice that I keep my house well-lit."

"Indeed, and a good way to ward off would-be burglars."

"Yep, I was robbed at gunpoint last year, and I don't want to experience that again. I'm saving for wrought-iron window bars and a door gate. It's a shame what this town is becoming. Anyway, once I turn in at night, I keep the coach lights and the porch lights on. There's a light above my back door, but it doesn't do much. After that incident last year, I installed motion sensor lights in my backyard. I got the expensive kind that won't trigger whenever a raccoon crosses the yard or a gust of wind rattles a tree. It has to be something big, like a human, to trigger the light. Anyway, the light woke me last night. My bedroom window faces the backyard, and I keep the blinds open just in case something unusual occurs." He took a breath and waited as J.T. jotted down his notes.

"Go on, please."

"Sure. Anyway, the light went on last night, and I jumped out of bed. I keep my old service weapon in my nightstand in case I ever have a need to use it. I looked out the glass and saw a man running through my yard. He cut through several yards and disappeared."

J.T. looked up from his notepad. "Which way was he going?"

"Toward Paul's Tap."

"*Toward* the bar?" I raised a questioning brow.

"Yes, ma'am. He was running from the east and heading through the backyards in a west-to-northwest direction. I ran to my front window and saw him cross the street and continue through the yards at Kinder Street."

"That's the next street north, right?" I pointed toward Jeff's front door.

"That's correct."

I looked at J.T. "We just cleared that street, but in the middle of the night with people that sleep soundly, I understand how they wouldn't realize someone had run through their yards."

"You did say a homeowner told you their dog was barking around bar time."

"I sure did." I pulled out my notepad and checked the house number. "Jeff, what is the house number here?"

"Two-two-eight Fillmore."

"And Mr. Lowell's house number is two-two-six Kinder." I looked up. "Do you know Mr. Lowell?"

"Sure do. Matt has lived there for sixteen years, and if Pearl barked in the middle of the night, something definitely caught her attention."

"I know it's a long shot, but did you see the person well enough to give us something?"

"Those motion sensor lights work pretty well. Granted, I saw the guy for maybe four seconds, but I did catch a few things. I could tell by his gait he was in a rush, almost frantic. I figured he was somewhat young by the baggy jeans. He wore a dark puffy jacket, probably goose down, and he had medium-length blond hair."

"Was it light blond or dishwater blond?" J.T. asked.

Jeff rubbed his chin. "I'd say medium blond. I'd put him at five ten or so. He easily ran under the lowest limb of my Crimson King Maple, and that's about six and a half feet off the ground. He had an average build from what I could tell. But with those baggy jeans and puffy coat, I could be off in either direction."

"You're pretty observant, Jeff. This is really good information."

He waved me off. "Comes with the territory after all those years in the police force. You know how it goes— second nature."

I smiled and understood. "So the man could have been coming from the block behind your home, cutting through yards, and traveling toward the street Paul's Tap is on?"

"That's correct, Agent Harper. Paul's is three blocks northwest of me on Jacobsen Street, the exact direction he was traveling."

I stood, warmed and comfortable. The information we had was enough for now, and we'd take a slow drive on the street behind us. There was a reason our assailant came from that direction. I gave Jeff my card and thanked him with a hearty handshake. J.T. did the same. Jeff told us to stay warm and stay safe as he closed the door.

J.T. jerked his head in the direction of the cruiser. "Let's get the car and check out a few of the streets behind us."

I pulled out my phone from my pocket and listened to Stone's message again. "Okay, we're going to have our eyes peeled for a white Civic or a blue Subie wagon."

"Got it."

We rounded the block and headed to the end of the street. We'd be back in the cruiser in under two minutes with the heat blowing at max force. My shoulders hurt from involuntarily hunching them as we walked.

"You know what every cruiser needs in winter?" I asked.

J.T. curled his lip until a grin formed. "I'm sure you're going to tell me."

"Damn straight—remote starts with the heat already set on high. That would be pure heaven."

"Come on, crybaby. We're almost there."

Chapter 33

Back in the cruiser, I stretched the seat belt over my coat, and J.T. turned the heater to the highest setting. I dialed Sullivan while we had a minute to spare. He answered on the second ring.

"Captain Sullivan here."

"Sir, it's Jade. We have a lead that's frankly the best we've gotten yet. A former police dispatch officer gave us a decent description of someone who ran through his yard last night at bar time. It matches the description given by Erin McNare—same height, build, and hair color."

"Great find. So what are you doing now?"

"We're going to patrol a few streets where the runner may have come from and see if anything shakes loose. Has anyone talked to Molly Davis's friend, Maddie Trapp? I just don't want anything overlooked."

"I'm pretty sure Andrews and Fitch are on that right now. There was something about a place called Penelope's too?"

"Yes, that's one of those new crossover coffee shops."

"That's right. They're going to stop in there too."

"Okay, we'll keep you posted." I clicked off and pocketed my phone.

J.T. looked up at the street sign. "This is Mayville Street." He pulled over and glanced through the backseat window behind my shoulder. "If the runner went through Jeff's yard at an angle going west to northwest, he had to be coming from that direction." J.T. pointed to his left and turned on Mayville. "Keep your eyes locked on the right side of the street. I'll watch the left."

J.T. drove at a snail's pace down the block. Neither of us spoke as we checked every parked car we passed at the curbs and in the driveways. He was near the end of the street. We'd have to make a decision to either go farther or turn and go south another block.

"Stop!" I yelled so loud we both jumped.

"Geez, Jade, you scared the crap out of me."

"Sorry, but there's a white Civic parked up ahead on my side. What was the plate number again?"

J.T. clicked on the dome light and pulled out his notepad. He handed it to me as he closed in on the vehicle.

I flipped to the last few pages. "Here it is, late model white Civic, plate number 429-FNP. We have a definite match, and we'll need forensics out here right away. They're going to have to open up the car. I hope to hell there isn't a DB inside."

J.T. found an open spot along the curb and tucked the cruiser in between two other cars. He grabbed a flashlight from the door pocket and got out. I called Sullivan again and told him what we needed as I watched J.T. shine the beam into the interior of the car. He craned his neck as he followed the light from the front seat floors and into the backseat area. He turned toward me and shook his head. I breathed a sigh of relief.

I closed the cruiser's door at my back and walked to the Civic, where J.T. stood. "Sullivan said forensics should be here in twenty minutes." I pointed a thumb over my shoulder. "I could go back and talk to Jen. There's no need for both of us to wait here."

"Yeah, let's do that. Hop back in the car. I'll drive you over."

J.T. dropped me off at the front door of Paul's Tap. The parking lot had filled considerably with cars as the night got later. I excused myself as I passed patrons huddled on the steps and smoking as they tried to stay out of the wind. My thoughts on that? Quit the nasty habit.

I opened the door and stepped into a warm, youth-filled bar. Jackson looked up as I entered, and waved me over.

"Hey, Agent Monroe, are you back to interview Jen?"

"I am. Could you point her out for me?"

"Sure thing. I'll have Abe cover for her. Do you know how long it'll take?"

"Hopefully not more than fifteen minutes. There's somewhere I need to be."

"Understood." He yelled out, and a cute brunette turned and faced him. "That's Jen."

I thanked him and approached her. With the introductions made, I asked if there was a quiet place where we could talk.

"Either in the storage room or outside. Take your pick," Jen said.

I'd had enough of the outside for a while and opted for the storage room.

"Sure, follow me." Jen led the way to a locked door. She reached into the pocket of her skinny jeans and fished out a key ring holding a half dozen keys. She thumbed through them until she found the one with a yellow happy face sticker on it. "Damn keys all look the same otherwise."

She grinned at me, and I instantly liked her. She pulled the old wooden door open and hit the switch on the wall. A flight of stairs leading to the basement was directly in front of us.

"Sorry, the basement is really dark and creepy. I usually don't go down here alone, but in the company of an FBI agent—hell yeah. No worries."

I chuckled and began descending. A musty, damp smell filled the air when we reached the basement floor. The small room was jam-packed with wooden crates and boxes. The more stable crates were stacked and nearly reached the ceiling. The basement was cool, but with my coat still zipped, I didn't mind.

"Sorry about the air quality down here." Jen shook her head as if disgusted. "I swear, if I was a smoker, I'd light one up right now just to kill the basement smell." She pointed at a crate. "Grab a seat."

I did. "Did Jackson give you a heads-up?"

"Not much, just said a couple of feds stopped by and wanted to talk to me about Kristen and Bethany. Where's your other half?"

I laughed. I loved the fact that she had very little filter when she spoke. She seemed forthright and uninhibited. Jen would do fine with the interview.

"My partner is busy at the moment. Anyway, Jackson said you waited on Bethany and Kristen last night?"

She snapped her gum. "Yep, I sure did, just like every Tuesday night. Those two are permanent fixtures here on ladies' night. Bethany always gets here first. Come hell or high water, nobody better take their table. She'd have something to say about that. Seniority, you know?"

"I bet. Did they stay until bar time?"

"Yeah, I think so. We were swamped last night because of the pay-per-view boxing match. It brings the guys in by the truckloads, which naturally brings the chicks in. The double banger was the ladies' night specials—two-for-one drinks. It was wall-to-wall people, but we stayed within the fire code limit."

I smiled. "I'm not here to bust your chops."

"Thanks, you're cool. Anyway, it's the same every night starting around two thirty. All hell breaks loose. Everyone wants their final few drinks before last call. The bar gets really jammed up at that time. The last time I glanced toward Beth and Kristen's table, they were nursing a couple of beers. They didn't look like they were too enthused to stand behind fifty people and get shoved toward the bar while they waited their turn to be served, if you know what I mean."

"So you didn't see them again after that?"

"Only from behind and for a split second when they

headed out the door. It was right when Jackson turned on the lights. That's fifteen minutes before we actually herd everyone out to meet the three o'clock closing time. We're pretty strict with that. We don't want fines or our liquor license pulled."

"Did the girls walk out alone?"

"Hmm." Jen massaged her eyebrows as I waited for an answer. "A guy walked out with them or maybe just the same time as them. I couldn't really say they were together given the number of people here at the time. It could have been nothing more than a coincidence, and they got mashed together at the door."

"Could you tell what he looked like?"

"Hell no. All I saw was a blond guy wearing a parka, and that was from the back."

"Could it have been a dark goose down jacket?"

"Yeah, I guess it could have been. It didn't have the fur around the hood like a true parka does."

"Did he look taller than the girls?"

"Hard to say, but he didn't tower over them at all. Keep in mind, especially when women are out for the night, they usually wear heels of some sort."

"True enough." I sighed and reached into my coat pocket. I pulled out two cards and handed one to Jen. On the other, I wrote down her full name and phone number then stashed it in my pants pocket so I wouldn't accidentally use it. "Okay, I think that should do it. I really appreciate your help, Jen."

"No sweat. It isn't every day I get to talk to a fed."

We headed up the stairs and parted ways as she thumbed through the keys again to lock the basement door. I thanked Jackson for his help and called J.T. as I made my way to the exit. "Hey, partner, are you able to pick me up, or do I have to hoof it?"

"Nah, the cavalry is on site, and they've already popped the trunk. Thankfully, it was empty. They're loading the car up on the flatbed as we speak. It's going to the evidence garage so they can give it a thorough once-over tonight. Sullivan dispatched a half dozen patrol units to check the neighborhood for Bethany's car, going out five blocks in each direction. If there's smoke, there's usually fire. We already spoke to the lookie-loos who were peering out their windows. Nobody saw the car being dropped off. So did you get anything from Jen?"

I chuckled. "What a character. I'll tell you all about it on our drive back to the station. Come get me."

"Yep, I'm a block away. Watch for my headlights."

Chapter 34

Sam busied himself in the corner of the workroom. He'd removed the tubes from Molly's body, and the plastic jugs containing her blood sat on the counter. With the jugs elevated upside-down, the lids tightly twisted on, and a hole in each lid large enough for a drain tube to fit through, Sam transferred the blood into sterile transfusion bags. He would use them for resale and for his mother. He managed to get four pints out of Molly before her heart stopped. He placed the bags in a plastic container, snapped the lid closed, and stepped from the workroom into the garage. With the container wedged under his arm, he pulled the key from his pocket and locked the door behind him. Back in the house, Sam placed the individual bags of blood next to the condiments in the refrigerator shelf space and closed the door.

The TV was on in the living room. Sam recognized the game show that played just by the host's voice. It was one of Adeline's favorites. He taped it nightly so she could watch it at her convenience. He peeked around the corner and saw his mother snuggled on the couch. The blanket was pulled up to her chin. "You okay, Mom?"

She didn't respond.

"Mom?" Sam pushed the coffee table out of the way, knelt on one knee, and stared at his mother's neck. His breath caught in his throat when he saw a pulse. She was breathing—just sleeping soundly. He gave a deep sigh of relief before he pushed off the coffee table and stood. Sam grabbed the laptop and took a seat on the recliner. He had to find a spot to dump Molly and somebody to sell her blood to because he was running out of cash.

He glanced at the clock—it was after ten thirty. The best time to dispose of a corpse was closing in. He needed to do it in the dead of night as he had with the others but at someplace where Molly wouldn't be found. Abandoned homes like the one he'd used for Taylor wouldn't work. She'd been found in a matter of weeks by junkies who regularly squatted in that drug house. He needed somewhere even more remote, preferably outside the city limits.

Another half hour passed. The eleven o'clock chimes sounded a few minutes ago.

Wait—what's this?

Sam stumbled upon pictures of an abandoned steel mill within a half hour's drive. He clicked on the images tab and studied the photos. The caption below several images of old newspaper articles showed the name of the place was Dasher Point. It had closed in 1987. The entire site was set for demolition years ago, but that had been put on hold. Recent articles noted the thirtieth anniversary of the closing of Dasher Point. The steel mill, standing in ruin, still hadn't been taken down. It appeared that even though it was an eyesore, the city couldn't afford to demolish it.

Sam zoomed in on the aerial view and saw several old driveways that still connected to secondary roads.

That place should work, and it's doubtful Molly would ever be found. But before I do anything, I have to get Mom to bed. I may be gone for a while.

Sam clicked on the map's image and hit Print. Then he pushed the handle on the side of the recliner to lower the footrest. He rose quietly and went down the hall to get the wheelchair and retrieve the map from the printer. He returned to the living room, moved the coffee table aside, and situated the wheelchair next to the couch.

"Mom." He gently tapped her shoulder several times. "Mom, wake up."

She cracked her eyes and squinted. "What's going on?"

"It's late, and I need to help you to bed. You've been asleep for hours."

"Oh, okay."

"Let's sit you up for a minute so you aren't dizzy." Sam helped her upright and sat next to her on the couch. "Tomorrow you're getting a pint of blood. You're going to need a little more than I originally thought, maybe a pint every other day. It's a work in progress, Mom, but I'll make you a good breakfast in the morning and get you well hydrated. Then we'll start the transfusion. Feeling okay to go to bed now?"

She nodded silently.

Sam held her under the armpits and lifted her to the chair. "There you go. Let's get you settled for the night."

By eleven thirty, Adeline was comfortable in bed, and Sam had said good night. He entered the garage and opened the sliding side door of the van. He tossed the map of Dasher Point on the passenger seat. He crossed the garage, reached up on the top shelf of the built-in cabinets, and pulled down the folded tarp he always used to transport bodies. The last thing Sam wanted was for blood traces to be found in the van if he was pulled over. He tucked the tarp under his arm, unlocked the workroom door, and stepped inside. Instantly, moaning sounded from the other side of the hanging sheets.

"Shut up. I'm not in the mood for you two tonight. Go to sleep." He kicked a stray two-by-four. It slid across the floor to their side of the curtain. The room temporarily quieted.

Sam shook out the tarp and spread it across the floor near the gurney. He turned to Molly and unstrapped the restraints that had imprisoned her since Monday. "There, no more straps. You're free again."

With a grunt, he lifted her from the gurney and placed her at the edge of the tarp. He folded the top and bottom over her then rolled the stiffened body until he came to the end of the fabric. "That should do it."

Sam lifted her a second time, pushed the door open with his foot, and carried her to the van. He slid the door closed. After returning to the workroom, he turned off the lights and locked the door.

According to the map he'd printed, the mill was about twenty-five minutes south. Sam turned the ignition in the van, pressed the garage door remote, and drove out. He peered out the windshield at the sky as he drove—no moon in sight. The night would only get darker once he was south of the city's ambient lights. A flashlight he kept in the van at all times would definitely be helpful that night. He'd leave the headlights on too once he got there. Sam knew nothing about Dasher Point or its current condition. He hoped to find structures still standing so he could hide Molly's body deep inside.

Sam listened to the radio as he drove. The quiet wasn't his friend—it made him think too much. He tapped his fingers against the steering wheel to the beat of the music as he made his way south.

His mind betrayed him, and he began to think, anyway. He thought about how he could continue to get enough blood for his mother's transfusions. It had taken only three days of blood draws before Molly's veins collapsed and were useless.

Maybe I could rob a blood bank or steal blood from somebody else that uses it regularly. I don't have enough, I'll never have enough, and Mom is only getting worse.

He slammed his fist against the dash and turned off the radio. He was getting closer to the mill. The drive needed his full attention, anyway.

Sam decided to take what used to be the main entrance. The aerial view had made it look like a straight shot in off two secondary roads. When he reached Countyline Road, he turned left and continued for three miles. The green street sign reflected off his headlights. Sam slowed and checked the street name. He was within a mile of the mill.

Okay, I'm almost there.

He turned right on Greenfield Street and continued. The hair on the back of Sam's neck bristled. Other than the headlights guiding the way, the night was as black as tar. He was going into an abandoned steel mill, no lights anywhere in the area, and he had a dead body in the back of his van. He sucked in a deep breath, trying to calm his anxiety. What he wanted to do was roll Molly out into the ditch and take off, but he knew better. She had to disappear for good, and so would everyone else he might have to kill going forward. Somehow he'd get through this rough patch, his mom's health would improve, and life would go on—at least he prayed it would.

A rusted-out, broken sign caught his attention near an overgrown driveway. It wasn't legible, but it had to be for the mill. Nothing else was out there. The area was devoid of any sort of building or house—he was definitely in the boondocks. Sam turned right and inched forward. He stared straight ahead. He pressed the brakes, shifted the van into Park, and craned his neck as he leaned against the dash and peered out the windshield. He pulled the lever for the high beams, and his eyes widened.

"Shit! How can there be tire tracks out here?"

It hadn't snowed for several days. Even then, it was only an inch or so of accumulation, but there they were—tracks leading down the driveway.

Now what the hell am I supposed to do?

He tried to make sense of it—rationalize it in a way. He wondered who could have been out there and why.

Cops, that's it. They patrol the area now and then, probably a few times a year at most. The place is a hazard, and they don't want anyone getting hurt. That's the only logical explanation.

With his mind satisfied, relief washed over Sam. He continued on. He'd place Molly deep within the belly of whatever building remained so she'd never be discovered. He crept a half mile farther in, extremely cautious. He didn't want to hit deep ruts that could cause a flat tire or, worse, cause him to get stuck. His high beams illuminated the path, and he finally saw the mill, or what was left of it, straight ahead. Rusted sheet metal, broken timbers, and skeletal remains of the structure were all that was left of what likely had been a thriving steel mill fifty years earlier. Sam stopped and took in his surroundings. "What the hell?"

In front of him stood what looked to be a recent but short-lived bonfire. Unburned timbers still stood upright, wedged against each other and shaped like a teepee. The lower pieces of wood were charred. The enormous ring of rocks and broken bricks that had kept everything intact was filled with ash.

Sam fumed. Nothing was going his way. He turned the ignition and shifted into Drive. Pulling ahead, he inched as close as possible to the largest standing structure. He killed the engine but left the high beams on. With the flashlight jammed in his pocket, Sam exited the van and rounded it to the passenger side. He slid the door open and rolled Molly toward him before picking her up and heading into the building. No doors remained on the structure, so the van's headlights cast light inside. Once he got farther in, he'd depend solely on his flashlight.

After rounding several corners, Sam noticed his light had diminished. He clicked on the flashlight and wedged it in his armpit. The old building squeaked, and feral critters scurried about. He needed to make it fast—anxiety was getting the best of him. A pile of broken and fallen beams, the size of a one-story building, lay straight ahead. Sam knew this would be Molly's final resting place, and he'd hide her within the rubble. He needed to make an opening—a crypt of sorts to place her in. He'd cover her with sheet metal and a few heavy beams so animals couldn't drag her body out. Coyotes and fox were prevalent in the remote areas of the county.

Sam lay the rolled tarp on the ground and began moving large pieces of sheet metal to the side. He dragged some of the lighter beams out of the way. When he'd created an opening large enough, he unrolled the tarp and pulled Molly's body out. He moved the tarp to the side, got down on his hands and knees, and pushed her into the void. Once she was hidden far enough inside, he tossed sheet metal over the opening and heaved beams on top of that.

Sam shined the beam of light around the area and couldn't tell anything had been disrupted. As a final precaution, he dragged the tarp behind him to make sure it rubbed out his footprints leading to Molly. With the flashlight guiding his way, he exited the building and climbed back in the van. His heart pounded. Exhausted, he gave the area a final look, drove away, and hoped for snow to cover any evidence he might have left behind.

Chapter 35

I pulled the door handle on the passenger's side of the cruiser and climbed in. J.T. had the heat already set to the highest temperature. I thanked him and rubbed my hands together in front of the vent.

"So, where are we off to?" I asked.

"Back to the station to regroup. Sullivan is expecting an update, and there are plenty of officers here, anyway." He gave me a thoughtful smile. "They're better dressed for the outdoor elements than you are. Where did you leave your warm gloves?"

"I think I left them in the bull pen. I was anxious to interview the employees at Paul's Tap and forgot to pick them up."

"Maybe we should pin them to your sleeves like they do with kids so you don't forget them."

I smirked and shot him a sneer. "You're a funny guy, Agent Harper."

We entered the parking structure and drove up to level four. We exited the cruiser and went inside the station.

Through the glass, I saw Sullivan sitting at his desk, a distressed look on his face. He placed the receiver on the phone's base and waved us in.

"Have a seat, guys. The officers on site just informed me that they found Bethany Kelly's car. It was about three blocks away from Kristen's vehicle. Forensics is going to tow hers too as soon as they do an initial sweep of the area and take photographs."

I groaned. "That's somber news. I'm sure the girls are together, but where? That's the million-dollar question. How soon do we want to alert the parents?"

Sullivan pressed his fingertips into his forehead and swirled them like a mini-massager. "We don't know an actual crime has been committed, but considering what has taken place in the last few days, the likelihood is high."

"For what it's worth, I found out a bit of information from one of the bartenders at Paul's Tap. I guess the girls go there often enough that the wait staff knows them by name. They usually show up on Tuesday nights. Jen, the bartender, waited on Bethany and Kristen throughout the night and said just before they closed last night, she saw them walk out with a blond-haired guy wearing a black parka." I drummed my fingers on the desk then waited. I didn't want to influence my colleagues one way or another, and I needed my recollection of what Jen said to come out correctly.

Sullivan stared at me. "Jade?"

I nodded. "Just thinking, sir. I want to word my comments cautiously. Jen did mention that the place was very crowded. The blond guy might have been walking out at the same time and nothing more. It could have been that innocent, and he was only another person leaving the bar."

J.T. scratched his chin as if something had just occurred to him. "Still, Erin McNare said the guy on the bench with Molly looked to have blond hair. Jeff Simmons said the same thing, and now, the bartender said the guy walking out with Bethany and Kristen had blond hair too. Jeff said the guy wore a black goose down jacket. The bartender described a similar jacket. Did she notice his build?"

"I think it was too crowded to see anything below his shoulders, but she did say he didn't tower over the girls. That would fit with the general description from Erin and Jeff as well."

Sullivan nodded. "Go with that as a starting point— blond hair, medium build, and a navy or black goose down jacket. Hopefully we can gather more information."

"We're assuming the guy is in the general age group as the ladies, sir."

"Go on, Jade."

"Well, the millennials seem to trust him enough to engage with him, and Jeff Simmons said the guy running through his backyard wore baggy jeans—something the younger generation does."

Sullivan glanced at the wind-up clock on his desk. "Good information for now. At least it's something we can work with. It's closing in on midnight, guys. Go catch some sleep. We'll reconvene in the morning and decide how to proceed after we hear from forensics. I don't want to cause undue stress on the parents, especially if there isn't any evidence of foul play in the vehicles."

"I assume you mean blood."

"Precisely."

J.T. and I left the police department and headed back to the hotel. I was ready to close my eyes and, with any luck, fall asleep quickly.

After an update text to Amber, I climbed into the snuggly hotel bed and turned off the light. My worries faded, and dreams took over.

A sound startled me awake. I sat upright in bed and checked the time—2:57. Had I dreamed it, or did I actually hear a noise? I waited and chalked it up to hallway chatter from late-night guests returning to their rooms. I snuggled deeper into the pillow and repositioned my head into a comfortable spot then heard the sound again. Knocking—and it was at my door.

"Damn it." I jumped from the bed and slipped my robe over my pajamas. I peered out the peephole. J.T. was pacing in front of my door with his hands buried deep in his pants pockets. Whatever had him there at three a.m. was serious enough that he didn't bother with his usual finger-over-the-peephole antics. I pulled the door open and ushered him in. "What the hell is going on?"

"I've been trying to call you, but you didn't pick up."

"Seriously?" I grabbed my phone off the night table. It was still set on vibrate. I had forgotten to turn the volume back up when I crawled into bed. "Shit. Sorry, J.T., my bad. Have a seat and tell me what happened."

"Sullivan called. The forensics team found blood in Bethany's car. They thought the location of the blood was odd, though."

I rubbed my eyes and yawned, even though I felt somewhat alert. "Where was it?"

"On the passenger side doorframe. That could give us a number of different scenarios. The first being, the assailant whacked her in the head, threw her in the car, and took her somewhere. But then what was Kristen doing during all of that? They didn't find any blood in Kristen's car, and both cars have dozens of fingerprints inside."

"I would imagine so. Young people are always catching rides somewhere with anyone who has an extra seat in their car. So now what?"

J.T. sighed. "Now we get dressed and pay the parents an unwelcome visit. Since we don't have DNA for either girl, we'll have to collect something of theirs to take with us. During their face-to-face interviews with the families, Stone and Mills got the description and plate numbers for both cars and a repeat of what the parents said earlier about the girls' plans for the night. Since there wasn't evidence of wrongdoing at the time, they didn't ask for DNA to take back to the station with them."

"This is the part of our job that's the toughest." I stood and opened the dresser drawer. "You have their addresses?"

"Yeah, Sullivan forwarded them to me from the interview reports."

"Okay, scoot so I can get dressed." I waved him toward the door.

J.T. turned the knob then looked over his shoulder at me. "Fifteen minutes?"

"Yep, I'll be ready."

As soon as J.T. left, I changed into a pair of black slacks and a beige sweater. I slipped on my cashmere socks and black Merrell boots. In the bathroom, I ran cold water over my face and brushed my teeth and hair. I still had five minutes, so I dabbed on a touch of blusher and a bit of lip gloss. I slipped on my coat, grabbed my purse, and then dropped my phone and room key into my pocket. J.T. knocked on the door just as I reached for it.

"Good timing," he said. "Got your gloves?"

I turned back and grabbed them off the credenza. "I do now, and thanks, Dad, for asking."

After a twenty-minute drive on nearly deserted streets back toward the city, we reached the home of Bethany Kelly.

I let out a deep sigh. "Ready to do this, partner?"

"Unfortunately, I'm getting used to giving families bad news. It seems we do that a lot more often than we report good news."

"Well, we don't know she's dead, so that's something." I jerked my chin toward the sidewalk that led to the front door. "Come on. It isn't going to get any easier with us sitting here."

We exited the cruiser and followed the sidewalk to the double wooden doors. J.T. rang the bell. I looked up and saw a second-story light go on.

I pointed upward. "Bedrooms must be upstairs. Let's give them a few minutes."

I pulled out my badge in preparation for the husband and wife peering out the window to see who woke them in the middle of the night. As the sound of footsteps got closer to the door, the porch light went on. Just as with every other late-night surprise visit, the curtains moved to the side, and Mr. Kelly stared out at us. J.T. and I turned our badges toward him so he could see them clearly. The dead bolt turned, and the door creaked open. A look of anxiety washed across the faces of him and Mrs. Kelly. She stood five feet behind him with her arms crossed protectively in front of her chest. They both wore nightclothes with robes over them.

I began the conversation. "Mr. and Mrs. Kelly, we're from the FBI. I'm Special Agent Jade Monroe, and this is my partner, Special Agent J.T. Harper. Sorry about the late hour, but we need to speak to you for a few minutes."

Mrs. Kelly wiped her eyes as the tears flowed freely. She led us into the family room. Her husband, with his arm around her shoulder, tried to comfort her as they took a seat on the couch. J.T. and I followed and sat on the love seat facing them.

"We know Officers Stone and Mills paid you a visit earlier in the evening and took your statements. What they didn't feel the need to do at the time was collect Bethany's DNA sample. Having the sample is standard procedure in a situation such as yours, especially when two girls go missing together. It doesn't mean anything directly other than the fact we need it on file to compare any biological evidence we may find," J.T. said.

"And have you? Why else would you be here at this time of night?" Mrs. Kelly asked.

I took over at that point. From my experience, women usually had a more delicate way of presenting bad news. "Ma'am, we found both vehicles in the vicinity of Paul's Tap. Right now the cars are being processed at the police department's evidence garage. Bethany's car came up positive for traces of blood."

"Oh no, this can't be happening." Mrs. Kelly sobbed against her husband's shoulder.

"Ma'am, at this time, we can't conclude that the blood belongs to Bethany or if it's even fresh blood. Can you think of any past incidents where somebody might have bled in, or against, her car? It was found on the passenger side doorframe."

"No, nothing she's ever mentioned."

I looked at Mr. Kelly, and he shook his head.

"Okay, as of now, we don't have any leads to the actual location of either girl. Do you know if Bethany had a male friend, someone in her general age group, with a medium build and blond hair?"

"Right now I can't think at all," Mrs. Kelly said.

"Understood." J.T. pushed off the love seat and stood. He fished two cards out of his wallet and handed them to the parents. "If anything rings a bell, please call anytime. Now what we'll need is Bethany's hairbrush and toothbrush in a plastic zipper bag."

Mrs. Kelly left the room to retrieve those items and returned minutes later. She handed the zipped bag to me, and I thanked her.

"We'll be in touch as soon as we have something new to tell you. Rest assured, we have plenty of people on this case," I said.

J.T. and I shook their hands and showed ourselves out. Now we had to repeat the process with Kristen's family and collect her DNA samples. At least we could tell them with certainty that no blood had been found in her car.

As J.T. backed out of the Kellys' driveway, I fastened my seat belt and pulled up the address I had programmed into my GPS for the Henry home.

"I'll keep my eyes peeled for an all-night drive-through restaurant. I'm going to need some coffee before we reach their house."

Chapter 36

The stress was getting to Sam, and his nerves were like a ticking time bomb. There wasn't enough blood for both Adeline and to sell to support the household. And they were still waiting on approval from the state-funded health insurance program.

Damn bureaucracy. Nothing is working out right, and the government is dragging its feet. Sam was about to take out his frustrations on Kristen and Bethany. He marched to the workroom at seven a.m. and flipped on the lights. Both girls woke with a start. Sam's expression said that nothing good was going to come out of that morning.

He cracked the plastic lids of two water bottles and pulled the tape off the girls' mouths. "Drink this. You'll get another bottle in a half hour, then we're doing the blood draws."

Kristen guzzled her water then took a deep breath. "Where's Molly? What did you do to her?" She yelled out her name. "Molly, answer me."

Sam snickered as he leaned forward within an inch of

her face. He exhaled hot air against Kristen's cheek. "Don't waste your breath. Molly can't hear you. She's left the house."

"Did you let her go? Where is she?"

"I'm in charge here and don't owe you an explanation. Now finish your water." He pushed the bottle into her mouth and tilted it. "Drink all of it." He did the same with Bethany before he taped their mouths again and left the room.

Back in the living room, Sam sat with the computer on his lap and a cup of coffee at his side. He searched the Internet for a person or group in the market to buy human blood. Adeline lay propped up on the couch with two pillows supporting her head. Sam had already served her breakfast. Now she relaxed with hot tea while she watched TV.

Sam knew finding somebody he could trust would prove difficult, and he was wary of those sites, which might be monitored by law enforcement. He'd be careful. He would write down the website URLs and contact information before private messaging anyone who might be helpful. He wouldn't use his own computer, either, but would correspond with them using the public library's computer lab. The alarm sounded on his phone. Sam closed his computer then stood.

"What was the alarm for?" Adeline could barely raise her head as she faced her son.

Sam noticed the increasingly dark circles around her eyes, and her skin had taken on an ashen color. "Time to give the girls more water and let them use the bathroom. I'll be back in a bit, Mom. Need anything?"

"Just a hug."

Sam knelt to the couch and gingerly hugged his mom. He was shocked at the way her bones protruded—she was getting weaker by the day. "We'll do your transfusion in about an hour, so just relax until then." He set the remote next to her hand and left the room.

Back at Kristen's side, Sam set the bags and tubes on a table and took a seat next to her. He opened another water bottle, removed the tape from both girls' mouths for the second time, and tipped the bottle between Kristen's lips. She clenched her teeth, and he swiftly slapped the side of her face. "Open your damn mouth and drink this, or would you rather have me knock out your teeth?"

She grudgingly opened her mouth, and Sam jammed the bottle in. Kristen gasped for air once the bottle was empty. Sam grinned and looked to his right. "Are you going to play nice, or am I going to have to show you who's the boss?"

Bethany opened her mouth. When the water was gone, each girl was allowed to use the facilities. Then Sam forced them back down on the chairs and bound them tightly.

"Why do you have four bags instead of two?" Bethany asked as she watched Sam prepare Kristen's arm for her blood draw.

"Because I'm taking two pints from each of you today."

Her voice cracked as she spoke. "That's too dangerous."

He laughed in her face. "I'm a lot more dangerous than the two pints of blood you're worried about giving. You'll live." He stood, grabbed the duct tape, and stretched a piece across her mouth. Then he shot her a threatening glare. "And if I want your opinion, I'll ask for it."

Sam snapped his fingers against Kristen's inner elbow and sank the needle deep into her vein.

An hour later and in a weakened state, both girls sat in the chairs as Sam watched them. Their heads, too heavy to hold upright, drooped against their chests.

"You two will be useless for the rest of the day." He shut off the light and locked the door behind him.

He entered the house and called out, "Ready for your transfusion, Mom?" Sam entered the living room and saw the remote lying on the floor. He was at his mother's side in two strides and knelt next to her. "Mom?" He pressed his ear against her chest and shook her shoulder. "Mom?"

Sam carefully lowered Adeline to the floor and tipped her head back. He listened again for breathing and heard nothing. He feared he'd break her fragile bones, but she was unconscious. He had to begin chest compressions.

He repeated aloud the instructions he had learned at the hospital. "Tilt head back, pinch nose, form a seal with the mouth, administer two rescue breaths, and continue chest compressions."

After three rounds of CPR, Adeline finally took a breath on her own. Sam leaned back against the couch in exhaustion and cried. "That's it." He stared at the ceiling in despair. "I have to sell the blood and get more women. I don't have a choice anymore."

With Adeline in his arms, Sam carried her down the hall

and placed her on the bed. He covered her with blankets and raised the side rails. He went to the kitchen. Sam pulled the refrigerator door handle and removed one of the pints of blood he had just put in the shelf on the door. It was still warm. With the bag in hand, he returned to Adeline's room and hooked it to the IV pole. After inserting the line into the needle port, he turned the valve. He scratched out a note and placed it on the roller table that he wheeled to Adeline's bedside. She couldn't miss it when she woke up.

He grabbed his coat and the information he'd gathered from the websites earlier, then he walked out through the garage. He had to contact somebody that day.

Chapter 37

J.T. and I headed to the police station. If we were lucky, we each might have gotten four hours of sleep at most last night. I always told myself I'd sleep between cases. Lately, that wasn't working out so well.

The cup holder held J.T.'s coffee as he drove the usual twenty-minute route from our hotel to the downtown precinct. I cradled my cup between my hands. The warmth felt good.

A powwow was scheduled for eight thirty with Sullivan, Fitch, Andrews, and the four officers who were helping the detectives in the investigation. Everyone was bringing the information they had gathered to the table. Hopefully, a profile of our killer would be delivered to the press later that day.

We entered the police station at eight fifteen and went directly to the conference room. A whiteboard had been set up at the far end of the table. Sullivan sat there with a half dozen sheets of paper spread out in front of him. Fitch had already taken a seat two down on Sullivan's left. We nodded our good mornings as we entered then waited for the rest of the group to arrive.

Stone walked in and closed the door behind him, and Sullivan began. "Okay, everyone, I want updates on everything we know so far, even if we've discussed it before. This assailant needs to be apprehended by the week's end."

"Sir," Fitch said, "today is Thursday."

"You're damn right it is, so let's get moving. I want to know what all of you have found, and then we'll see if we've missed something and left a gaping hole that should be filled in." He turned to Stone and Mills. "What have you got?"

Officer Stone began from earlier that week with the search for Heather Francis's car. "Nothing ever popped with that, boss, even though her death was the most recent. Her car was never seen in Indiana, Illinois, or Michigan, at least as far as tollbooth cameras or plate readers. No law enforcement or private tow company has her vehicle."

Mills added, "As far as monitoring the incoming tips, the only one that panned out was the clothing tip on Molly that came in from Erin McNare. That led Agents Monroe and Harper to Molly's boss and finally to Mitchell Carter, a tip that fizzled out. His employer and wife corroborated his whereabouts on Monday, and the description of the man seen with Molly doesn't fit Mitchell."

Stone added, "Then I took the call from Bethany's mom, and Clark here"—he pointed at Officer Mills— "took the call from Kristen's mom. That's where we're at right now."

After Sullivan finished jotting notes on the whiteboard with a green dry-erase marker, he turned his focus to Jeffries and Christopher. He jerked his chin at Jeffries. "You're up."

"Yes, sir." He glanced at Officer Christopher and spoke for both of them. "We've been conducting extensive interviews with neighbors, friends, and acquaintances around the college Taylor went to and all of the places the young ladies frequented. We've gone through their social media sites with the tech department and re-interviewed best friends and the parents. We've also looked for connections between the girls, such as hobbies and clubs they might have had in common. Nothing popped. The only girls that knew each other were Kristen and Bethany, the latest abductees."

Sullivan groaned and took a sip of the coffee that had been sitting on the table since we arrived a half hour earlier. "Fitch and Andrews, what have you got?"

Mel spoke up. "I did the initial phone interview with Erin McNare then gave that to Agents Monroe and Harper to follow up on. We went back to Marquette Park, where Heather was found, and to the running trails where Molly Davis went missing. Between six officers and ourselves, we didn't find any additional evidence or clues. There aren't any good leads coming in, sir. We've gone through all of them, and they're dead ends."

Sullivan placed a check mark on the whiteboard next to every lead that had been checked numerous times, then he turned to us.

I began by saying the only common link in the abductions

of Molly, Kristin, and Bethany was a vague description of the possible assailant. J.T. and I weren't in Indiana to assist in the abductions and murders of Corrine and Taylor. As far as we knew, no leads had surfaced and no eyewitnesses had come forward in their cases.

"The common thread we've discovered is a blond-haired, medium-built man, average height and probably in his twenties. He was with Molly and was possibly sighted with Kristen and Bethany. The same man was described running through a backyard on the night the latest girls went missing. He would have been coming from the location where Kristen's car was abandoned. We've been told blood was found in Bethany's car, but it's still being analyzed. We're comparing it to Bethany and Kristen's DNA. As of right now, Molly Davis, Kristen Henry, and Bethany Kelly are missing and possibly injured or worse."

J.T. took over. "What we need to do is focus on any man these young ladies might have known who fits the description we just put out there. It's the only common thread that we know of. The girls might not have known each other, but that doesn't mean they didn't know the assailant. Has anyone heard interesting chatter on Alex Everly's phone line yet?"

Andrews spoke up. "Charlie in tech said no phone calls have come in from anyone wanting to sell blood."

"Did Alex mention on his vampire rave sites that he was in the market to buy blood, like he agreed?" I asked.

"Excuse me, I'll find out." Andrews stepped out of the conference room with his phone in hand and returned a minute later. "Charlie is checking out the websites. He's going to call me right back."

Sullivan's phone rang while we waited. "Yes, are you sure? Okay, thanks, Bob." He clicked off the call and rolled his neck. He let out a long frustrated sigh.

"You look like you're about to give us bad news," I said.

"The blood came back positive for belonging to Kristen Henry."

J.T. whistled. "Wow, that isn't what I was expecting. We have to guess how that played out."

I raked my fingers through my hair and tried to figure out why Bethany's car was found blocks away from Paul's Tap with Kristen's blood on the passenger door. Since each girl drove herself to the bar, I could think of no reason Kristen would have been at the door of Bethany's car, as if she was going to get in.

I voiced my thoughts while images filled my mind. "The forensics guys said the blood was on the doorframe, correct?"

Sullivan nodded.

"Then that sounds like the door was open, but why? Kristen and Bethany would have parted ways at whoever's car was the closest to the bar's exit."

"Okay, I'll play devil's advocate," J.T. said.

Andrews's phone rang just as J.T. started to speak. "Sorry, but it's Charlie calling back." Andrews hit Talk and answered. "Larry here. What did you find out? I'm putting you on speakerphone. We're all in the conference room."

"I went through all the sites frequented by Alex, or

Massimo, as he likes to be called. I even hit the dark web just in case he's trying to hide something from us. There's no mention anywhere of him hinting around about being interested in buying human blood."

"That was our agreement with him—do it or be locked up. I guarantee we could dig up something on him that would stick," I snarled. Alex Everly had wasted precious time we didn't have.

Sullivan slapped the table so hard that I grimaced. I could almost feel the sting. He told Andrews, "Get someone out to Alex's house and pick him up. I want a face-to-face with that punk."

"I'm on it, boss." Andrews pushed back his chair and left the conference room.

Sullivan was fuming, and his face glowed red. He poured himself a glass of water from the pitcher centered on the table. "Okay, where were we?"

J.T. spoke up. "We were trying to figure out how Kristen's blood ended up on the passenger side doorframe of Bethany's car. There wasn't blood evidence in Kristen's car, so we know she didn't return to it after she was injured."

"Yet both cars were moved to different areas, and both girls are missing," Mel added.

"What about that accomplice theory?" I said. "What are the chances that one guy could subdue both girls, move both cars at some point, and take the girls away without being noticed?"

Sullivan loudly swallowed some water. "The chances are slim but possibly doable. You said that bartender saw the girls leave, but only one guy walked out next to them."

I doodled on my notepad as I thought. "True, and maybe they were impaired. Tuesday was ladies' night—two-for-one drinks the entire time the girls were there."

Mills added his take. "Okay, how about this scenario? The drunk girls walk out with the friendly stranger. He escorts them to Bethany's car. Maybe hers was the closest to the bar, who knows? Anyway, Bethany gets in behind the wheel, and Kristen is too drunk to drive herself home, so she's going to catch a ride with Bethany. She's standing at the passenger door with Mr. Kidnapper, and he whacks her in the head and tosses her inside."

I frowned. "Then what? Bethany doesn't scream for help or try to run? She calmly gets out, climbs into the backseat, and lets him drive the car several blocks away? He'd still have to move Kristen's car and transport both girls in something else without anyone noticing. That theory doesn't work."

Stone piped in. "I think our guy drugged both of them and took them somewhere in Bethany's car. Think about it. Kristen got there much later than Bethany, meaning she was likely less impaired from alcohol and maybe more combative. That's why she got slammed against the car."

I nodded. "I think you're onto something, Stone. Keep going."

"Okay, so he whacks Kristen and throws her in the car. If he did drug them and Bethany had enough alcohol in her already, she was useless to fight back. He drove them somewhere, dumped them off, and came back to move the

239

cars. That's why Mr. Simmons saw the assailant running through his backyard."

"Bingo." I reached out and fist-bumped Stone. "I think that's exactly how it went down. The kidnapper obviously had his own vehicle there too. He blitz attacked Kristen, tossed her in Bethany's car, and took them somewhere. Then he drove Bethany's car back, dropped it off, ran back, and moved Kristen's car too. When that was all said and done, he leisurely took his own vehicle home."

Sullivan leaned back in his chair and exhaled a deep, pent-up breath. He stared at the ceiling tiles. "At least if we run with that scenario, we could eliminate the accomplice theory. I like it, but it isn't helping us solve the case, only the mystery of how the cars were moved."

Andrews returned a few minutes later. "Alex Everly is here. Officer Putnam has him sitting in interrogation room number two. There was a situation, though."

Sullivan stood. "I don't like situations. Care to explain?"

"Alex saw Putnam and Reynolds approaching in the squad car and made a run for it. Putnam said Alex was just climbing into his own car when they rolled up. He jumped in and gunned it down the street."

"That sounds like a man with a guilty conscience if I ever heard of one," I said. "I wonder why he felt the need to run."

Sullivan's face turned a deeper shade of red with every play-by-play detail. "Then what?"

"Then they pursued with lights and sirens engaged. Apparently Alex went over several curbs, sped through red lights, and finally smashed into the side of a guard rail right after taking out another vehicle."

"Son of a bitch. Was anyone hurt?"

"No, sir, but there's quite a mess out at the intersection of Fayette and Stevenson Roads. We have several patrol units out there cleaning up, and the tow truck was on its way when Putnam and Reynolds left. Alex is cuffed and waiting. He isn't a happy camper, sir."

"Neither am I, and I think it's time to have a word with Elvira." Sullivan tossed his notes and pen in the desk drawer and slammed it closed. He waved us toward the door. "That's it for now, everyone. Keep doing what you're doing, and let's reconvene later today to complete the profile. I'll schedule a press conference for tomorrow."

"Sir?"

Sullivan turned just before he exited the room. "Yep?"

"I'd like to join you. Actually we both would. Alex needs to know this is his one and only chance, if releasing him is even on the table. You can always hold him on obstructing justice, fleeing, erratic driving, and endangering the life of a motorist if he doesn't update those websites today. He'll be sitting for a while, and he can stew all he wants behind bars."

Sullivan jerked his chin toward the door. "Let's go, then."

Chapter 38

We took the elevator down to the first floor, where the city jail was located. That time, Alex sat in box two. I was too pissed off to bother watching him through the one-way glass. J.T. and I stormed into the interrogation room right behind Captain Sullivan.

Alex raised his head from the table and groaned when he saw us. "Not the head pig and the wannabe cops again."

I grinned when I saw the cuts across his nose and the swollen lower lip. "Eat a steering wheel lately?" I leaned over his shoulder and talked into his ear. "We missed you, Massimo." I puckered a big kiss and smacked it next to his cheek.

He pulled back angrily. "Get the hell away from me, bitch."

"That's Ms. FBI Bitch to you. Get it right, punk."

Sullivan took a seat across from Alex. "Looks like we have a breach of contract here, Alex. You didn't live up to your end of the bargain."

"Yeah, what bargain was that?"

"Don't act coy. It doesn't become you." J.T. rubbed his chin. "Actually, nothing becomes you with that greasy, stringy hair. Take a shower, man. Anyway, you reneged on advertising that you were in the market to buy human blood. You know, on your vampire websites, or rave sites, whatever you call that foolishness."

Alex snarled. "That's why your asshole cops chased me down the street? My lifestyle isn't any of your business, and it isn't foolish."

J.T. looked at me, I looked at Sullivan, and we all laughed.

"What would you call a grown man who likes to wear fangs, has a god-awful hairstyle, only wears black, and drinks human blood? I'd call him foolish, or better yet, a horse's ass. I mean at some point in life, don't you want to grow up and act like a real man, or is that too tough for you, Massimo?" I wanted to get his goat, and I was succeeding. I saw the veins pop bright blue along his temples. "Am I making you mad, Elvira?" Alex jerked his head forward and tried to head-butt me but missed. I laughed. "Now that's what I'm talking about. An attempted assault on a federal agent is a one-year prison stint. We can even throw in a thousand-dollar fine as a chaser. You're lucky your aim sucks because that would have been an automatic eight-year stay in the house of corrections. We can haul your horse's ass away now or you can cooperate. You have thirty seconds to decide or it's off the table. If you think I'm joking, go ahead and try me."

Alex pounded the table with his fist. "Nobody can know I'm working with you."

J.T. piped in. "You don't call the shots, we do." He glanced at the clock above the door. "You have fifteen seconds left."

"Fine! What do you want?"

Sullivan pushed back his chair. "I'll be right back. Hey, Alex, why don't you entertain the agents with some knock-knock jokes until I return?"

"Go f—"

I leaned across the table. "Excuse me?"

Alex placed his head on his arms and turned away without saying another word.

While we waited for Sullivan to come back, I texted Amber. At that time of day she was at work, likely running radar, but sitting in a patrol car still afforded her time to read a text. I let her know we hadn't made the progress we had hoped for and said I'd try to call her later and catch up. I hit Send and tucked the phone back into my pocket.

J.T. stepped out momentarily and said he would update Spelling on the case.

Five minutes later, the door opened. J.T. walked through first. Sullivan followed, and Charlie from the tech department, who had a laptop tucked under his arm, came in last.

Alex huffed when he looked up. "What—now the whole gang is joining in?"

Sullivan dragged a chair across the floor and placed it at the table, just inches from Alex. "You try anything funny and I promise you won't see the light of day for years. You're going to tell Charlie every website that you frequent as

Massimo or Alex Everly, whether it's on the World Wide Web or dark web. You're going to advertise on every one of those sites that you're looking to purchase human blood and if anyone has some to sell, they should PM you. Charlie will set up the private messaging link that will come directly into the police department. That way you can't intercept the messages and delete them. Everything you do and say will be monitored, so don't try anything cute. If we see you're violating the agreement, you'll be in lockup for a minimum of a year. No more chances."

"How long do I need to do this shit?"

"As long as it takes. Go ahead, Charlie. Set it up and buzz us when you're done. Officer Putnam will sit in here with you." Sullivan cocked his head at Alex. "You'll recognize him, right? He's one of the cops that chased you down earlier. Just an FYI, Alex, Putnam wears a Glock 22 and he's a crack shot, so don't piss him off."

We left interrogation room two and walked to the bank of elevators. Two were on one side of the hallway and two were on the other. We waited and watched as the light above the doors indicated where the elevator had stopped. Sullivan crossed his arms over his chest, and J.T. paced. I stared at the light. The elevator was making a slow but continuous descent. Finally, the bell dinged at level one, and the doors parted. Inside, J.T. pressed the button for the fourth floor. We rode up in silence.

Sullivan pushed off the back wall as the elevator stopped and the doors opened. "Let's go in my office. We'll do some brainstorming of our own."

We walked down the hall and passed through the bull pen. After we reached his office, J.T. and I dropped down in Sullivan's guest chairs. He closed the door and rounded the desk. I heaved a frustrated sigh.

"Jade, have something to say?"

"Only that we've done everything and followed up with everyone I can think of. We're putting in the time—hell, we all are—but nothing has surfaced. J.T. and I have been here for four days, trying to add our expertise. The guy is a ghost."

"Nah, don't beat yourself up. He's human just like the rest of us, and he'll make a mistake."

"Hopefully he does sooner rather than later."

"Maybe we're looking at this the wrong way and it isn't about selling blood to make money," J.T. said. "If that were the case, the guy would have been doing it ever since Corrine was murdered. Maybe he actually needs blood."

Sullivan furrowed his brows, which touched at the center of his forehead. "You mean like a hemophiliac?"

"Possibly."

"Then what, he'd transfuse other people's blood into himself? That isn't even safe. He'd need plasma, not whole blood, wouldn't he?"

"And what about health insurance?" I said. "Why not go the usual route where you aren't killing people to get medical treatment? And, he wouldn't need blood unless he was injured, would he?"

J.T. shrugged and rubbed the back of his neck. "I'm just throwing ideas out there since most hemophiliacs are male."

Sullivan's office phone rang, and he jerked his chair forward and reached across his desk. "Excuse me for a second."

While we waited, J.T. pulled out his cell and checked messages. I checked my cuticles.

"Hell no! Son of a bitch! Tell them not to touch a thing. We'll be there in twenty minutes." Sullivan slammed down the receiver. He picked it up again and pressed a few buttons. "Mary, call Jane Felder at the ME's office and get her out to Dasher Point. Call the sheriff and get some deputies out there too. I'm not sure if that location is within the city limits or not. Tell forensics to head out and call Mills and Stone. I want everybody there now!"

I was already standing and ready to bolt out the door. "What the hell is going on, Captain?"

"A man walking his dog discovered a body at Dasher Point. What are the odds?" He dialed Putnam downstairs. "Bruce, it's Sullivan. Throw Alex Everly in a cell and leave him there until further notice."

I jerked my head at J.T. "Come on. Let's grab our coats. We'll meet you at Dasher Point, sir."

With our coats in hand, J.T. and I pushed through the doors to the parking garage and climbed into the cruiser. I slammed the passenger side door at my back.

"Do you remember how to get there, or should I pull it up on the GPS?" I asked as I snapped the seat belt over my left hip.

"I remember. We should probably go in the front entrance, though. I don't know what road leads in there. Check that out on the map."

"Yep, I'm pulling it up now. Okay, make your way to Franklin and go south like we did the first time we drove there. When you come to Countyline Road, you'll turn left. We'll have a three-mile drive, then it looks like we go right on Greenfield for a mile or so. The main entrance was originally off Greenfield."

"Okay, just remind me as we go."

I watched the street signs as J.T. drove. "Do you think Alex has anything to do with this?"

J.T. raised his brows as he glanced toward me. "Maybe, or maybe it's one of his groupies, coven, or whatever the hell they're called. Alex isn't a blond, but I bet we can find some of his followers who are."

"Good point. It looks like the left-hand turn for Countyline is coming up in a quarter mile."

J.T. clicked his blinker and made the turn.

"Okay, three miles and then a right on Greenfield. That'll take us to the mill. I'm sure somebody is ahead of us. There's probably a half dozen people there already."

Chapter 39

With his hand on the rearview mirror, J.T. adjusted it and squinted. "I'm pretty sure that's Sullivan behind us."

I twisted in my seat and peered out the back window. "I think you're right. Let him pass."

J.T. rolled down his window and waved for the vehicle closing in on us to lead the way. It zoomed by and pulled in ahead. "Yeah, that was Sullivan. I'm sure he knows exactly where the driveway is."

"And the daylight helps. We'll be able to see the mill, anyway."

J.T. scanned the horizon then checked his mirror again. "A few more cars are closing in on us."

I glanced through my side mirror and saw four squads almost at our rear bumper. I pointed forward and to my right. "We're almost there. I can see what's left of the mill up the road. Sullivan just turned in."

We followed the unmarked black cruiser down the narrow, overgrown driveway. New ruts had already formed in the snow-packed path.

"Watch out for those deep ruts. You don't want a flat tire along with the rest of this shit storm."

The path widened when we reached what used to be the parking lot, now reduced to bare ground with chunks of gravel, rock, and rubble mixed in with the patchy snow. J.T. parked away from the squad cars, coroner's van, and forensics van already on site. Sullivan parked near what had been the bonfire a few nights earlier. He killed the engine, climbed out of his cruiser, and slammed the door at his back.

Two sheriff's deputies stood with a man at the south side of what remained of the building. The man held a leash in his right hand, with some type of spaniel standing at his side.

J.T. and I headed toward them, twenty feet behind Sullivan. Sullivan extended his hand. I heard the deputies make the introductions and assumed that since they were already on site, this had to be county land.

We reached them and introduced ourselves. Sullivan took the lead.

"So, Mr. Abbens, I know you've given your statement to these deputies, but would you mind going over it again for our benefit?"

"No, I don't mind."

I pulled out my notepad and pen.

"Sadie"—he looked down and gave the dog a pat on the head—"and me go for an hour walk every morning. She's a hunting dog and needs the exercise. We always find a spot out in the country where it allows her the opportunity to run."

"Understood, and then?" Sullivan asked.

Mr. Abbens rubbed his forehead then pulled the stocking cap lower over his ears. "Well, I knew this old mill was out here. I mean, I didn't notice any 'No Trespassing' signs when we got here, so I pulled in and let Sadie out." He pointed to his left. "I was only going to throw the ball for her out in that field and let her get some exercise, but I guess she had other plans. She loves to run and fetch but not today. She bolted for the building like a bat out of hell as soon as I unsnapped the leash. I've never seen her behave that way."

Sullivan looked toward the area that had once served as the main entrance to the building. These days it lacked any doors and windows. "She went in that way?"

Mr. Abbens turned and glanced over his shoulder. "Yep, right through there. I had to go after her because she wouldn't come out. I called and called and heard her barks echo from deeper in the building. I didn't intend to trespass, but I had to get my dog."

"That doesn't matter to us other than the building being unsafe." Sullivan swatted the air dismissively. "Go on, please."

"It was the strangest thing I'd ever seen her do. I guess she smelled something. Although, as a human, I didn't. She was scratching and pawing, yelping and barking up a storm at a pile of rubble inside. She spun in circles and yelped some more. There was obviously something there that had her all excited. I wasn't sure I wanted to know what, but at that point I needed to satisfy my curiosity and get the leash back on Sadie's collar." He shook his head as if to wash away the image in his mind.

"Mr. Abbens?"

"Sorry… I just can't get it out of my head. I pushed a couple of large boards and debris out of the way—Sadie was frantic—then I pulled a piece of sheet metal from the opening and saw human legs."

I reached for the man's shoulder in the best comforting gesture I could muster at that moment. "We sure appreciate your help, Mr. Abbens. Can you excuse us for a few minutes?"

He nodded.

Sullivan instructed an officer to take Mr. Abbens and Sadie to his squad car to warm up. Mr. Abbens was visibly shaken. I wasn't sure whether his trembling was from the cold or from what he had witnessed, but either way, I wanted him comfortable, and we needed to get inside the building to investigate. Eventually, Mr. Abbens would need to come to the station to give a formal written statement.

"Give me a second here, guys. I don't want this to become a territorial dispute." Sullivan left us and walked over to the sheriff's deputies.

I gave one of the police officers a questioning look. He raised his hands—palms up. "This is the county's jurisdiction. They'll have to figure things out between the departments on their own."

Sullivan returned moments later. "Okay, let's go ahead. The sheriff's department and I will address the location later. Right now, we have permission to go ahead as long as the deputies escort us." He turned to the officer nearest us. "Norman, have you been inside?"

"Yes, sir."

"Then show us the way."

The three of us followed Officer Norman and the two deputies into the belly of the building. Without the daylight peeking through the nearly roofless structure, it would have been dark inside. We walked quite a distance. The lighting was dim at best, but with the aid of our flashlights, we managed well enough. What remained of the window openings on the outer walls of the building was far behind us, and directly ahead stood only the cold remnants of a building that creaked in the wind.

Norman pointed at the marks on the ground. "Please keep to the sides. Forensics wants to check out those drag marks." He shined his flashlight at the area.

"Will do," Sullivan said.

"Over here." Norman waved us toward a heap of rubble in the middle of a large open space. "Anything else, Captain?"

"I think we're good for now. I want everyone that isn't busy to start scouring the ground directly outside and along the driveway."

"Yes, sir." Norman turned and walked out the way he had come in.

Jane Felder, the ME, wore a dark blue jacket over her office attire. The back of her jacket had Medical Examiner stamped across it in yellow. Her assistant, standing to the side, wore the same type of coat. Three people I recognized from the forensics team were on site as well. They gave us a quick glance then continued taking notes, measurements, and pictures. Jane gave us a nod of recognition when she saw us approach.

"Jane."

"Captain Sullivan, agents."

"So, what have we got?"

"A dead female, I'd say in her twenties. Without her out in the open, I can't give you much yet. Forensics needs to get in here and take pictures, then we'll pull her out. We literally got here five minutes before you."

"Okay, let's get forensics over here to snap some pictures and go over the scene." Sullivan called out to Chad Nellis. "Chad, can you get a few pics of the DB so we can get her out into the open?"

"Sure thing, Captain. We were trying to get a few pictures of the marks on the floor before too many people entered and kicked up dust. We have to preserve the evidence, you know."

Sullivan nodded and backed out of the way. Jane Felder moved to the side as well. Chad, the daytime lead in the forensics department, crawled into the small opening and began taking pictures of the dead woman. I crossed my arms over my chest and tucked my hands in my armpits to stay warm. I followed the sounds above me with my eyes. A half dozen pigeons flew in and out of the structure, some perching on beams three stories above us. Their wings echoed in the hollow building. This young woman— whoever she was—had met her fate and been discarded like trash, left alone in this shell of a structure.

Dozens of flashes lit up the makeshift tomb as Chad took pictures. He finally backed out of the space, stood, and took more pictures of the rubble and the opening that led to the body. He gave us the go-ahead and stepped away. "Okay, she's all yours."

Jane called the assistant ME to her side. "I'll need the body board, a body bag, and several tarps."

"Right away." The young man hurried past us but stayed to the outer sides of the coned-off path. He headed toward the entrance, where the coroner's van was parked.

Jane stood and brushed the dirt off the knees of her pants. "This isn't going to be pretty, meaning there's no good way of getting her out of that space. She's in full rigor, literally stiff as a board, and frozen. We can possibly pull some of this garbage back, but I don't want anything collapsing in on her. I may have to grab her by the ankles and drag her out."

I grimaced at the images of her extraction that played through my mind. "How was she jammed in there, then?"

"My best guess would be she hadn't died too long before she was stuffed in there. If her body was still flexible at the time, the killer could easily have pushed her in."

Tom Knight, the assistant ME, returned five minutes later with a backboard pressed between his body and his left arm, his hand cupped under the bottom to hold it steady. Several tarps were draped over his right arm. He placed the items down and knelt next to Jane, who was on the floor and assessing the opening. "How do you want to do this?" he asked.

She seemed to be judging the amount of space inside the opening, and she glanced over her shoulder. "Let's spread one tarp behind us just to keep the area and her dirt-free once we get her out. The other tarp, I'm going to push in as close to her as possible. Maybe I can get her body partially on it and then pull the tarp toward us. There isn't enough room inside for both of us to pull her out."

"No offense, Jane, but I'm probably stronger than you. Let me give it a shot."

She backed away and gave Tom room. "Okay, see what you can do."

Jane stood with the captain, J.T., and me. Tom crawled into the opening with the tarp in front of him and explained what he was doing as he went along. With only Tom's feet exposed, we needed to hear his commentary to know whether he was having any success.

He called back to Jane, "This isn't going to be easy. Something might snap, if you get my drift."

Jane looked at each of us and waited. Sullivan gave her the go-ahead nod.

"Do the best you can, Tom. Take it slow and easy. Try to position her limbs so they don't catch on anything."

"Okay, I'm working on it."

"Excuse me, folks. I'll be right back," Sullivan said.

When Sullivan walked away, I jerked my head at J.T., who shrugged and turned his focus back to Tom. I watched as the captain disappeared around the corner.

"I think I'm ready to inch her out." Tom slowly backed out of the hole with a hand on either side of the tarp. "I don't have her fully on it, but maybe with a little room, I can reposition her." He stopped, made some adjustments, and continued backward. His feet had reached the second tarp, and the lower part of her body was now exposed.

Dirt and blood covered her bare legs. I fidgeted as we waited. Tom reached in and made more adjustments. He'd said her right arm was tangled in debris. "Okay, she's coming out."

He continued crawling backward, and her knees came into view. I noticed how her skin was not only white from blood loss but also wore a coat of crystallized frost from exposure to the weather. I swore under my breath and squeezed my eyes closed for a second to calm myself. I opened my eyes in the dim light then clicked on my flashlight. I saw a full set of legs and red bikini underwear but nothing else from the waist down. The deep purple bruise at her femoral artery was more than obvious. I knew we were dealing with the same person who'd killed Corrine, Taylor, and Heather. This girl was drained of blood while she was alive too.

Jane knelt and grabbed the left side of the tarp and pulled. Inch by inch, more of our Jane Doe was exposed.

My voice caught in my throat when I yelled out, "Oh, hell no!"

J.T. jerked his head toward me then back at the body. The purple running jacket with the lime-green-and-black stripe down the sleeve gave her away. Even with the dirt and the poor lighting, the color and design of the jacket told us who we were staring at. When she was finally out of the hole, the red hair confirmed it. Our search for Molly Davis had just ended.

Chapter 40

Sam slid the van into the two-hour parallel parking spot across the street from the Gary Public Library. He dropped eight quarters into the slot on the meter. He'd pulled the change out of the jar on the kitchen counter before he left the house. After looking both ways, he crossed over to the side of the street where the two-story dull cement structure took up the corner block of West Fifth and Adams Streets. Sam had never been to the library. Once he passed through the vestibule and into the main room, he was surprised to see how few people were inside. He asked where to find the computer lab and was directed to an area fifty feet to his left. There, he found long counters separated by wooden dividers, with a computer stationed in every third booth. Uncomfortable looking armless office chairs sat in the compartments that held the dated, well-worn computers. Sam assumed that at one point, all of the spaces must have held computers. With the city in decline and experiencing budget cuts, the chances of replacing equipment had likely fallen by the wayside. He took off his coat and placed it in the empty space next to him.

"Sir?"

Sam turned in the chair.

"You aren't going to get online unless you pay in advance."

"Oh, sure. How much is it"—he looked at her name tag—"Jean, and who do I pay?"

"It's three dollars for every hour of use, and you pay me at the counter over there." She pointed directly behind her.

Sam stood and walked with her to the counter. He fished three singles out of his wallet and slid them across the laminate surface.

Jean smiled as she accepted the money and printed a receipt. "You don't look familiar. First time here?"

"Yeah, I have midterms. Have to study, you know."

"Really, what are you going to school for?"

"Phlebotomy, the study of blood. Going into the medical field."

She handed him the receipt. "That sounds exciting. You're in booth three. If you need more time, let me know in advance so the computer doesn't shut you down before you're ready. Good luck."

Sam took the receipt, tucked it in his wallet, and walked away. He muttered under his breath, "I'll need all the luck I can get."

He repositioned himself at the computer in booth three. There was barely enough room to scoot in and still have elbow space. With all of the empty areas between computers, he was surprised they hadn't thought of removing some of the dividers. He huffed his discomfort and pulled the slip of paper out of his front pants pocket.

Sam typed in the search bar the first URL he had written down before he left the house. Vampireravesonline popped up on the screen, with dozens of related sites listed down the page. That particular URL directed him to all the vampire raves and clans throughout the United States. He needed to narrow it down to Indiana, Illinois, and Michigan. With Adeline so ill, Sam couldn't leave the house for any length of time. Five hours was about as long as he felt comfortable being gone. He scanned the site but didn't find a local chapter of the group. The nearest Indiana location was on the southern edge of Indianapolis, a two-and-a-half-hour drive from Gary. That wouldn't work.

"What's this?" he whispered as he narrowed the search even more by typing *blood cults near Gary Indiana* into the search bar. Up popped a local site consisting of witch and warlock groups within a fifty-mile radius of Gary.

I know they use blood for their rituals, but they probably just snatch and kill people's pets.

Sam clicked on the link that took him to the web page. Locations popped up on a map, and the calendar of upcoming events was posted as well. Sam browsed the locations and found a chapter called Spiritual Awakenings only fifteen minutes east of his home. He clicked on the link, which directed him to their home page. There, he found information about the coven, its members and activities, and a "Contact us" page.

Bingo. This is just what I need, but I wonder how long it'll take for somebody to respond?

There was no other way to contact this group, and Sam

didn't want to have a face-to-face yet, anyway. He'd ask a few generic questions through the contact form and see what response he got.

He began typing, made up a fake name, and asked about the group and whether they really considered themselves witches and warlocks or were nothing more than people dressing the part. He said he had recently moved to the area from the west coast. He claimed he had been involved with a well-known group in LA and enjoyed participating in blood sacrifices.

That ought to get their attention. They may be pissed off enough to respond quickly.

He kept the tab open and went back to search for vampire sites. If anyone used human blood for their rituals, it would be them. If they were actually drinking it, they would probably pay more for the blood.

Chapter 41

Sullivan returned to our side. "What have we got?"

I growled, "We have Molly Davis, that's what. Captain—"

Sullivan interrupted my rant as he ground his fist into his eyes. "Son of a bitch. Give me a second."

We watched as he paced, perhaps to blow off steam. He returned seconds later. "Okay, I talked to Putnam back at the station a few minutes ago. Alex is in a holding cell, and he gave us the names of all his cohorts and where to find them. Let's just say he didn't have a choice. It wasn't going to come out good on his end if he didn't cooperate. I told Putnam to let him know in no uncertain terms that I'd make sure he got that yearlong incarceration otherwise. His groupies are being rounded up and hauled in as we speak. Every one of those sons of bitches will be interrogated separately and in depth, especially anyone with blond hair."

"Then what's the point of gauging their interest in buying blood on the websites? If one of his own guys is committing the crimes, that information will be of no use," I said.

"But if the killer isn't one of his people, that interest in buying blood is still out there as a lure. Charlie told Putnam all of the sites are live and linked back to the station."

Jane interrupted. "Guys, I'm going to have forensics take a few more pictures while she's still here. I did an initial exam, and her condition is just like the others. Maybe I should say closer to Heather's simply because she hasn't been dead and out in the elements for an extended period of time like Corrine and Taylor were. Either way, the signs are identical. Enough blood was drained from her carotid and femoral arteries to stop her heart from beating. Any loss beyond 2.24 liters is nearly guaranteed death. I'm sure the killer took everything he could until her heart stopped pumping."

"Anything that was atypical?" J.T. asked.

"Actually, yes, take a look."

We knelt next to Molly's side and watched as Jane pushed back Molly's jacket sleeves. Jane shined the flashlight on both of Molly's arms and pointed. "See the puncture wounds and bruises along her inner elbow veins? Both arms look about the same, plus she has pinch marks six inches higher, right there and there, likely from the tourniquet that's tightened on the arm before blood draws. Her shins show signs of restraints too. Once I get her jacket off, I'll be able to see if there are more marks from restraints across her chest area. How long had she been missing?"

"Since Monday," I said.

"That means the killer took a number of blood draws before he decided to finish her off. This isn't killing for killing's sake, it's all about the blood."

J.T. nodded. "Same conclusion we came to a few days back."

"If there's nothing else, Tom and I will get her loaded up and take her back with us. I need to know how cold her body actually is before I do anything with her. She may be slightly frozen or completely frozen. Everything depends on how long she's been outside. I should have definitive information for you later today."

Sullivan thanked Jane and Tom. We watched as they carried Molly away, zipped in the body bag and strapped to the backboard.

"What's going on in your head, Jade? I can almost hear the wheels spinning."

I looked at Sullivan in surprise. "You're getting more and more like J.T. every day we're around you. How come everybody knows when something is bouncing around in my brain?"

"Might be that curled lip and twisted eyebrow thing you do when something is weighing on your mind," J.T. said. He gave me a wink when I reached up and touched my eyebrow.

He got a smirk in return. "Okay, here's what I was thinking. What if—and it's only my initial thoughts—but what if Alex and his group actually put Molly in the building Tuesday night when they were at Dasher Point? Maybe they had already killed her and were performing their ritual with some of her blood. We didn't compare the human blood to anyone's DNA. We only had it tested to see if it was indeed human. Do you think some of it could have been hers?"

"Shit, you have a good point, Jade. I'll see if the lab can run a test against Molly's DNA sample we have on file. That group could have gotten there long before us. Hell, just because their ritual began at eleven o'clock doesn't mean they didn't arrive earlier and hide her inside the building. How many people were there that night?"

J.T. answered. "Twenty-six including Alex."

"Okay, let's get back to the station. We're going to have our hands full doing interviews with only three interrogation rooms to work in."

"If I could add my two cents, sir?"

"Sure. You haven't been shy before. Why start now?" Sullivan smiled. "Go ahead. I'm just giving you shit."

"I know, and I appreciate your candor, Captain. Let's begin the interviews with blond men that fit with the parameters our witnesses gave us. They'd be medium height and weight, and their age would likely be under thirty. It might make things go faster, especially if somebody actually lets their conscience get the best of them and fesses up."

"That'll work. Let's go."

Chapter 42

Sam's phone vibrated on the tabletop of the empty cubicle next to him. Nobody ever called him except Adeline. Something had to be wrong. Sam reached around the corner and grabbed the phone. It was his mother. He was thankful the phone was voice activated. All his mother had to do was tell it to call Sam and it autodialed his number. He picked up and tried to speak in a low voice even though his anxiety level had just gone through the roof. "Mom, what's wrong? Are you okay?"

"I don't think so, honey. I got out of bed to use the bathroom, and the entire room began to spin. I fell to the floor, and I think I'm too weak to stand up."

"Stay put, Mom. Don't even try to stand. I'll be home in fifteen minutes. You aren't short of breath or feeling chest pains, are you?"

"No, but everything is blurry and spinning."

Sam grabbed his coat and deleted the sites he had visited. He powered down the computer and rushed out the door. "I'm leaving now, Mom. Just don't move."

Inside the van, Sam checked his side mirrors and squealed out of the parking space. He'd get home, help his mom back into bed, and give her a transfusion. Both girls were going to give another donation that day, whether they liked it or not.

Chapter 43

"What are we going to hold the people on?" I asked as we hurried back to our cars.

Sullivan dug the cruiser's car keys out of his pocket. "I told the officers rounding them up to charge all of them with aggravated trespassing and starting an illegal bonfire on private property. It's just petty bullshit charges. I doubt if any of them know the difference between something we can actually hold them on or not."

"Sounds good to me. We'll see you back at the station," I said.

J.T. climbed in behind the wheel. I sat shotgun and clicked the seat belt over me.

My phone vibrated just as J.T. turned onto the road. I dipped my hand in my coat pocket, pulled the phone out and glanced to my left. "Spelling is calling." I clicked Talk. "Hey, boss. We're driving right now, so I'm putting you on speakerphone. What's up?"

"Just wondering how the investigation is going. I had to send Moore and Delgado to Grand Rapids on a case. We're spreading ourselves pretty thin here. Cam and I are the only agents left at the office. Until you four get back, we may have to call in help from the downtown headquarters if needed."

J.T. groaned and rubbed his forehead. "I bet Val hated leaving her boy."

"Yeah, but sometimes duty calls us out of town whether we like it or not."

"Understood."

"So, what's the latest?"

"Unfortunately, another body was just discovered. Molly Davis, the young lady who went missing on Monday while out for a jog, was found this morning by a man walking his dog. It was purely coincidental. I doubt she would have ever been located otherwise."

Spelling cleared his throat. "So you have a positive ID?"

"Not yet, but from her appearance and the clothing she wore, yes. We'll let you know as soon as it's confirmed with the DNA profile we've collected for her."

I heard the disappointment in Spelling's voice. "So, you're no closer to finding the perp?"

"We're hauling in the entire group of so-called vampires that hang out with Alex Everly. Molly's body was found at Dasher Point, the very place Alex and his clan held a blood-drinking ritual two nights ago. That abandoned steel mill is so off the beaten path, it's too much of a stretch to think her being found there was a coincidence."

"That's where the man and his dog found her?"

"Absolutely, and that sounds fishy at best."

"Okay, keep me posted on the outcome of the interviews."

"Will do. Goodbye, sir." I clicked off and dropped my phone back into my coat pocket.

J.T. turned in to the station's parking garage twenty minutes later, right behind Captain Sullivan. He pulled into one of the few visitors' spaces and parked. We were five cars beyond the reserved spot that had a tin plaque with the captain's name on it bolted to the wall.

After he climbed out of his cruiser and slammed the door behind him, Sullivan waited for us to catch up. "I talked to Putnam as I drove. He's staring at eleven of the remaining twenty-five people that patrol rounded up. They're downstairs in a holding cell, waiting to be questioned."

J.T. frowned. "What about the female followers?"

Sullivan pulled off his gloves and pocketed them. He raked his scalp. "Everyone is getting talked to. Even if they didn't take part in a crime, they may still have valuable information they'd be willing to share for a pass from us. Let's not assume they're innocent just because they're female. Somebody like Alex could have anyone do his bidding." Sullivan held the glass door open, and we crossed into the police department lobby. He jerked his chin toward the hallway that led to the bull pen and his office. "Let's head into my office. I'll call downstairs and have Putnam get us a count on the blonds in custody. We'll begin with them and go from there. We have to plan these questioning sessions too. At this point, none of the people we're holding actually know why they're here."

As we passed through the bull pen, we made a pit stop at the coffee station along the back wall of the room. Each of us needed a cup of the hot brew before we started the interviews. I poured creamer into mine and J.T.'s and gave them a quick stir. Sullivan drank his black.

A few minutes after we got settled in, a knock sounded on Sullivan's door. Officer Putnam peeked around the glass wall. Sullivan waved him through.

"I have an update." He tipped his head at each of us.

Sullivan pointed at a guest chair under a window overlooking the city. "Take a seat, Bruce. What have you got?"

"Well, sir, first off, the lab is comparing Molly Davis's DNA sample to the residue left in those bottles. They should have the results in a few hours."

"Good, and what else?"

"And out of the eleven people being held downstairs, five have various shades of blond hair, but two of those five are women."

"I don't care if they're monkeys. Everyone is getting interviewed. We'll take turns with them in the three boxes, and the blonds will obviously go first. As long as they have no idea why they're here, they can't make up a story that they'll all stick to. After each interview we'll separate the ones that have been questioned from the ones that haven't. That way no one gets a heads-up."

I crossed my right knee over my left leg and rearranged myself in the chair. "So we should keep the questions the same for all of them. If somebody expounds on their answers, it'll all be recorded and on video, anyway."

"That's correct, and we'll keep the questions simple. Ask when they arrived at Dasher Point Tuesday night. I want a minute-by-minute playback of the entire night up to the point where we stepped in and took over. We're only gathering information right now to see if everyone's account matches up. Any person that deviates from their rendition of that night's activities will be kept aside and talked to again. The second time around we'll press them a little harder." Sullivan gave me an odd look. "I'm not trying to be sexist, but since you're the only woman here, would you mind pointing out to us brain-dead men which people are the blonds? I don't know the difference between dark blond and light brown."

I grinned. "Sure, and I don't take offense at your question." I turned toward Putnam. "What I want to know is who told you there were five blonds?"

"Myra in lockup picked them out for me."

At least we got one good chuckle before it was time to get down to business. We rose and headed back to the elevators with our notepads ready.

Chapter 44

The van jumped the curb when Sam overshot the driveway. The vehicle had barely come to a stop when he slammed into Park and opened the door. He ran up the sidewalk of the tired looking Cape Cod and turned the key in the knob. "Mom, Mom."

Sam ripped off his jacket. He tossed the keys on the coffee table and ran down the hall. Lying on the floor alongside her bed, Adeline was nearly unconscious. He checked her pulse—slow but constant.

"I'll be right back." Sam raced to the kitchen and pulled open the refrigerator door. He grabbed a single-serving box of orange juice, punched the straw through the hole, and ran back to the bedroom. With the juice box on the floor next to him, Sam carefully lifted his mom to a sitting position. "Mom, can you hear me?" He put his ear close to her face.

A barely coherent voice, almost a whisper, responded, "Sam, is that you?"

"It's me. Try to drink this orange juice. You need more

sugar in your system. Here, I'll help you hold it." Sam noticed how weak his mother looked. Her hand shook as she held the juice box. Her skin appeared grayish and bruised from all the transfusions. Her veins were flat and nearly invisible. "You aren't getting enough liquids."

"Just let me die. It'll be easier on you. The cancer will have its way. It'll kill me no matter what. You're only prolonging the inevitable."

"Don't even say that. I promised to take care of you when Dad walked out on us. I'm not going back on my word. I'll get you through this." He steadied her against the bed and stood. "I'll be back in a second."

Sam disappeared down the hallway. Minutes later he returned with a warm, damp washcloth cupped in his hand. He folded it twice lengthwise. "Here, let me put this cloth on your forehead. It'll feel good." He placed the cloth above her brows and pressed it against her skin.

A brief smile crossed her lips. "Thank you, honey. You try really hard."

"I need to help you into bed."

A slurping sound indicated that Adeline had finished her juice. "I'm afraid I wet the floor. I'm so sorry, Sam. Cleaning up after me isn't your job."

He waved away her comment. "I'll get you a dry nightgown. Don't worry about it."

Once Adeline was changed and lying in bed, Sam took the empty juice box and got her another. He punched the straw into the hole and set the juice on the roller table. He took a seat in the chair next to her. "Has the dizziness gone away?"

"It's better, but lying here helps. So does the juice. Thank you, honey."

"No worries. I'm going to make you dinner. How about a bowl of chicken noodle soup?"

"That sounds good."

"Okay, you rest, and I'll be back soon." Sam closed the bedroom door and checked the blood supply in the refrigerator. Four bags remained in the door, and two were earmarked to sell. He was already a month behind with the electric bill, among others. If he didn't catch up, the power would be turned off at the next billing cycle, and the blood supply, if there was any, would be ruined. After dinner and another blood draw from each girl, Sam would scour the local vampire rave sites on his own computer. He couldn't risk leaving Adeline home alone again in her weakened condition.

Chapter 45

The short ding indicated that the elevator doors were ready to part. I glanced up at the lit numbers. We had reached the first floor. We walked down the long corridor that had more hallways branching off the main one. Through a secured and gated door, we entered another wing with the city jail. Sullivan signed us in at the counter. We passed by the visitors' waiting room, where a TV hung on the wall and several snack machines were lined up next to each other. We crossed through a second set of gated doors into the actual jail area where inmates were held. On the left corner of the hallway was a plaque that read Interview Rooms, and an arrow on it pointing ahead. Three doors stood side-by-side, and they were marked as Observation Room 1, 2, and 3. Beyond the observation rooms—on the other side of the one-way mirrors—were the usual interrogation rooms, or boxes as we fondly called them. Around the left corner were two holding cells, each a twenty-foot-long by fifteen-foot-wide space. Three women sat in the cell to the right. Eight men waited on a bench in the other cell.

I cupped my hand and leaned closer to Sullivan and J.T. "Let's get the women's interviews out of the way. Since there are three of them and three interrogation rooms, nobody will realize we wanted to talk to the blondes first. They'll just think we're questioning the women before them." I jerked my head to my right. "We'll pull the blond men out after we talk to those ladies."

Sullivan rubbed his chin and stared at the women. "But one woman is a brunette."

"No matter," I said. "They all have to be interviewed, anyway. What's one brunette in the beginning? We'll make it fast unless she has something interesting to say."

Sullivan waved the guard over. "Let's get these ladies into the interrogation rooms."

"Yes, sir." The guard opened the cell and hustled the women out one by one. Each woman was placed in an interrogation room, and the door was locked behind them.

Sullivan jerked his chin at Putnam. "Get Detectives Andrews and Fitch down here to help with the interviews. Stone, Jeffries, Christopher, and Mills can help me cover the observation rooms."

"You got it, boss." Putnam headed to the nearest desk phone and picked up the receiver.

"Either of you have a preference?" Sullivan asked.

"Nope, I'm good with anybody linked up across from me," I said. J. T. echoed my sentiment.

"Okay, then. Let's get that camera equipment set up and head in.

A half hour later, I sat across from Chris Brant, a twenty-year-old blonde who wore a huge chip on her shoulder—just my type. "So, Chris, why the vampire world? You never considered joining a group a little less controversial like the Girl Scouts?"

"No. They're my brothers and sisters."

"Literally?"

"I don't know what that means."

I stared at her. "Right. Okay, let's move on to the questions you may understand. What time did you get to Dasher Point Tuesday night, and why that place?"

"We do what Alex, I mean, Massimo, says. He said to go to Dasher Point, and we did. We followed the van in our cars."

"What time did you arrive?"

"The blood ceremony was at eleven. You pigs were watching us. You know damn well what time it was."

"I asked what time you went there. Please listen to my words. Are you capable of doing that?"

She stared at the table and didn't respond. The tension in the room was thick enough to slice.

I slapped the table, and she jumped.

I smiled. "I thought you drifted off there for a minute. Are you on something? Do we need to piss test you?"

"I want to leave. This is harassment."

"You don't have a clue what harassment is. I'd suggest answering my questions or you'll be finding a cozy place on that hard cell floor to spend the night. I don't have all day, either. I asked what time you got to Dasher Point."

She spewed her response. "I don't know, around ten thirty, I guess."

"Tell me the minute-by-minute playback."

"We met at the Kwik Stop gas station on Evanston. Massimo was in the lead van, and we all pulled in behind him and waited until everyone got there."

"And that was?"

"Tenish."

"Then what?"

"Then we followed the van to Dasher Point."

I rearranged myself on the hard steel chair. "Go on."

"We got there, and Massimo said to start gathering wood for the fire. Some of us did that while others found rocks and bricks to make the fire ring."

"So you're responsible?"

She smirked her one-word answer. "Yeah."

"What was Massimo doing all that time?"

"Standing around."

"Did you see anything unusual? Did anyone go in the building?"

"No, I mean, I don't think so. That place is creepy. It looked like everyone stood outside and waited for the fire to build up. It was cold that night."

"Did anyone bring anything out of the vehicles?"

"The table, chairs, and the ritual supplies."

"Nothing else?"

"No."

A knock sounded on the glass. I pushed back my chair and stood. "I'll be right back." I walked out and closed the door behind me then entered the observation room where Sullivan sat.

"She doesn't know shit," he said.

"What's the word from the other rooms?"

"About the same. I think we should move on to the guys."

"Yeah, I agree." I folded my arms across my chest and looked at the floor.

"Is something cooking upstairs, Monroe?"

"Yeah, I think we can speed up this process, but we should still talk to all of the blond men. Get Reynolds or a patrol officer out to the Kwik Stop station on Evanston. They can pull up the parking lot footage from Tuesday night. If everyone met there at ten o'clock like Chris said, and it's nearly a half-hour drive to Dasher Point from there, at least we'll know when they arrived."

"True, but even if they got there at ten thirty, they still had time to hide Molly's body in the building."

I tried to rub the frown lines out of my forehead. "I don't know about that, Captain. She was well hidden under that rubble. That in itself would take nearly a half hour to do. We got there shortly after ten thirty ourselves."

Sullivan turned to Mills. "Get somebody to the Kwik Stop station immediately. I want them to check the videos from Tuesday night beginning at nine o'clock."

"I'm on it." Mills hurried out and closed the door behind him.

"Okay, let's just continue with the blond men."

"What do you want done with the women?"

"Cut them loose."

I nodded then walked back to the interrogation room

and released Chris Brant. She had papers to sign, and I had the guard make a copy of her driver's license before I released her.

After opening the door to the main hallway, I had someone show her out. "I'd suggest staying off private property from now on. Next time you'll be looking at a hefty fine along with an overnight stay or two."

I heard a grumble mixed with several curse words before the door closed at her back. The other two women were released shortly after Chris.

"Take fifteen minutes and grab some coffee and a bite to eat. I'm sure we've all missed dinner. We'll start fresh with the men"—Sullivan looked at his watch—"at eight o'clock."

"Got it, sir. I'm going to run upstairs and see how far along the guys are with the DNA match for Molly."

Sullivan nodded and headed to the snack machines.

I exited the elevator and took the west hallway to the forensics lab. I pulled the handle on their door. Chad Nellis turned and gave me a nod.

"You're still here?" I asked. "There is a night shift, isn't there?"

"Yeah, but the captain said he needed that DNA compared tonight, so I stuck around. I wanted to follow it from start to finish."

I gave him an appreciative pat on the back. "Dedication to the max. So, speaking of Molly's DNA test, how's it coming?"

He glanced at the clock. "We should have the results in about five minutes."

"Perfect timing. Mind if I grab a seat and wait?"

"Nope, I'll sit with you. I've been running the prints on that receipt, but nothing has popped yet."

"What receipt?"

He tipped his head at the bagged slip of paper on the desk next to him. "That one. One of the patrol officers brought it in from Dasher Point. I thought they showed you everything they found there."

"Hell no. I don't even think the captain saw it or was told about it."

"Well, like I said, nothing has popped."

"Who found it?"

"Officer Martin brought it in. He's a rookie, though, and maybe misunderstood the protocol."

I grabbed a pair of latex gloves from the dispenser. "May I?"

"Yeah, no sweat."

I carefully opened the sealed bag and slid out the receipt. The store name listed at the top was Second Life Resale. An address and phone number were printed below the name. Everything about the receipt seemed sadly ironic. A dead girl had been placed in a makeshift tomb at a location where so-called vampires were celebrating their second-life ritual—drinking human blood to sustain their entire existence, at least in their messed-up minds.

The receipt showed two upholstered armchairs were purchased late Tuesday. I assumed that Alex or somebody in his group had dropped the receipt that night at Dasher Point. I took a picture of it then slipped my phone into my back pocket. "You said no hits on the prints, though, right?"

Chad shook his head. "Nothing in the system."

I gave that some thought and remembered Sullivan's description of Alex the first time he spoke of him. He'd told us Alex had an extensive rap sheet. The prints couldn't be his. They would have shown a match when Chad searched the database.

"Here we go. The DNA comparison test is complete."

I waited anxiously as Chad looked over the results.

"No match, Jade."

"You're absolutely sure?"

"There's no human error involved. It's all science. None of the blood residue from the bottles matches Molly's DNA."

My shoulders dropped with disappointment. We were back to square one. "Okay." I sighed and gave Chad a smile for his effort. "I appreciate your help. Now go home and have a beer."

He flashed his pearly whites. "Yes, ma'am. Actually that sounds really good about now."

"Yeah, and I wish I could join you."

Chapter 46

J.T. had already begun the interrogation in room one with a guy named Steven Dawson. Steven was the first of three blond men to be interviewed that night. I stepped into the observation room and saw Sullivan leaning back in a chair, his hands folded behind his head. He was watching the interview through the glass. He turned and nodded when I entered then cracked his neck from side to side.

"Captain, I have to discuss some things with you and J.T."

Sullivan pushed himself forward off the chair and knocked on the window.

J.T. stood and told Steven to hang tight. A few seconds later, J.T. opened the door behind us and stepped in. "What's up?"

Sullivan said, "Not sure yet. Jade, go ahead."

"First off, Molly's DNA doesn't match any from the bottles."

Sullivan rolled his eyes and let out a long breath. "Guess we struck out on that one. Just because they didn't drink her blood that night doesn't mean they aren't responsible for her death, though."

J.T. cracked the seal on a bottle of water sitting on the counter and took a deep swig. "And Alex did say they store their own blood. That sounds like he may have some at his house. I think we need to get a warrant to search his premises."

Sullivan agreed. "I'll make the call."

"One more thing, and it may be insignificant to the case, but patrol found a receipt on the ground at Dasher Point during their search."

"And this is just coming to light seven hours later?"

I shrugged. "Here." I opened the gallery to the picture I had taken and passed my phone to J.T. "Chad said he checked the fingerprints from the receipt. Nothing came up in the database."

"Then it can't be Alex that handled it."

"Right, but twenty-five other people could have. The point is, two armchairs were purchased on Tuesday from the resale shop listed at the top of the receipt."

"Makes sense," J.T. said. "Those must be the chairs they had out at the bonfire."

"That's what I thought too, and they were armchairs, just not upholstered armchairs."

J.T. frowned. "Nah, that's splitting hairs, Jade. I think they just have it worded wrong."

I smirked. "Don't be so sure. Ask Steven where those chairs came from."

"Yeah, okay. Are we done here?"

Sullivan tipped his chin toward the window. "Go ahead. I'll get on the warrant after I hear his response."

I dropped down in the chair next to Sullivan and cracked open a bottle of water for myself. We watched as J.T. returned to the interrogation room and took his seat across from Steven.

"So, Steven, why did you guys decide to take a couple of chairs along to your hoedown Tuesday night?"

"What the hell does that mean?"

"Chairs—you know, like, that thing you're sitting on."

Steven smirked. "Do you guys go to comedy school before you get your dollar store plastic police badges?"

I looked at Sullivan and laughed. "He's pretty funny and quick. Should I go in and slap him upside the head?"

Sullivan's jowls jiggled when he chuckled. "Now who's being funny? Let's see how J.T. handles him."

J.T. tipped his chair back and crossed his arms over his chest. We couldn't see his face, but it appeared that the two men were having a stare down. J.T. finally broke the silence in a slow and methodical tone. "Don't make me ask you a second time."

"Shit, he's scaring me," I said with a grin. "I wish I had a bag of popcorn right now."

We turned our focus back to J.T. and Steven.

Steven finally spoke up. "Fine. I don't know what the hell you're getting at, but those chairs and that table go with us everywhere. They're part of our ritual. As far as I know, those chairs were part of a dining room set Massimo's grandma gave him years ago. He's had them as long as I've known him."

"And how long has that been?" J.T. asked.

"Three years."

Chapter 47

Sam balled his hands into fists and ground them into his red, swollen eyes. Adeline was fading. She knew it, and he did too. She was all he had, and now she was dying. He couldn't fix her no matter how hard he tried. They were both exhausted. It was just a matter of time—weeks, maybe, if they were lucky—but if he was a realist, probably only days. Sam was angry. Life for the last twenty years had been cruel and unfair.

Another threatening letter had arrived that day. Power would be turned off soon, and he knew eviction notices were on the horizon.

Fix this, fix that, pay the overdue bills—blah, blah, blah.

He was sick of it and threw everything into the trash can, but the threats lingered in his mind. He couldn't sleep at night.

Sam pulled the wooden lever on the side of the recliner and dropped the footrest. The back came forward, and he rose. With soft steps, he walked down the hallway to Adeline's room and listened to her labored breathing as she slept. He knew Kristen and Bethany didn't have long to live, either. He could tell they were in a severely weakened state after the last blood draw that evening. He was lucky to have found viable veins. His own energy was dwindling from lack of sleep, and he didn't have the ambition to go out and hunt for another woman. Adeline couldn't be left alone for any length of time. With the cold night and blustery wind, he wasn't prepared to roam the streets in hopes of snatching a woman walking in the elements.

Sam returned to the chair with his laptop in hand and powered it up. He needed to sell the remaining blood in the refrigerator so he could buy food. Sam pulled the slip of paper out of his pocket and typed a URL into the search bar. While at the library earlier that day, he had written down the URL of a local vampire rave site. As foolish as vampires sounded to him, Sam was desperate to find someone to sell the blood to.

He clicked on the images, the home page, and the member information. He'd have to fill out a form and be interviewed by the head person, someone who went by the name Massimo, if he wanted to join their clan. He'd have to create a log-in name to go much further into the site.

I don't want to join your stupid clan. I just want to sell blood to you, if you really even deal with human blood.

With a tap of his index finger, he clicked on the profile for Massimo and began reading. The man's written words were nonsense and way too deep. Massimo's talk of the underworld and his spiritual gibberish nearly bored Sam to death. He was impatient and ready to look elsewhere. As he was about to click off the site, his eyes fell on a paragraph about human blood and how it nourished Massimo's body and restored his sense of well-being. The man wrote of how he needed it on a daily basis. It was his drug of choice, but he didn't have access to it as often as he liked.

Sam perked up and read that part again. His interest was piqued. He'd have to be careful with his words and show merely a vague interest in selling blood. He'd ask more questions first. He began typing then stopped. He didn't want to use his personal computer for something illegal like that.

Sam kept that tab open and scoured the Internet for any of the area's all-night coffee shops that had a business center. He found one only five miles from his house. Apprehensively, he slipped on his shoes and coat, raised the hoodie over his head, and grabbed the van keys off the kitchen counter. He climbed into the van and left.

I'll make up some vague log-in name and send a quick note directly to Massimo's contact page, offering to sell blood. Then I'll wait until tomorrow to see if he responds.

Sam hoped to be home within the hour. He'd head to the library in the morning and check for a private message.

Chapter 48

Sullivan gave the window another tap. J.T. rose and left the interrogation room. Within ten seconds, J.T. opened the door to the observation room where we sat.

"Captain?"

"He doesn't know anything," Sullivan said. "Start with the next blond."

"I have a good idea," I said.

They turned toward me, and J.T. spoke. "Yeah? Then spill it."

"It may speed up the interview process. Let's get Jeff Simmons down here and see if he can pick out from a lineup the person who ran through his backyard."

"Right, but we only have three blond guys to choose from at the moment."

"It's a start, though. We can toss a few cops wearing their street clothes in the mix."

"Not a bad idea. Okay, let's do it. Jade, call Simmons, and I'll get that warrant for Alex's house under way. J.T."—Sullivan tipped his head toward the wall—"how about giving Andrews a hand in box three?"

"Sure, no sweat." J.T. pointed at the mirror. "Steven can enjoy some solitude for a while."

We parted ways at the door.

"Take a break, Monroe. We'll reconvene in observation room two in a few minutes." Sullivan's phone rang as we reached the elevator. He picked up on the second ring. "Sullivan here. Yeah, Reynolds, uh-huh. Okay, make sure you get a copy of that tape and drop it off in the tech department when you get back." He clicked off and pocketed his phone. When the bell dinged and the doors parted, we entered the elevator.

"What did Reynolds say?" I pressed the button for the fourth floor.

"The Kwik Stop video shows five vehicles lined up along the edge of their driveway at ten o'clock Tuesday night. The lead one was an extended van. Reynolds is bringing a copy of the tape back with him to see if tech can pull up the plate number."

"So Chris's story is true."

"Seems that way. Okay, give Simmons that call."

"I think I ought to call that resale shop too and ask if they have a surveillance camera at their store."

"You're one sharp agent, Monroe." The elevator doors opened, and Sullivan gave me a wink and disappeared into his office.

After I pulled my notepad out of my purse, I took a vacant seat in the bull pen. I dialed Jeff Simmons first since we needed him at the station as soon as possible. I assumed I'd get a voicemail recording at the secondhand store, asking me to leave a message.

Jeff answered on the third ring. "Hello."

I gave him the brief version of why I'd called. He said he could be at the station in thirty minutes. I thanked him and hung up. I clicked the Gallery icon on my phone and pulled up the picture I'd taken of the receipt from Second Life Resale. I wrote the phone number in my notepad and dialed. As I'd imagined, I heard a recorded message giving a brief description of their merchandise, store hours, and location. I hung up and planned to pay them a visit tomorrow as soon as they opened for business.

I filled my coffee cup and rode the elevator back to the first floor. With a quick stop at the security desk before I buzzed through to the jail area, I asked to be called as soon as Jeff Simmons arrived.

Sullivan watched from observation room number two as Fitch questioned a man on the other side of the glass. I took a seat next to Sullivan and sipped my coffee. I tipped my head toward the window.

"Anything interesting going on in there?"

He rubbed his nose, then he scratched something that apparently irritated him along the base of his jaw. "Nah, same old shit. I think we're barking up the wrong tree. These jokers don't know a damn thing other than what Alex tells them. No matter what, none of them seem to know about a woman being stuffed under the rubble inside the building."

I slapped the surface of the tabletop. "Shit, I didn't even think to ask."

"What's that?"

"Molly. What's the deal with notifying her family?"

Sullivan let out a deep groan. "Jane took care of it. Earlier she matched up the DNA from Molly's file to the body and confirmed the identity. It was Molly, but we already knew that. The mom and dad are going to the coroner's office tomorrow to make a positive ID. Jane wanted Molly to look as presentable as possible first."

I jotted down a reminder to pay the family a visit sometime tomorrow. "That has to be horrible for them." My mind drifted back to the night that my own dad had died, but my vibrating phone interrupted my thoughts. I was thankful. "Agent Jade Monroe speaking. Yes, I'll be right out." I clicked off.

Sullivan stood. "Time to get the lineup together?"

"Yep, Jeff Simmons just arrived. I have no idea if he'll be able to tell us anything, but it's another check and balance."

"Good enough. I have several officers waiting in their street clothes to pitch in. I'll get them over to the lineup room."

We gathered behind the glass with Jeff Simmons as six men, each with a different shade of blond hair, were ushered into the room. Each one held in front of his chest a piece of cardboard with a number on it—one through six.

Jeff stood nearest the one-way glass and peered through. He fidgeted, seeming unsure of what to say.

J.T. tried to reassure the nervous man. "Jeff, don't force yourself to choose somebody. Just think back to what you saw that night. If nobody fits, they don't fit. If somebody seems like a possibility, point them out."

"Can you have them turn to the side? I never saw the man face-to-face."

"Sure thing," Sullivan said. He called through the intercom, "Everyone turn to the side and face the east wall."

Jeff stared again. "I'm sorry, guys, but I'm not confident enough to pick out anyone. I'd say the hair color on number three is about what I remember, and the height and body type of number five seems right, but that's all I can give you."

I patted his shoulder. "Thanks for coming down, Jeff. You've been a big help." I had an officer escort him out. We paused our conversation until the door closed at their backs.

"Well, other than Steven's hair color, we have nothing. Number five is Officer Lewis." Sullivan reached deep in his pocket for the ringing phone. "Captain Sullivan here. Yeah, Charlie, what's up? No shit? Meet us in my office in five minutes."

J.T.'s brows rose, and I'm sure mine did too. I grasped the doorknob, ready to head upstairs.

"Charlie has information." Sullivan looked back at Andrews and Fitch then jerked his head toward the men still standing on the other side of the glass. "Throw those three in the holding cell for now. We'll get back to them later."

Chapter 49

We turned the corner and saw Charlie leaning against the door to Sullivan's office. He held a laptop pressed against his chest. A wide grin crossed his face when he saw us approaching from the end of the hallway.

"You really have a hit?" I couldn't hide my enthusiasm.

"Hell yeah. I was about to call it a night and shut down the computer. That's when I saw the alert. Looks like it came in about an hour ago."

I felt my forehead crease. J.T. pointed at it, causing me to frown even harder. "That means the likelihood is low of any of these fools in lockup being our perpetrator. Even their cell phones were taken away temporarily. To be honest, the only thing I think they're guilty of is trespassing on private property and starting a bonfire."

"And being weirdos," J.T. said.

"Yeah, there's that, but if every weirdo was in jail, there wouldn't be many people left in the free world."

"Okay," Sullivan said, "let's go inside and you can show us what you have."

Charlie burrowed in on one of the guest chairs and opened the laptop. He powered it up, and the home screen came to life. "Okay, here we go. First, I traced the IP address, which is a simple task. The perp was smart enough not to use a personal computer to send the message."

I dropped my shoulders. "Damn it. I was hoping to charge into his house and arrest him on the spot."

"Not quite that simple. You'll have to do a little legwork tomorrow."

"I'm okay with that. Go ahead."

"Anyway, the IP address belongs to a computer at an all-night coffee shop east of here about ten miles. I looked up the place online, and it's called Insomnia."

"Clever. So it's an Internet cafe?" Sullivan asked.

"Of sorts, but more of a coffee shop and snack food kind of joint. The photos give a vibe of where the young, after-the-bar crowds congregate for a cup of joe before they drive home."

"Got it. What else?" J.T. asked.

"Here, I'll pull up their website, and you can see for yourself." Charlie tapped a few keys and typed in the web address for Insomnia. An image of their establishment lit up the screen. Along the left side, a drop-down menu appeared. Charlie tapped on the button showing the computer area. The image bounced over to the bedroom-sized room with three tables, each holding two computers. The price for using the computers was two dollars for every half hour.

"Go back to the coffee shop area," I said.

Charlie clicked back to the still shot of the main room.

"Yeah, I don't see any security cameras against the walls." I looked at the time on the lower right side of the laptop—9:15. I turned to J.T. "Want to take a ride?"

"Sure, why not?"

"Oh, by the way, Captain," I said as I stood to leave, "the secondhand store was already closed for the night when I called, but they reopen at nine a.m. That'll probably be the first place we hit tomorrow."

"Sounds good. There's no need for you to come back here after the coffee shop unless they have an ID on our suspect. Get some sleep. We'll touch base in the morning."

I pulled out my coat from the hall closet near Sullivan's office then peeked back in the doorway as I slipped it on. "Sure thing, but I'll still let you know how it went when we leave Insomnia."

By nine thirty, we were in the cruiser and exiting the precinct's parking garage. With my phone in hand, I pulled up directions to the coffee shop and let the GPS guide us during the ten-mile drive. Optimism finally gave me a reason to smile. I hoped this would be the lead we needed to solve the case by tomorrow.

"The person who contacted Alex was in the coffee shop just over an hour ago. Whoever took his money should be able to give us a pretty accurate description of him."

J.T. glanced my way. "You'd think so."

After a fifteen-minute drive, J.T. pulled into the coffee shop's small lot that was jammed between two buildings. The one-story stuccoed building held two individual retail spaces. Insomnia was closest to the parking lot. It shared a center wall with a shipping service store.

With the cruiser tucked neatly between a compact car and the dumpster near a fence, we exited our vehicle and walked to the front of the building. Insomnia appeared to be a recently remodeled storefront that might have been some other type of retail space not long ago. Building permits, still taped to the front window, looked torn and ragged, as if the wind caught them on a regular basis. We entered the coffee shop and approached the counter clerk. The room held wall-to-wall tables, likely to accommodate the late-night crowd once they showed up. Even for that time of night, the coffee shop was surprisingly busy. The constant hum of voices filled the space.

J.T. took charge, and I hung back and checked out the crowd. Insomnia seemed to be the perfect place for our perp to pick out his next victim. That was one possible reason he had been there. Everyone looked to be in their twenties— "young and innocent" to predators like the one who had visited Insomnia that very night.

"Psst."

I turned around to see J.T. give me a head jerk. I walked over. "What have you got?"

"Somebody who may know something. Jade, this is Gina Figoli. She said she's been working here since seven o'clock. She didn't personally talk to the guy we're asking about, but she said she saw him. And just a side note, there aren't any cameras in or outside this building."

"Figured as much. Okay, Gina, we're going to need you to answer some questions for us."

She looked around. "Yeah, and now is better than later.

I think Denny can handle things for fifteen minutes or so. Can you give me a second?"

"Sure, go ahead." Gina walked over to a young man taking an order at a table. He nodded, which I considered a positive sign.

"Okay, we're good. Follow me. We can use the office."

The small room consisted of a desk and one side chair. J.T. nodded for me to take a seat. I'd ask the questions, and he would take the notes.

"So, Gina, who waited on the guy who asked to use a computer?" I assumed if it was Denny, we needed to be talking to him instead of her.

"Like I told Agent Harper when he asked, it was Sue, but she's already left for the night."

J.T. apologized for not mentioning that tidbit.

"Okay, no problem. Let's start with the upper part of his body and work our way down. That will actually give us a better description to work with."

"Sure. He left his hoodie pulled up, but these days everyone does, and it's cold outside."

"Right. What color was it?"

"Black, and he wore a black coat over it. His hair was straight and medium blond. It kind of looked like it was all one length, you know, like he had to tuck the sides behind his ears. I noticed that because his hair fell in his face when he signed in."

"He signed in?"

"Yeah, we only ask for the time you sign in and out and your initials, though."

J.T. jotted that down then looked at Gina. "We'll need to see that sheet before we leave."

"What did his face look like?"

"I mean, he was cute and everything."

I smiled at her youthful language. "How about details? Beard, mustache, monobrow, rotten teeth, that sort of thing."

"Um, he had a clean-shaven face and blue eyes. He glanced at me and kind of stared for a few seconds."

That comment made me shudder. I was sure I knew why he was checking her out. "How about age?"

"Humph. I'd put him between twenty and thirty."

I dropped my shoulders. "Gina, everyone here is between twenty and thirty."

She pressed her temples with her fingertips and rubbed as if that would clarify the image in her mind. "Yeah, sorry. I'd put him closer to thirty. He didn't have a baby face."

"Okay, you said he wore a black coat and hoodie. What kind of pants?"

"Baggy jeans, but not like he had to hold them up or anything. I guess more like carpenter jeans."

"Okay, lastly, his build."

"Geez, that's tough with a coat and baggy pants on. I'd say he was built like Denny. Yeah, just like Denny."

I looked up at J.T., and he nodded. "Okay, thanks for your time, Gina. All we need now is a peek at that sign-in sheet."

"Sure, it's back at the register."

We followed her to the front and waited at the counter

as she stepped behind it. She pulled out a clipboard with a sheet attached to it.

"We change out the sheet every night when we close." She checked it before handing it to us. "Here you go. His was the last entry, but the ink is kind of smeared. Sue probably had wet hands when he passed it back to her."

Gina slid it across the counter, and J.T. picked it up. He squinted at the initials then handed the clipboard to me. "Can you tell what they are?"

"Hmm… a *J* and *R*, maybe? Could be a *J* and a *B* or an *S* and a *B*. Honestly, I can't tell. The only thing I can read is the check-in and -out times. I'll take a picture and see if anyone at the station can make heads or tails of it. Maybe the tech department can sharpen it." I pulled out my phone, snapped a few close-ups, and then slid the clipboard back across the counter.

J.T. handed Gina his card. "Please call if you think of anything else," he said.

I approached Denny and asked him his height and weight before we walked out.

Back in the car, J.T. closed the driver's door while I buckled my seat belt.

"Write this in your notes while it's fresh in my mind," I said.

He pulled his notepad out of his coat pocket. "Okay, shoot."

"Denny said he was five eleven and weighs one hundred eighty-two pounds, give or take."

"Got it. Hungry?"

"Yeah, I'm starving, and a fast-food joint works for me. I'm too tired for a sit-down restaurant." While we rode, I called and updated Sullivan on our visit to Insomnia and forwarded pictures of the sign-in sheet. "Can you get those shots to the tech department, Captain? Maybe they can sharpen them up so the initials are more legible."

"Will do, Jade. I'll see you two in the morning."

J.T. hit the drive-through, and we took our burgers and fries back to our hotel rooms and parted ways for the night.

As I lay in bed eating my late-night burger, I saw a text had come in earlier from Amber. All she wrote was that she had good news, but I wouldn't find out what it was through a text. She'd call sometime tomorrow and try to get me on the phone.

"That's interesting."

I finished my meal and brushed my teeth. Then I clicked off the nightstand lamp as I crawled into bed.

Chapter 50

I craned my neck beyond J.T.'s shoulder and through the driver's side window as we stared at the entrance to Second Life Resale. I checked the time on my phone. "There must be an alley entrance, otherwise we would have seen somebody walk up and unlock the front door."

We sat in the cruiser and sipped coffee as we watched the door and windows for signs of life. A light should go on soon, and somebody would have to turn the Closed sign around.

I stared at the run-down buildings on either side of the street. The neighborhood looked rough at best.

"Why the hell would somebody choose to have a business right here?" I asked, more rhetorically than anything else. "I'd have my sidearm locked and loaded twenty-four seven."

J.T. chuckled. "You already do."

I checked the time again—8:55.

"Queue the lights," J.T. said. "Somebody is inside and headed toward the door. Got everything you need?"

I smirked as I climbed out of the cruiser. "You mean my gun?"

We crossed the street and approached the building just as the sign on the door was spun to indicate the store was officially open. Past experience had told us it was best not to give potential witnesses a heads-up that we were coming. They wouldn't have time to think of anything but the truth, in most cases.

A woman gave us a surprised smile as we neared the door. She pulled it open and allowed us in. "Wow, my assistant must have marked everything down. We never have customers right out of the gate."

Once we were inside and she had closed the door behind us, I stuck out my hand to introduce myself. "Sorry, but this is an official visit. We aren't here to shop. I'm FBI Agent Jade Monroe, and this"—I pointed at J.T.—"is my partner, J.T. Harper." We pulled out our IDs. "Are you the store owner?"

"FBI? Is something wrong?"

I noticed how her eyes darted from left to right out the floor-to-ceiling windows on either side of the door.

"Believe me, this is an iffy neighborhood on its best days, hence the bars on the door and windows." She paused and looked at us apprehensively. "Oh, sorry. Yes, I'm the owner, Jan Severson. What seems to be the problem, agents?"

"We're looking for information on a purchase made late in the day on Tuesday. I have a photo of the receipt right here." I dipped my hand into my coat pocket and pulled out my phone. She waited as I tapped the Gallery icon and scrolled to the picture. I handed my phone to her.

"Okay, yes, Emma told me she sold several chairs the other night."

J.T. spoke up. "So you weren't here during that transaction?"

"Sorry, but no. I work Monday, Wednesday, and Friday until three, and then I have part-time employees pick up the other weekdays and cover the weekends. Was there a problem with the chairs?"

I smiled. "We didn't buy them, ma'am, but we are very interested in the person who did." My eyes scanned the interior walls. I pointed. "I see you have a camera near the register. Are there any more?"

"I'm afraid not. There's really no concern over theft since most of our items are too large. It's the till I worry about."

"We noticed a few cameras outside along the rooflines as we walked over here. Are any of those yours?"

"No, but given the quantity of security cameras in the neighborhood, most of them overlap and cover my doorway too. That's why I didn't bother installing my own. We don't have a lot of markup on the furniture here, so I tend to cut corners in other areas where I can."

J.T. nodded. "How about letting us take a look at the register video from Tuesday? We'd like to see the person who purchased those chairs."

"Of course, but do I need to sit in there with you? I may get customers, and until noon, I'm the only one here."

"We only need you to set it up, ma'am," I said. "We can handle it after that."

Jan led us to a closet-sized office where the camera footage was installed on a laptop computer. We watched as she clicked the camera icon on the desktop. The live feed came up and showed an empty counter where the cash register was located.

"There you go. It's all ready. I'll back it up to where the tape begins on Tuesday. It switches to the next day at midnight. That's the best I can do. You'll have to advance the footage to get to the precise minute that's on your copy of the receipt."

I gave her a thank-you nod. "I think we can handle it from here. We appreciate your help, Jan."

"Holler if you need anything." She walked out and closed the door.

"Okay"—I double-checked the picture on my phone— "we're looking for five-fifty according to the receipt."

The process was much more tedious than we had anticipated. The camera taped a full twenty-four hours before kicking over to the next day, so we had nearly an eighteen-hour length of tape to get through before we reached five-fifty p.m. Even pushing the slider bar ahead, we found it took about ten minutes to get through each hour of tape.

I groaned. "At this rate, it's going to take three hours to get to the time we need. This system must be ten years old. How about I stay here and you knock on the doors of some of the other buildings? Maybe their outside cameras caught the guy entering the store."

J.T. pushed back from the desk. "Yeah, good idea.

There's no point in both of us sitting here like Tweedledee and Tweedledum."

I rolled my eyes. "Did you really just say that?"

"I'm afraid so. Keep your phone handy in case I find something."

"Will do." I called Sullivan as I watched the minutes pass on the video. I manually inched the scrubber bar forward with the computer mouse.

Sullivan picked up his office phone on the first ring. I assumed he had to be sitting at his desk. "Captain Sullivan speaking. How can I help you?"

"Hey, Captain, Jade here. J.T. and I are at the secondhand store. I'm reviewing their slower- than-molasses video feed from Tuesday, and J.T. went out to see if any neighboring stores had videos that are from the twenty-first century."

He sighed. "So are you saying you'll be there for a while?"

"Afraid so unless J.T. finds something helpful soon. Any news on that sign-in sheet?"

"I talked to Charlie ten minutes ago. He said they were getting close."

"Good to know. At least that's something."

"Yeah, I can only hold Alex for forty-eight hours before I have to charge him with a crime or cut him loose. We've rounded up a few more people from his clan, and Fitch and Andrews are conducting the interviews. Something has to surface today, or everyone will have to be let go."

"We're working on it, sir. I'd suggest getting somebody

to start compiling the initials of everyone that has been interviewed. It'll speed things up once Charlie and the tech department definitely figures out what's written on that sign-in sheet from Insomnia."

"Great idea. I'll get Stone and Mills on that immediately. Keep me posted, and I'll do the same."

I hung up and slid the scrubber bar to the right again. This process was inefficient and time-consuming. I paused the tape and pushed back the chair. I needed to talk to Jan. I stepped out of that stuffy room to brighter light and fresher air. I saw Jan at the back of the store and called her over.

"Agent Monroe, what can I help you with?"

"This process is going to take a long time. My partner is seeing what we can get from the outside cameras." I rubbed my forehead in thought. "Okay, here's what I want you to do. Call the woman who worked Tuesday night and get her over here. You said her name was Emma, right?"

With her cell phone already in hand, Jan scrolled the contact list with her index finger. She looked up at me. "Yes, Emma is the one who sold the chairs to the man in question."

"Good, get her here now. I need more information."

"I'm on it, Agent Monroe."

Chapter 51

"Son of a bitch, wake up." Sam slapped Kristen across the face. He gripped her cheeks between his thumb and fingers and squeezed hard. He shook her face and slapped it again. She didn't move. "I said to wake up, damn you!" When he let go, her head dropped to her chest. He felt for a pulse. She was dead. "You stupid bitch, this wasn't supposed to happen."

Sam kicked over the chair that stood in his way and checked on Bethany. Her head bobbled when he called her name. She gave a nearly inaudible moan. He slapped her inner arm to check for viable veins—they were almost invisible. "There's no way I'm going to let you die before I get more blood out of you."

Sam quickly set up the equipment. He wiped her inner elbow with a cotton ball dipped in rubbing alcohol and placed the empty transfusion bag on her lap. He connected the clear tube to the end of the bag. Next he tightened a rubber tourniquet around her upper arm. With a couple of snaps of his thumb and index finger against her skin, he was able to see a faint blue vein. He jammed the needle deep into the vein and taped it in place. With the end of the tube inserted in the needle port, he flipped the valve and watched as new blood seeped out of Bethany's arm and into the bag. Sam sighed deeply then got back to work.

He cleared the area around the gurney. After he set up the collection jugs beneath it, he pulled the tape and ropes off Kristen. He carried her lifeless body to the gurney and dropped her on it. He had no idea how long she had been dead, but rigor hadn't set in. He'd drain her blood. That was what he'd sell.

There's no way in hell I'm going to transfuse a dead person's blood into Mom. Kristen's blood is what I'll sell.

That thought reminded him that he needed to take a trip to the library. As soon as he had Kristen set up and her blood draining into the jugs, he'd head out to check for a response from Massimo.

Chapter 52

"Anything yet?" I asked with a long sigh into the phone.

"Nah, mostly undesirables milling around on the sidewalks in the general area," J.T. said. "They're probably waiting for drug buyers or sellers to show up. There's a dozen or so vehicles parked along the curb on both sides of the street, but I haven't seen anyone entering or exiting any of them."

"Damn it. What store are you in?"

"I'm two doors north of Second Life at a corner bodega. Some of these places, given the fact that they're dumpy neighborhood bars, don't open until mid-afternoon."

I walked to the window and looked out. "Hey, some guy just went into the store across the street. Hang on. Jan?" I pointed out the window. "What's that place over there?"

She looked at where I was pointing. "The yellow building?"

"Yeah, that one."

"It's a check-cashing place. They're stocked with cameras since they need to keep a lot of cash on hand." She glanced at the time. "Yeah, they just opened."

"Great, thanks. Okay, J.T. leave the bodega and go to the yellow building directly across from Second Life. Jan said it's a check-cashing store with plenty of cameras. I guess they just opened."

"Got it. I'm on my way."

My phone rang just as I returned to the office and clicked the arrow to restart the video. Sullivan was calling again. I leaned back in the chair and answered. "Hey, Captain, what have you got?"

"Charlie is pretty confident that the initials are an *S* and an *R*."

That's awesome, and our guesses were close, but close only counts—well, in my opinion, close doesn't count at all. Anyway, J.T. is checking out a business across the street as we speak. We were told it has a decent number of cameras since it's a check-cashing store. Have Stone and Mills started compiling names of everyone interviewed?"

"Yeah, and now that we're relatively confident of the initials on that sheet, they can speed through the list."

"Okay, I'm waiting on the night clerk to arrive so she can go over everything with me. I should know something soon. I think we're getting somewhere, sir. I have a good feeling about today. Has Charlie replied to the message from last night?"

"Yeah, he's taking it slowly, though. We don't want to spook this guy. A couple of back-and-forth emails should do the trick. It'll make our perp less suspicious and more likely to set up a meeting. Charlie will let us know the minute another message comes in."

"Perfect, and I have to go. It looks like that girl I need to speak with just walked in." I caught a glimpse of J.T. out the window as he entered the building across the street. I approached the young lady standing with Jan and introduced myself. "Would you mind sitting in the office with me where we can talk privately, Emma?"

The bell above the door rang, and Jan left and greeted the customer who had just entered.

Emma looked worried. "Sure, but did I do something wrong?"

I smiled to ease her mind. "Not at all, and to be honest, we could really use your help."

I closed the door behind us as we squeezed into that tiny office. I pulled my notepad out of my purse that hung from the chair back and offered Emma the one and only seat. Leaning against the wall, I had my pen, notepad, and questions ready.

"Emma, I need to know everything you can remember about Tuesday evening around six o'clock. I believe that's the time you sold two chairs to a male customer. Can you take it from the first contact you had with him?"

"Oh, okay." She situated herself in the chair and folded her hands in her lap. "He called first and asked if we had any upholstered armchairs. He specifically mentioned that type. I asked if they needed to match, and he said no. I told him we had five in the store. He said he'd come in and take a look. About twenty minutes later, I saw somebody standing near the chairs, so I assumed it was him." Emma paused while I caught up.

"Thanks. Okay, go on."

"I think I scared him when I asked if he needed help. He said he was deep in thought. He ended up taking two mismatched heavy chairs. He mentioned something about wanting the arms to be wide enough. I asked for what, and he just said for comfort."

"Okay, I need you to think hard about his appearance. Take your time and only tell me the things you remember for sure."

Her forehead wrinkled as she seemed to dig deep into her mind's eye. "It isn't like I study the customers' faces, although I do remember thinking he was cute."

"That's good, Emma. I do realize it's difficult several days later to remember everything about a customer. Just do the best you can."

"He wore a sweatshirt with a jacket over it. It was chilly that night, and I remember feeling the cold air blow in every time the front door opened. He had the sweatshirt hood pulled up."

"What color was his hair?"

"Sort of a medium blond."

"Was he tall, short, heavy, or thin?"

"Average, just like a regular guy."

"Okay, that works." I gave her a reassuring nod. "Did he happen to mention his name?"

"No, not that I remember."

"And he paid with cash, correct?"

"Yes."

"You said he took two heavy chairs. What did he put them in?"

"I don't know. I told the guy to pull around to the alley and Jerry would give him a hand loading them. He did and then came back inside a few minutes later and paid the bill. That was the last time I saw him."

"Jerry should remember the vehicle, though. Right?"

"Sure. I'll give him a call right now."

J.T. entered the store as I waited in the retail area for Emma to make her call.

"Find out anything?" He blew on his hands to warm them up.

I jerked my chin at him. "Where are your gloves?"

He stared down at his hands. "Yeah, I left them in the cruiser."

I smiled. "Humph. Emma, the night clerk, is here, and she's making a call to the man who helped our guy load his vehicle. We ought to have a description of it any minute."

"Good to know. The lighting was dim in the video from the check-cashing store, but I did see several people get in vehicles and leave the area during that time. One person came out of the store, but they were empty handed."

"That was probably him. Emma said she told him to pull around the back to the loading dock. What kind of vehicle did he have?"

"A van, and I know your next question. I couldn't tell the color except that it was dark, but it wasn't the extended van Alex's clan uses." J.T. tipped his head. "Is that Emma?"

I turned around. "Yeah, that's her. What did you find out, Emma?"

She approached us, smiling. "Jerry remembered the

vehicle. He said the guy had a charcoal-gray van that had sliding side doors. He said it was completely empty from the front seats to the back. That's the only way the chairs fit inside. Oh, and he said the van seemed older just because it looked a little run-down."

"He didn't happen to see the plate number, did he?" J.T. asked as he took notes.

"He said he didn't even think to look, but he remembered seeing a parking pass sticker on the windshield."

"That ought to help." I gave J.T. a hopeful glance. I let out a long breath. "Okay, anything else at all that you can remember, Emma?"

"Just that he said he was artsy and wanted to reupholster the chairs. That's why he didn't care if they matched."

"Okay, thanks. You've been a big help." I handed her and Jan my contact card. "We'll be in touch. I have to find out from our tech department if there's a way to pull Tuesday's footage from the camera. That way we can review it at the precinct. We may be sending someone over to take a look."

J.T. and I headed back to the station with the information we had gathered. As J.T. drove, I pulled out my notepad to give everything a thorough review.

"Did Charlie get anywhere with those initials?"

"Yeah, he says they're an *S* and an *R*."

"That rules out Alex. How about the rest of the people in his group?"

"Fitch and Andrews are going through the names of everyone interviewed." I flipped through my notepad in reverse.

"Looking for something in particular?"

"Yeah, we did interviews too, you know. I may as well go through those names while I'm sitting here, anyway."

Chapter 53

She could barely hold her head up. Adeline's energy level had faded dramatically overnight. Sam had a hard time keeping her alert.

"Mom, please drink the juice. You need vitamins and liquids in your body. You have to keep up your strength so I can give you a transfusion today."

She whispered in a raspy voice, "Just let me die. I'm going to no matter what."

"No you aren't, and don't talk that way."

Sam held the straw to her mouth and willed her to take a sip. With a quick glance at the clock on her nightstand, he checked the time—ten thirty. He needed to get to the library to see whether Massimo had responded to his message from last night.

Kristen's dead body lay on the gurney in the back room, and her blood was filling the jugs. He'd bag it as soon as he returned home. His mind was consumed with thoughts of finding another dump site for a body. Chances were he'd have two bodies to dump this time. Sam was sure Bethany's death wouldn't be far behind.

Adeline's fresh blood supply would dwindle quickly now that Kristen was gone. Sam would be lucky to get a few more draws from Bethany before her veins were completely useless and her blood supply depleted.

"Mom, don't try to get out of bed. I'll be back as fast as I can, I promise."

She nodded and closed her eyes. Sam grabbed the keys and left through the garage. He backed the van down the driveway, lowered the overhead, and sped off, heading to the library. He planned his next steps as he drove. He'd sell Kristen's blood to Massimo to free up some cash. Then he'd search for a new donor. His mind went back to the clerk from Second Life Resale. She was a good possibility.

Chapter 54

"No shit! You have to be kidding me." I sat up straight and focused on the page in my notepad.

"What?" J.T. jerked his head toward me.

"I got it. I swear I know who he is." My head nearly hit the passenger door window as J.T. cranked the steering wheel and swerved the cruiser into a grocery store parking lot.

"Show me."

"Geez, I think I have whiplash." I handed him my notepad with the page folded back. "Look at the name of the last person we interviewed at the hospital where Heather worked. Think about it, J.T. You do remember what he looked like, right?"

J.T. stared at my notes. "Sam Reed. The initials are right, and he has blond hair. A well-mannered, polite guy if I remember correctly."

"Yeah, a good act if I do say so myself, and he said he barely knew Heather. His hair color, age, and body size fits the descriptions we were given. Now we need to know what he drives. Hospital employees usually have parking passes on their vehicles too, just like Jerry described." I grabbed my cell and called Sullivan. I tapped the speakerphone icon as the phone rang. He picked up before the third ring. "Captain, I think we know the guy. We need a DL for a Sam Reed and his vehicle registration information. If he drives a dark gray van, we have him dead to rights."

J.T. pulled back out onto the street and continued toward downtown.

"Who the hell is Sam Reed?" Sullivan asked.

"He works at the same hospital Heather did. We interviewed the punk ourselves, damn it." I checked my notes again. "He's local and said he lives in the vicinity of Second Street but avoided giving me an exact address."

"Okay, Charlie sent off a return message earlier, posing as Massimo, and the seller has already replied. He must be getting desperate. He wants to meet at twelve forty-five today at Franklin County Park. We can't arrest somebody based on their initials, so we need to catch him in the act of trying to sell human blood. I'll have tech pull up Sam Reed's DL and vehicle registration. How far out are you guys?"

"We're here and pulling into the parking garage right now."

J.T. parked. We hurried through the door then headed straight for Sullivan's office.

"Did tech get a hit on Sam Reed's DL?" I asked as I took a seat in a guest chair.

"That name doesn't come up in the system with any driver's license at all."

J.T. ground his fist in his right eye. "How the hell is that possible?"

"Maybe Sam Reed isn't even his real name." I checked the time. We had an hour and a half to come up with a plan. "Who's meeting this guy in the park?"

Sullivan huffed. "Who do you think? It has to be Alex. It's his picture on that website."

"Shit. Has anyone briefed him yet?" J.T. asked.

"Andrews is putting him in interrogation room two right now. The rest of the clan has been released."

"Okay, I'll call the personnel department at the hospital and get Sam's address." I gave J.T. a glance. "You're going to be the person briefing Alex, right?"

"Absolutely, and come downstairs after your call. Just don't get your hopes up that the hospital is going to give you confidential information over the phone."

"I know, but it's worth a try. Maybe I'll get a newbie on the line."

Sullivan pushed back his chair and joined J.T. at the door. "Use my office to make your call. At least it's quiet in here." He pulled the door closed behind him. I watched through the glass wall as they walked away.

I looked up the hospital's number on my phone and dialed. I waited as the phone rang four times.

"St. Mary's Hospital, how may I direct your call?"

"Hello. I need the personnel department, please."

"One moment."

I listened to smooth jazz for a solid minute before somebody picked up.

"Personnel, how may I help you?"

I went through the usual introductions with no luck. Unless I went to the hospital and showed them my FBI ID in person, they weren't obligated to give me any employee's personal information over the phone. I hung up and flipped through my notes again. I remembered Joan Miller being talkative and helpful during her interview. She was the one who gave us information about Heather's infatuation with Adam Drake. She could very well be the perfect person to talk to. I called again, altered my voice a bit, and asked for the lab. I was transferred to the receptionist there.

"Lab, Deb speaking."

"Hi, Deb." I recognized the voice of the not-so-helpful, gum-snapping young lady who sat behind the glass window in the lab's registration area. I thought I'd play it nice and see whether I'd have better luck with her, but I wasn't about to let on who I was. "I have an urgent message for Joan Miller. May I speak to her, please?"

"Give me a sec."

I waited as Deb put me on hold for nearly a minute. A rustle on the other end told me she'd returned. "Joan just left for her hour-long lunch. I'll give her your message when she returns."

"No, thanks, but you can give me her cell number."

I could imagine her smirking on the other end. "I don't think so. That's against hospital policies. You'll have to try back after lunch."

I hung up. "Damn it, I'm not getting anywhere."

I pocketed my phone and headed to the elevator. Down

on the first floor, I made my way through the security doors to the interrogation and observation rooms. I opened the door and entered observation room number two. Sullivan's elbows rested on the counter. His head was propped in his open palms as he watched J.T. through the window. Andrews leaned against the wall with his arms folded over his chest. Fitch sat in a folding chair.

"How's it going?" I asked. I stuffed my hands deep into my pants pockets and watched through the mirror with the others.

"J.T. is coaching him on everything to say and every move to make," Sullivan said, "and Alex isn't liking it one bit."

"What other choice does he have?"

Mel grinned. "None, and he knows it. We can charge him with obstructing justice, fleeing an officer, speeding, erratic driving, and endangering the life of a motorist."

I rolled the knots out of my neck as I joined Andrews against the wall. "That ought to convince him to cooperate."

Sullivan asked how my call to the hospital went.

"Yeah, no luck with the personnel department—they're tight-lipped—but I may have a chance with somebody after lunch. Isn't it time for your guys to head out?"

Sullivan leaned forward and knocked on the window. J.T. rose and left the interrogation room.

Seconds later, J.T. entered the room and stood at my side. He sucked in a deep breath. "I think we're good to go. There isn't much more I can tell Alex before he goes into brain overload. How many of us are staking out the park?"

"I already have Stone, Mills, and Jeffries out there in street clothes. They're parked several blocks away in their personal cars. They're watching the area to see if the seller shows up early. It isn't the time of year to be strolling through a park, and that's likely why our guy picked it. He would definitely notice an unusual amount of people milling around and get suspicious, so it's up to Alex to pull this off. The rest of us have to hang back."

J.T. coughed into his hand before talking. "Jade and I can't be seen if this man is actually Sam Reed from the hospital. He'd recognize us from the interview and know it's a setup. We'll stay back and watch through our binoculars."

"I think I'll take a pass on this one. I'm heading to the hospital. If the only way I'm going to get an address for Sam Reed is by flashing my badge, then I need to be there in person."

"Okay, keep us posted," Sullivan said. He jerked his head at Andrews. "Get someone from impound to bring a clunker around to the side entrance. It's for Alex to drive. He has to look the part of a low-life wannabe vampire. We need to get a wire on him too. Let's saddle up and get this pony show on the road."

I parted ways with the rest of the group and wished them luck. After I took the elevator to the fourth floor and crossed the footbridge to the parking structure, I left in our cruiser and headed to the hospital.

Chapter 55

Sam kept his eye on the time as he pulled into the driveway and parked. He pulled the E-brake, killed the engine, and went in through the front door. He had forty minutes before he had to leave for the meetup. Luckily, the park was only a ten-minute drive from his house. He needed to pack Kristen's blood in double zipper bags first so they'd be ready to go when he was. Then he'd pull the transfusion bag from Bethany and get it set up for Adeline.

Sam fished the keys out of his front pants pocket, unlocked the door, and flipped the light switch on the wall. He entered the workroom and headed straight for the gurney. There was no time to waste. He removed the tubes from the jugs and placed them next to Kristen. Then he carried the jugs into the kitchen and set them on the countertop by the sink. Sam knelt at the bottom cabinet drawer and slid it open. He pulled out four gallon zipper bags from the dispenser and double bagged them. With each doubled bag in the sink, he carefully poured the blood in until the bags were half full. He zipped the inner bag, pressed the air out of the outer bag, and zipped that one too. He placed both bags in a large plastic trash bag so they'd be ready for transport.

Sam quickly glanced at the clock and returned to the workroom to retrieve the full transfusion bag from Bethany. He had just enough time to give Adeline one much-needed pint before he left the house.

Bethany sat quietly with her chin slumped against her chest. Sam flipped the lever on the valve and removed the tube from her arm. He followed the length of clear plastic to the bag on her lap. It was nearly empty. "What the hell? Did I miss her vein?" Sam jerked his head back and gave Bethany a suspicious look. "No, no, no, no." He spun around and pressed his index and middle fingers against her inner wrist but felt nothing. He tried her neck. It felt the same. He screeched, "Son of a bitch, you can't be dead!" Sam kicked the chair aside and leaned in. He lifted her head and pulled her right eyelid up. Her eyes were glazed over and glassy. "Shit! I can't give Mom Kristen's blood, and there isn't enough in the house to hold her over!"

Chapter 56

I entered the hospital through the automatic glass doors and approached the woman flipping through a magazine at the information desk. I cleared my throat and she looked up.

"May I help you?"

Knowing there wasn't time for pleasantries, I whipped out my badge and showed it to her. "I need to get to the personnel department. Which way do I go?"

"Oh dear, is someone expecting you?" She looked from left to right. "Ma'am, it's hospital policy to have an escort if you're going into restricted areas without an appointment."

I jerked my chin toward the doors behind her. "I have an escort—you." I took a quick glance at her name tag. "Come on, Sylvia. We don't have time to waste."

She looked apprehensive but rose, anyway, since I insisted. Sylvia led me through a set of automatic doors, down a long hallway, and through a second set of doors. We entered an area that resembled a typical office. It was filled with small rooms and cubicles. The hospital vibe had all but vanished. Sylvia looked over her shoulder at me. "We're close."

We went down two more hallways, then a placard on the wall told me we had reached our destination. The personnel department was just beyond the set of doors in front of us. We entered the large office space. Sylvia hung back and took a seat in a guest chair against the wall. I approached the first counter and pulled my badge from the lanyard. I slid it across the laminate surface to the only woman stationed there. "I need information on an employee, and I don't have time to mess around."

The woman looked at me, then my badge, then at me again, as if she were comparing my face to the image in the photo.

"It's me, and I need you to pull up the employee file for Sam Reed."

"Yes, ma'am," she said. "What department does he work in?"

"The lab."

"One moment, please."

I stared at her as she tapped the keyboard. She frowned at the screen and leaned in closer.

"What's wrong?" I asked.

"We don't have a record of a Sam Reed that works in the lab."

"Okay, then just pull up his personnel file."

"There isn't one. We don't have an employee named Sam Reed in the entire hospital. Are you sure he isn't an outside vendor?"

"Yes I'm sure, and I interviewed him several days back in the lab. He has to be in the employee database."

"I'm sorry, ma'am, but he isn't."

I spun toward Sylvia. "Let's go. You're taking me to the lab." I checked the time on my phone as we followed the double yellow lines on the floor to a bank of elevators. Sylvia pressed the button. We waited until the bell dinged. I looked at the large arrow that illuminated as the doors parted, and we slipped in. Sylvia pressed the button for the fourth floor. The doors closed, and we rode up in silence.

I knew the way from there, but Sylvia apparently felt the need to escort me. I'm sure she feared her job could be on the line if she didn't. I pushed through the doors, which opened to the lab's waiting area and the small check-in window where Deb sat. She glanced up, rolled her eyes, and huffed.

"Don't start with me and don't talk. I need you to get Joan Miller out here right this minute."

She shoved her chair away from the counter and disappeared through the door at her back. Minutes later, as I paced the floor, the door between the lab and the waiting area opened. Joan walked through.

"Agent Monroe," she said in a whisper, "what's this about?"

"Come with me."

"But I'm working."

"It'll only take a minute." When Sylvia began to stand, I pointed at her. "Stay put. We're just going out in the hallway, and it's a private conversation."

Joan followed me then leaned against the wall when the door closed at our backs. "What's going on?"

"I need information, Joan. It's urgent."

"Sure, if I can help."

"You know Sam, right? The guy that files the blood samples?"

"Yeah, slightly, but he was fired the other day for missing too much work."

I nodded. Now it made sense that personnel wouldn't have his file anymore. It had been expunged from their database. "What did you know about Sam?"

"Not much since his position kept him pretty isolated, but he was a cute guy. Somewhat quiet but nice enough."

"Sam Reed, right? I'm sure that's what he said his name was."

"Sam Reed? No, you must have misunderstood him. His name is Sam Ryan."

I scribbled that down on my notepad. "You're positive?"

"I mean, as positive as I can be since that's what he told me. I can only go by his word."

"Do you know if Sam drives a charcoal-gray van?"

She looked surprised. "Yeah, he does."

"Good, that's really good. Do you know what the plate number is, or even a partial number? I need to locate him. It's urgent. Do you know where he lives?"

"No, he never mentioned it. But I do know the plate number. It was easy to remember, and I asked him about it once. We arrived to work at the same time and parked nose to nose. That's when I saw it. I asked Sam what it meant as we walked in together."

"Yeah, what was it?" I was getting anxious. "Hurry, just tell me."

"*Addie* was written across the plates. That's it, just the name. He said the van belonged to his mom."

"Spell it." Joan did, and I wrote it down. I squeezed her shoulders and took off toward the elevators as I pulled my phone out of my pocket. I yelled back before Joan crossed through the lab doors. "Tell Sylvia I showed myself out."

I dialed as I waited for the down elevator. Sullivan answered immediately. "Captain, I have the plate info. Have the tech department pull it up right away."

"Go ahead, Jade."

I rattled off the name and made sure he had it spelled correctly.

"Good work, agent. Just so you know, the seller is a no-show. We're going to give him fifteen more minutes then call it off."

I climbed into the elevator and hit the button for the first floor. "I'll come and meet you guys. What street are you sitting on?"

"We're two blocks away from Franklin Park. J.T. and I are sitting on East Seventeenth and Cumberland."

"I'll find it." I wrote down their location as I wedged the phone between my cheek and shoulder. "I'll program it into my GPS as soon as I hang up. I should be there before our seller's fifteen-minute deadline."

I raced out of the hospital and jumped into the cruiser. With government plates on the car and nobody to question me, I hit the lights and sirens and headed to Franklin County Park. Two miles out, I silenced the sound and turned off the light bar. I didn't want to spook our killer, if indeed he actually showed up. I called J.T. as I got closer.

"What's the word, partner?"

"Andrews and Fitch are a half block from the meet-up point. They said nobody has arrived. Alex is hanging out in the parking lot and waiting in the car we borrowed from impound. We're about to call it quits. Our guy either chickened out or smelled a trap."

"Maybe, but I'm calling Charlie to see if they've pulled an address on the van yet. If Sam—as in Sam Ryan, not Sam Reed—isn't coming to meet Alex, he may be at home. Don't forget, if he's our guy, he's still holding Bethany and Kristen prisoner. Apparently, he was fired from the hospital for not showing up at work when scheduled. There has to be a reason for that."

I clicked off the call and arrived a few minutes later behind the cruiser J.T. and Sullivan sat in. I killed the engine and tucked the car keys in my pocket. I quickly walked over and climbed into the backseat of their vehicle.

"Nothing yet?" I asked. I had positioned myself between their seats, dead center behind the console.

J.T. spoke up. "Alex is wired and ready to go, but according to him, no calls have come in, and he hasn't seen any movement nearby. The buyer, known only by his log-in name, Seller4567, is in the wind. He's twenty minutes late, and Alex had no way to contact him other than through the website."

The radio squawked in Sullivan's cruiser. "Sullivan here. What's up?"

Andrews spoke from his location near the park. "Alex called me. He wants to know what he should do."

Sullivan groaned into the phone and turned to J.T. then back to me.

J.T. checked the time. "Give him five more minutes, then tell Alex to leave and drive four blocks south to Hickory. Stone and Mills can escort him to the station. Let's head back and reconvene in the conference room. Once we have Sam's address, we'll make our move."

Chapter 57

Sullivan reached up and pulled the finger loop on the roller map of the city. He lowered the map and secured the loop to the hook on the wall. He turned and tipped his head at me. "The floor is yours, Jade. What did you find out from Charlie?"

I stood and approached the map. "Sam lied about where he lived. His actual home is only ten minutes from the park." I pointed at the street where the house was in relationship to Franklin County Park. "According to the personalized plates on the van, the address on record for Adeline Ryan is 4062 Montgomery Street. I checked the satellite imagery, and it isn't going to be easy to sneak up on the house. The residence is at the end of a secluded cul-de-sac and on a large parcel of land surrounded by woods. If he's hunkered down with a good visual of the street, he'll see us coming. We won't have the surprise factor on our side."

"Could you tell how many doors lead into the house?" Sullivan asked.

J.T. responded. "I looked at the satellite image with Jade. We're pretty confident in saying there's three points of entry. There's the front door to the right of the driveway, the overhead garage door, and a side yard door on the left leading into the garage."

Andrews cleared his throat then spoke up. "What about neighbors?"

"None close by." J.T. jerked his chin at Fitch. "Pull up the address on your laptop so you guys can take a look."

Mel opened her laptop and powered it up. "Okay, the address again."

I rattled it off. She clicked on the bird's-eye view tab. An aerial view of the property came up. J.T. leaned in and explained to the group what they were looking at.

"The neighborhood is thick with woods, although this time of year, we don't have cover from foliage. Still, we can access the property through the woods and make entry at the side door that leads into the garage. The noise buffer from that side of the house should help. We can station officers at the overhead garage and front doors."

"Do we have enough probable cause to break in?" Stone asked.

I nodded. "You bet we do. There was no reason on earth for a receipt for the purchase of two armchairs to be at Dasher Point. The receipt was from Tuesday. According to everyone we spoke to, Alex has had his two chairs forever, plus they aren't upholstered armchairs. I'm sure it wasn't a coincidence that Sam bought two chairs just before Kristen and Bethany went missing. Also, he lied about his last name and where he lives, and his description matches the account from the bartender at Paul's Tap, Jeff Simmons, and the employee at Insomnia. We have enough circumstantial evidence and two missing women to find. There's the mother to take into consideration too. We have no idea if she's part of his diabolical actions or if she's a prisoner like the others. What I do know is, it's time to go." I turned to Sullivan. "Captain, do you want to join in on this? Otherwise, the six of us can handle it." I glanced around the table. "Are we all in?"

Sullivan stood. "We're all in, but that makes seven of us."

"Good to hear. That means we need to plan our approach right now."

Thirty minutes later and with everyone assigned an area to cover, we headed out. Our approach would be from the nearest parallel street behind the house and through the woods. Everyone gathered radios, earpieces, and vests and put them on. Our service weapons were ready, and each of us had extra ammo. Well-armed and ready to go, we filed out of the parking garage with sirens squealing and lights flashing.

"Thank God we both brought our boots along," I said to J.T. as he drove. "According to the GPS coordinates, driving in a southeast direction, we should arrive at that side street in twenty minutes."

"Got it. Just guide me in."

I took off my street shoes and reached to the backseat floor and grabbed my Merrell boots.

Adams Street was the road that ran parallel to Montgomery. The roads were a half mile apart, meaning we'd be trudging through a half mile of woods. I was thankful only a few inches of snow covered the ground. Adams Street was rural too, which helped keep curiosity seekers away. The only house on that road was a good three hundred yards back in the direction we came from. We drove in on Adams about the same distance as the Ryan house was on Montgomery, then we parked our cruisers ten feet apart in case we had to make a quick exit in the cars. The ditch to our right separated the road from the woods.

The lights and sirens had been disengaged three miles back as a precaution. We exited our cars, each of us with a set of binoculars hanging from our necks. In a wide stance to steady ourselves, we leaned against the cars and peered in the direction of the Ryan home. We saw the roofline from where we stood but nothing more.

J.T. gathered the group one last time before we moved out. "Okay, people, let's go. Everyone has their area to cover. Any questions?"

We kept silent.

"Then let's do this. Remember, we take him alive unless we have no other choice. There are likely hostages in there. Once we breach the house, we have to act swiftly, find the women, and apprehend him. Everyone, watch your partner's back and be careful. We don't know with one hundred percent certainty that Sam is our guy, but we're going in as if he were. If he's the killer, we know what he's capable of."

We moved in quickly until we reached the ridge behind the home. Once we cleared that ridge, our only cover would be trees. We'd do our best to stay out of view of any windows and reach the doors unseen.

I pressed the button on my earpiece and spoke through my radio. "Everyone give me a hand signal if you can hear me." I looked around and counted six thumbs-up. "Good enough. Once we clear this ridge, stay low and hightail it for the side of the house. Get to your locations, take cover, and wait. On our go, you'll breach the house. Okay, move in."

Seven of us ran through the woods toward the house with two football-field lengths to go. We crouched behind trees, checked for movement, then continued on. With a final hundred feet to go and a burst of adrenaline, we reached the house and gathered at the side garage door. All was quiet. As far as we could tell, that meant we had gone unseen. With hand signals, I motioned for everyone to take their positions. Fitch and Andrews headed for the front door. Stone and Mills were positioned at the overhead, and Sullivan, J.T., and I stayed at the side door.

With my hand on the doorknob, I was ready to give it a turn when a voice came over Sullivan's radio. He held up his hand for me to wait while he listened to the message from Andrews. Sullivan responded then pressed the button on his earpiece.

"The van is in the driveway, and there are several lights on at the back of the house. Andrews thinks it's the kitchen and hallway light, but he hasn't seen any movement."

J.T. whispered, "Tell him to stay out of sight until we clear the garage."

We waited as Sullivan gave the order. I continued at the door and turned the knob. Surprisingly, the door opened until the chain lock caught. I gave J.T. a questioning frown and stood to the side. He shouldered the door with a quick thrust and snapped the chain. We pulled our weapons and entered the darkened room. The garage was the typical older, unkempt room with one bay for a vehicle. Dark wooden walls held multiple shelves, mostly bare. Several buckets, mops, and brooms lined a far back wall. I tapped J.T.'s shoulder and pointed at them. A few miscellaneous tools lay scattered about. The cracked cement floor wore years of oil stains and caked dirt.

With the outer door open, we had just enough daylight streaming in to help us find the wall switch. Sullivan gave me a nod, and I flipped it. The garage lit up. I turned slowly and looked around. A closed door at the back of the garage stood next to the mops and buckets.

"Over here," I whispered as I jerked my head toward the door. From our perspective, we could see that the room had been added to the garage and altered to be a separate, private space. I turned the knob—it was locked. Since it was a hollow core door, I knew it couldn't withstand much force. "You guys ready?"

J.T. nodded. "Go for it."

He stood next to Sullivan, both with their guns drawn, as I gave the door one of the best Taekwondo kicks I could deliver. The doorframe splintered and broke free from the wall. J.T. pushed the door in. We rushed the room. Sullivan hit the wall switch and yelled through his radio to breach the house. The dead young woman lying on a gurney in front of us needed no explanation. Sam was the killer.

I punched the wall. "That son of a bitch."

J.T. grabbed the sheets dividing the room and ripped them down. "We have another girl over here. They have to be Kristen and Bethany. He ran to her side and felt for a pulse. He turned to me and shook his head. "She's cold."

"Where the hell is that bastard?" I turned back to the garage and took the two steps that led to the house. I pulled the door toward me right as Andrews reached us.

"Holy shit, you guys have to see this."

Chapter 58

The sight in front of us was beyond comprehension. We stood at the doorway and stared. I shook my head, stepped back, and left the room. I needed a minute to process what I had just seen. No matter how horrible and inexcusable Sam's crimes were, what we had all just witnessed gave me a split second of understanding. Everything came into focus.

Sullivan pulled Andrews to the side. "Call the ME and forensics and get them out here right away. Now we know why he didn't show up to make the sale."

J.T. found me sitting on the couch. He unzipped his jacket pocket and pulled out several pair of latex gloves. He handed a set to me. "We better put these on if we're going to spend any time here." He took a seat at my side. "You okay, partner?"

"Yeah, I'm good. Just stunned, that's all." I slipped the gloves over my hands. "How can I feel sad for someone who committed such horrible acts against at least six young ladies? I'll never understand people." I shook my head again. "I just never will."

Sullivan asked Andrews, Mills, and Stone to bring the cruisers around to Montgomery Street. "Park down the road a bit so you don't block the ME and forensics vans."

Andrews nodded and collected the keys. "Will do."

A half hour later, Fitch pulled the curtain aside and looked out to the driveway. "The ME is here." When the chime rang out on the mantel clock, I checked the time—two o'clock.

Jane Felder entered through the front door, her equipment in hand. Tom Knight followed. They both nodded when they saw us waiting in the living room.

"What have we got?" Jane asked.

"Plenty." I stood. "Follow me. I'll show you."

"You sure, Jade?" J.T. asked.

I waved his comment away. "Yeah, I got this." I led the way down the hall to the mother's bedroom. Inside, one dim lamp lit the room, casting shadows on the walls. I opened the curtains to bring in more light.

Jane rubbed her forehead. "Wow, I've never—"

"Me, either."

She walked around to the far side of the bed and assessed the scene. "I don't want to disturb anything before forensics takes their photos."

"So this is why all of the young ladies were drained of their blood. He was transfusing it into…?" Jane stared at the dead woman lying in bed.

"I assume she's Adeline Ryan, Sam's mom."

"And I take it Sam is the dead man with the needle in his arm and the tube direct-lined to the IV port in the mother's hand?" Tom asked.

"That would be correct."

Tom scratched his head. "He transfused all of his own blood into his mom until his heart stopped pumping?"

I grimaced and sucked in a deep breath. "It appears so, but apparently she was too far gone for it to help."

"You know transferring whole blood into another person is very dangerous, right, Agent Monroe?" Jane said.

"Of course I know that, but this scene tells me a couple of things. One, that Sam completely went off the deep end out of pure desperation. And two, that he loved his mom so much that he sacrificed his life in hopes of saving hers. This is one of the saddest crime scenes I've ever witnessed."

I turned and saw the forensics team coming down the hall. I stepped aside to give them room and motioned for Jane to follow me.

"There are two dead girls in a room off the garage. I'll show you where they are." I led them to Kristen and Bethany. Then I went to the living room, where I found J.T. and Sullivan sifting through stacks of mail they had dumped out of the garbage can.

"Everything is starting to make sense," J.T. said.

"Yeah? Enlighten me."

"It looks like Sam was trying to get medical help for his mom through the state, but you know how slow government bureaucracy can be. Apparently, she didn't get the help she needed in time. It looks like the bills were all past due, and the house was going into foreclosure."

"Maybe with all the problems facing him, he wanted to die with her."

Sullivan nodded as he dragged his fingertips through his hair. "Maybe so, but I know one thing for sure."

Fitch tipped her head. "What's that, sir?"

"Nobody came out a winner in this case. I guess I'll call the station and tell Reynolds to cut Alex loose. He may be a weird one, but he didn't commit any serious crimes."

Andrews, Mills, and Stone were back. They walked in through the living room door. "The cars are out front, Captain."

"You four stick around and collect evidence after forensics does their job. Tell Jane to call me on her way back to her office. We have to notify the families." He jerked his head toward the door. "Ready to head out?"

I looked at J.T.

"Yeah, there's no need for us to stick around," he said.

We drove back in our cruiser. Sullivan, in front of us, drove alone in his. We arrived at the station and parked in the visitors' spot on the fourth floor, five spots away from Sullivan. He was already parked and placing his vest in his trunk. We got out and did the same. The captain leaned back against his car and waited for us. "You two heading back to Milwaukee today?"

"Yeah, we still have plenty of daylight left. We'll wrap up our paperwork with you, gather our stuff, and head out."

Sullivan patted my shoulder as we crossed the footbridge together. "It was an honor getting to meet both of you."

"And likewise, sir," I said. "That goes for your entire team. I hope the families can find some peace when it's all said and done."

For the next hour, J.T. and I filled out paperwork about

the case. Finally, after making a dozen copies, we headed to Sullivan's office. I knocked, and he ushered us in.

"Wrapping it up?"

"Yeah, we're about done here." I counted out six copies and handed them to Sullivan. "Here you go, sir."

"Thanks, Jade. Got your case files?"

"Yep." I patted the folders under my arm. "We've got everything. Now to check out of the hotel we didn't spend much time in." I grinned. "It's been a pleasure, sir."

Sullivan shook our hands, and we followed the hallway to the main entry.

J.T. nudged my shoulder. "How about you driving for a while?"

"Sure thing, partner."

I climbed in behind the wheel and drove south to our hotel. It took only fifteen minutes to gather our belongings and check out. We returned to the cruiser with our go bags in hand. I tossed the keys to J.T.

"What the hell is this?"

"I drove for a while, so I'm good."

He shook his head. "Women."

We hit the interstate twenty minutes later and were on our way north to Milwaukee. I was anxious to get home. I had barely spoken to Amber the entire time we were gone, so I sent a quick text saying we were on our way back.

As J.T. drove, I called Spelling. Even the condensed version of events took a good fifteen minutes to relay. I said we'd give him our detailed report at the regular meeting in the morning.

"Go home and get some rest. Sounds like you two have had a busy week. I'll see you tomorrow."

"Sounds like a great idea. I'm beat. Good night, sir."

"Good night, guys."

I clicked off speakerphone and hit End Call. My phone rang just as I dropped it in my pocket. I pulled it back out and looked at the screen. A wide smile crossed my face.

J.T. grinned. "Must be Amber."

"It sure is." I clicked Talk. "Hey, little sister, how have you been?"

"I'm good. Can you talk?"

"Sure. Is it private, because I have you on speakerphone?"

"No, it's okay. Remember a few nights ago when I said I had a surprise to tell you but wouldn't tell you in a text?"

"Yes, I do remember, now that you mention it. What's the surprise?"

I suddenly heard two voices chime in at once, "We've been promoted!"

I laughed. "Is that Kate I just heard squealing with you?"

"Damn straight."

"You've been promoted to what?"

Another voice took over the conversation. It was deep, manly, and very familiar.

"Jack? What the hell is going on?"

He chuckled. "They're both moving into the bull pen under my wing and supervision. I'm their new boss. If everything works out right, these two ladies will be detectives by next summer."

I had to pull the phone away from my face to avoid a broken

eardrum. I laughed again. "It sounds like congratulations are definitely in order."

"That's why I'm calling. Please meet us at the Washington House when you get to town. We'll be there celebrating."

I recalled the last celebration we had there back when Kate and Amber got accepted into the police academy. We all had a hell of a hangover the next day. I knew better, but she was my little sister and I'd do anything for her.

I chuckled. "You got it, hon. Sleep is overrated, anyway."

THE END

Thank you for reading *Donors*, Book 3 in the new Agent Jade Monroe FBI Thriller Series. I hope you enjoyed it!

Follow the complete Jade Monroe saga starting with the Detective Jade Monroe Crime Thriller Series. The books are listed in order below:

Maniacal
Captive
Fallacy
Premonition
Exposed

The Jade Monroe FBI Thriller books follow on the heels of the conclusion of *Exposed*, Book 5 in the Detective Jade Monroe Crime Thriller Series. Currently available books are listed in order below:

Snapped
Justified

Stay abreast of my new releases by signing up for my VIP email list at: http://cmsutter.com/newsletter/

You'll be one of the first to get a glimpse of the cover reveals and release dates, and you'll have a chance at exciting raffles and freebies offered throughout the series.

Posting a review will help other readers find my books. I appreciate every review, whether positive or negative, and if you have a second to spare, a review is truly appreciated.

Again, thank you for reading!

Visit my author website at: http://cmsutter.com/

See all of my available titles at:
http://cmsutter.com/available-books/

Made in United States
Orlando, FL
05 February 2024

43308426R00214